Tales of
Naybor Manor

JOANN KEDER

Tales of Naybor Manor

Edited by: Debbie Lombardo See and Sara Williams
Cover Design by Molly Burton with Cozy Cover Designs

Publisher: Purpleflower Press

ISBN: 978-1-7336639-8-4

First Edition October 2020

Publisher: Purpleflower Press

OTHER BOOKS BY JOANN KEDER

Be the first to hear about new releases! Sign up for my newsletter here:
http://www.joannkeder.com

For
My Wonderful Family

ACKNOWLEDGEMENTS

Each successful writer needs not just one but many people in their corner, helping at all stages of development. I'm especially fond of the team of people I've assembled; each an expert in their own way. I'm fortunate that you are willing to share your personal areas of expertise with me. Keder Readers, you are the best Advanced Reader team. I'm certain you are the cream of the crop when it comes to marketing and passing the word about new publications. Special thanks to Doug, Mackensie and Meghan for your help with all sorts of odd questions and for being supportive of my chosen writerly lifestyle. Please don't ask to look at their search histories. Glenn, your detailed stories and willingness to help are deeply appreciated. Dayle, you devote time you don't have to help me and I am immensely grateful. Laurie, Barbara and Jamie, you are always quick to offer advice when I need it most. Debbie, you are, as always, a treasure in so many ways.

"I don't have to listen to rumors about a man when I can judge him for myself."

Stephen King

Chapter One

Pookie

1946

Dearest Diary,

This was the most darling gift I've ever received on my birthday. Last week I turned twelve. Daddy says I'm the most mature girl he's ever met, and that's why I should have something of such significance. He would know. Daddy has been all over the world and knows just about everything of importance.

The Second War is over and evil was soundly defeated. Life for everyone is so much better now, but even so, we must be ever vigilant. I must document everything I see, as Daddy says I must do my part to preserve history. When my thirteenth birthday arrives, however, I'll be called upon to make a much bigger contribution to Naybor Manor. I'll be a woman of great means and also great responsibility. That's also what Daddy says.

I will include the most colorful descriptions of my charmed country life.

Happily Yours,
Pookie A. Naybor

"What will his name be this time, Daddy?" Pookie loved the feeling of the wind gently lifting her long, brown braids as they bumped down the dirt road. "Will we leave the top down, or should we put it up, so he doesn't think we're being boastful? Most people don't have a convertible automobile and we don't want them to feel bad. Isn't that right?" She turned her large, brown eyes to her stately father, Welcome, who beamed.

He often told her the story of how he came to be called 'Welcome.' His parents, being kindly and generous to all, wanted him to know how desperately loved and wanted he was. They often reminded him of how important it would be to live up to his moniker; being kind and 'welcome' to others his entire life.

"You're right, Pookie. We don't want our new help to feel uncomfortable about his unfortunate circumstances. We'll put the top up when we get to town. You must also remember that young girls who chatter on and on may also be considered prideful to someone who doesn't have much to say."

Pookie lowered her eyes. "Sorry, Daddy. I get so excited when we have new hired hands. They have such interesting stories from their lives on the road!"

She folded her thin, tanned arms over each other and sat silently for ten minutes. The rest of the ride into the center of the scenic, coastal town of Flanagan, Oregon. When she glimpsed a familiar sight, she forgot her sorrow and began bouncing in her seat. "There it is, Daddy! The movie theatre!"

Welcome laughed. "Pookie, my darling. You are always the brightest sunlight in every day. Any father should be so lucky to have a daughter like you." He began their usual game. "Which actress is on the marquee today, my girl?"

"Oh, Daddy!" Pookie squealed. "Tulip Sloan! She's the best actress in all of Hollywood! So beautiful and glamourous!"

"S'that so? Well, don't keep me wondering, which picture is it?"

"*Hasty Engagement*. It's her newest one! Oh, Daddy!"

Welcome laughed a hearty belly laugh, making his short body shake with barely suppressed mirth.

"Don't tease me. You know Mr. Acorn only shows Tulip Sloan movies when he's forced." They pulled up in front of the Flanagan Majestic, Welcome taking care to put the roof up on their cherry-apple-red Packard Darrin. He pulled five quarters from his pocket and held them in his palm.

"These two are for you." He pointed to the first two silver circles. "These are for Fred. And this one is for your sour candy. But only a few. I don't want you up all night with a sick stomach."

Pookie reached across the seat and kissed her

father's pale cheek. "Thank you, Daddy. You're the kindest, most wonderful, most perfect–"

"Mornin', Welcome."

A man wearing a white fedora and brown pants with suspenders, resembling every other man in Flanagan as far as Pookie was concerned, tipped his hat. "Mornin' Pookie. Looks like you're off to the picture show. Good to stretch a girl's imagination before she's grown and lookin' for a proper husband."

Welcome straightened his jacket. "Nice to see you, Rogers. What's brought you out on this glorious August day?"

Welcome's friend stepped aside, revealing a thin, blond-haired man with hollow cheeks and a long, pointed nose. His shirt was torn and dirty, and he smelled like he'd spent more than one night under the stars bedded down between farm animals.

"Welcome, this here's Raymond. Found him sleeping in my barn night before last. I can tell he's a decent sort of fella. Just down on his luck. I know you can always use the help on your farm. Raymond, please meet Welcome Naybor, a man of great in-te-gri-ty."

Raymond put grubby hands to his mouth, concealing a girlish giggle. "Never heard of a man with that sort of name."

Welcome got out of the car and buttoned the

jacket on his compact, rotund body. He straightened his round glasses and walked around to shake Raymond's hand, just like he was any important person in the town of Flanagan, Oregon. "The last name is Nah BOR. Welcome Nah BOR. Pleased to meet you, Raymond. What did you say your last name was? We can always use the help at our estate."

"Raymond Dockley." He put his hand in Welcome's while keeping a healthy distance. "Don't want to get your fancy suit dirty, sir. Come out here ten years ago from Oklahoma. Worked on the ships for a time, hauling things to Canada." He scratched his dirty head with his free hand. "The pay was good, but my feet need dry land for a while. Now that my belly's been empty a bit, I need to work."

"Have you done farm labor?"

Pookie opened her door and stood beside her father, her eyes almost able to peer over the top of his head. "I'm Pookie Naybor. It's not my real name, but my Daddy says it's better than the one my mother gave me. She left me on the doorstep."

"This isn't an appropriate topic of conversation now, Pookie." Welcome shook his head. "You can conversate with Raymond on our way home. Run along and find your friend now."

Pookie kissed her father on the cheek. "Okay, Daddy. We shall discuss all glorious things on the way home. Nice to meet you, Raymond!"

"And you too, Miss!" he called after her, as she skipped down the street.

When she reached the ornate, gold swirls that outlined the entrance to the Flanagan Majestic, she stared at its magnificent shape, imagining herself as a famous actress pausing to wave at adoring fans as she walked through the doors to her premier.

"Thought you'd never come." Her dark-haired pal slugged her in the arm, his usual greeting. He squinted, the late-morning sun bouncing off the deep, red birthmark covering one side of his face. "What took you so long?" He held his hand out expectantly.

Pookie reached into the pocket of her blue jean overalls and pulled out two shiny quarters. "Another farm hand. Daddy liked him well enough. He'll be coming home with us today. I think he's rather dreamy. Looks a little like Johnson Hobarth in *Wind Over My Shoulder*."

"You think every hired hand is dreamy." Freddie shivered. "Gives me the dern willies."

They settled into their plush, red-velvet seats with one box of Tart Chewies and one box of popcorn. "You dumping today?" Pookie asked, offering her box of sour candy to her friend.

"Sure." Freddie took the box from her hand and dumped it into their popcorn, shaking gently to mix their favorite concoction.

"Why do you think your daddy likes those bums? Is it cause he don't want them to make fun of his name? 'Cause everybody does, you know."

Pookie turned to face her friend. "Freddie Browler, no one makes fun of my daddy. He's the most charitable man in the entire county. He gives work to people who need it. He even shares our crops with those who need them. In the trunk, we brought four bushels of vegetables to town today."

"Welcome Naybor chops up his workers when he's tired of 'em. That's what my buddy says and he don't lie."

Pookie sighed. "Nah BOR. And nobody's ever been chopped up. Don't be thick. Be quiet now, the movie is about to start and I won't miss a Tulip Sloan production to listen to your silly babbling."

"Why don't you go to school with the rest of us? You're smart enough for a girl."

Pookie sighed loud. The man in the seat beside her tapped them both on the shoulder and put his fingers to his lips.

"I told you. Daddy says I'm much too bright for the local school," Pookie whispered. "He'd miss me terribly if I attended boarding school. It's better for him to teach me; he and Miss Dandridge. Besides, I'm so far beyond everyone my age, I'd be bored. Now hush."

The newsreel began. Stories of happy living after

the war and new industry growing every day played on the screen, but all Pookie could think about was Tulip Sloan. Her silky, blonde hair curving gently around her face and her large, weepy eyes. A velvety voice using words like "daahling" and "duhuty." Just like how she imagined her mother would speak.

At the end of *Hasty Engagement*, Tulip, the heroine, saved herself from peril as per usual. At the end of each movie, she turned to movie goers and told them to hug and kiss the ones they loved dearly, because the world was not always roses and sunshine.

The lights came up and everyone in the theatre stood and cheered. Pookie looked over at Freddie, who stubbornly sat in his seat. She kicked him, but he shook his head firmly, staying seated.

"Get up!" she hissed. "People will think you don't understand theatre."

"Well, maybe I don't much. How is it Miss Sloan is always outsmarting the men? Everybody knows a woman ain't near as smart as a man. At least once the man should get the better of her."

Pookie sighed and yanked on his arm, hard. "You're backwards, Freddie. In just about every way. Girls can do anything boys can do. Let's get outta here before we get in trouble."

Reluctantly, he stood and followed her outside. "Your daddy give you enough for a Grommy's

Grape Soda today? I'm parched."

Pookie, while staring directly at Freddie, bumped squarely into a man dressed too formal for a Saturday afternoon at the picture show. When she looked up at his face, she noticed he had a large scar over one eye. "Sorry, Mister. I wasn't paying attention." She tried to move around him, but he anticipated her move and stayed in front of her.

"You Welcome's girl?" he yelled more than asked.

Pookie nodded, too afraid to speak. She looked for a way to move around him, but there was none. She nodded toward Freddie, who took that as a sign to run instead of coming to her aid.

"Are you looking for work, Mister?" She gulped, mustering all of the Tulip Sloan heroism she could. "My Daddy can give you a job. He's always hiring the less–"

The man grasped hold of her arm. "Your life is in danger, little miss. Best to keep your eyes open and know when to run."

Luckily, Pookie's arms were pliable enough to wriggle free from his grip. She ran, but her curiosity got the better of her. She stopped halfway down the block. He wasn't following her. Instead, he stood in place, his wide-brimmed hat tipped back exposing his scar. His gaze never wavered. Was he sad? Or was that anger? He was well-dressed, like Daddy. He held no resemblance to the men they'd hired to work the farm – no hollow eyes or clenched mouth.

Something compelled her to wave at him. Maybe he was just a lonely man who needed a friend. "I'll be fine, Mister!" she called.

He raised his hand slowly to the brim of his hat, tipping it in response before disappearing behind the theatre.

CHAPTER TWO

Lanie
Piney Falls

"PIPER'S ON THE phone. She's wondering if you're coming in today?"

Cosmo is sprawled across our new Fancypants Foam Mattress wearing a lumberjack shirt and boxers, a sight that would have made me melt last year. Those boxers look strikingly similar to the pair he wore yesterday, and I know the shirt hasn't seen the washing machine since last month. He rolls over onto his stomach and stares out my bedroom window.

"Maybe. It's been a few days."

"Six. If I was counting, which I'm not." I push his feet to the side and sit down beside him, touching his muscular back lightly. "I'll tell her you're coming in today. After a good shower and change of clothes."

"I can hear you, Lanie!" a disembodied voice calls from the receiver.

I put the phone to my ear and roll my eyes. "I'm sorry. He's coming in today. He'll help you with the lunch menu and–"

"You know I'm here to help him, not to run the place by myself. I don't mind baking and serving customers, but it is called Cosmic Cakes and Antiquery for a reason."

Piper Moonlight, Cosmo's chief baker, current manager, and one of my favorite twenty-somethings in the world, has stepped up to fill a rather large void. Ever since Cosmo's sister, Cedar, left for her new job as marketing coordinator at Sleepy Sounds corporate headquarters in San Diego, Cosmo hasn't been himself. Though he's a rugged, self-made businessman who survived twenty years in prison – and before that, life in a cult – losing his sister's constant companionship has brought him to his knees. Were it not for Piper showing up and running things daily, his business would have closed months ago.

"We'll be there by ten. I promise this will happen today."

I put the phone down and stare at my fiancé; the muscular, blue-eyed, silver-haired hunk of my dreams. I expected him to struggle when the other half of his soul moved on, but it's dragged on for so many months I'm doubting he can pull himself out of the doldrums.

"I'll pick out some clothes while you shower. I've got to check on the progress of the hotel, so I can drop you off."

His body wiggles, just slightly.

"I'll call November if I need to. You know how strong she is. She'll put you over her shoulder and throw you in the back seat. That's not an experience you want to enjoy twice."

Two weeks ago, my chromatically-dressed, quirky, best friend and neighbor, November Bean, came tromping through the house, picked up Cosmo and put him in her car. She kidnapped him for an hour, taking him to the beach and forcing him to listen to her Mantra for Meandering Souls. She even spent time in preparation scouring her vast music collection beforehand, choosing just the right steel drum sound to accompany her well-rehearsed twerks and spasms. When they returned, his mood was no different. The fact that he wasn't the slightest bit irritated by her shenanigans worried me the most.

Cosmo sighs and slides off the bed, disappearing into the shower. We used to laugh about adults who pouted like teens. Now he could be their eye-rolling spokesman.

My phone rings again and the name *Sassy Lasses* displays on the caller ID.

"Is this Lanie Anders?"

"Yes...if you're calling about our luxury resort

and spa, things are moving slower–"

"I'm Marveline Pherson, part-owner of Sassy Lasses Winery. Last month we discussed featuring our wines at the new resort." Her voice is smooth and soothing, just like a public radio gardening program.

"Of course! Marveline! Our timeline has changed – you know: a construction set-back here, or a zoning issue there – but I'm sure they are still interested."

"That's not really why I'm calling though. I did some research on you, Miss Anders. I'm told you're a top-notch detective and engaged to be married soon. Both of those things interest me."

"I wouldn't call myself a detective. I solved a few–"

"Miss Anders, I need someone to look into the history of our winery. Our neighbors were happy when this property was vacant. They believe it is cursed; some nonsense having to do with the previous owner."

"I'm very busy right now. As you know, I'm the marketing coordinator for the Inn and Spa at Fallen Branch Resort and trying to plan my wedding. There are always too many irons in the fire it seems." I pause after delivering the speech I usually give when I'm asked for the thirtieth time to head a new social group. "However I have a hard time turning down a good mystery." I struggle to hide my glee. Solving local whodunits excites me more than I'd ever admit, even if lifting a curse is more November's specialty. "I'd be happy to look into that for you." I glance in the bathroom, where Cosmo has achieved his first shower in days and is staring blankly in the mirror. "Can I ask how my fiancé factors into this equation?"

"Ever since my sister and I took over this property, we've struggled. The neighbors made it abundantly clear they don't want us around and are spreading ridiculous rumors trying to shut us down. They sabotage every event – well, we've only had three. But no one wants to come to place with negative buzz. I'd love for you to consider our property for your wedding. We would give you a big discount for helping us."

Cosmo has been resistant to my attempts to plan our wedding; not so much resistant as non-compliant. He's had no reaction to anything I've suggested, so reluctantly, I just gave up.

"The winery is located thirty miles inland from Piney Falls, on a large estate known for its beautiful views and bountiful harvest. We include all the amenities of a bigger resort. I'm sure if you'd visit, you and your fiancé would find it to your liking."

I sigh. I knew there would be a catch. "That's kind of a drive for our friends. I was thinking we would celebrate our wedding at the resort when it's finished."

"Oh." Her voice lowers two octaves. "Well...it was just an idea. We thought it would be a great way to show off our location and get people enthusiastic about our wines. We've just had such bad luck."

The slow process of getting the resort going, and Cosmo's mood, have got me in a bit of a slump, too. Maybe a change of scenery is what we both need. "You know what? I am interested. My fiancé and I will make a trip out there tomorrow to check things out."

"Oh, thank you, Miss Anders! You're wonderful! We will make sure you enjoy every minute of your experience!"

As I hang up, I realize getting Cosmo to agree to a trip out of town may be harder than I imagined. When I turn around, he's standing in clean clothes with the car keys in his hand. "Are we leaving or are you just going to stand there?" He winks, the old Cosmo charm sneaking back in.

"I...I don't know if you overheard, but I've made plans for us tomorrow," I say, flustered by this sudden change of heart. "We're going to tour the Sassy Lasses Winery as a possible wedding venue." I look at him hopefully, wishing there was a way to ensure his full functionality 24 hours from now.

"What I heard was your cheerful voice. That tells

me you've found another mystery that needs the Lanie Anders Hill touch."

I hug him and rub my face back and forth on his clean-smelling chest. "Soon-to-be Hill. But that will only happen if you go with me tomorrow and get things started."

"Your wish," he kisses the top of my head, "is my command. Let's get to my bakery and make sure the kid hasn't burned it down."

"Your bakery has been in capable hands, Cos. Please make sure you tell her that."

Driving down the hill from where my rental house sits and into the oceanfront community of Piney Falls, Oregon, I consider what to say next. "Have you given any more thought to the plans for our new home? I liked the latest revisions with the two-level patio."

Cosmo rubs his chin. "We've got plenty of time to figure that out. Can we wait until Cedar comes for her visit over Christmas? Let her look those over and give us her input?" As much as I love his sister, she has no business planning our dream home. He promised me we would move in together and start our lives as a twosome. Instead, day after day, he contributes less to our lives together and his business.

From four hours to three, his interest in the bakery slipped away until he eventually stopped going in altogether. After months of worry, I decided he needed to be under my watchful eye each and every day. November and I moved all of his things into my place and he followed silently behind us, like a puppy. There was no further talk of building our dream home together, on the property donated by other former members of the cult Cosmo grew up in.

I'd like to tell him that Cedar has begun a new life; a well-deserved chance to spread her wings. I want him to realize that we've got to solider on in our own way. Instead, I swallow my feelings to make sure he doesn't change his mind about meeting with Piper. "In a few months, then." We pull into a parking space in front of Cosmic Cakes and Antiquery to find a line of people snaking down the block, waiting to get in.

Cosmo jumps out of the car and runs up to the person closest to the door. "What's going on? Is she having trouble with the cash register?"

The elderly gentlemen shakes his head. "Today is the first day of Pied Piper's Pies. She's randomly picking one person who buys one of her mini pies and posts a picture on social media. That lucky schmuck wins a trip to Hawaii!"

Cosmo's mouth drops open.

"Let us through, please!" I demand, pushing Cosmo through the door and into the tiny, crowded space. When we get to the counter, I see two unfamiliar faces working frantically beside Piper, boxing up miniature berry pies.

A round-faced young woman with dark hair pulled back in a ponytail looks up and smiles when she recognizes me. "Hi Lanie! We could sure use some help! Want to throw on an apron?"

I point behind me to Cosmo, who has a hurricane-sized storm brewing on his face.

"What in the blessed biscuit have you done to my bakery?" He explodes. The busy space becomes quiet. Everyone in town is familiar with Cosmo's volatile temper, though most know he's more bluster than anything.

Piper's face turns bright red, and her violet eyes fill with tears. "I'm running a special to test out a new product. I called you and left messages about it last week, but you never responded."

"Let's take this outside, shall we?" As I firmly pull on Cosmo's arm, Piper runs to the back door and out into the alley.

When we reach her, she is sobbing. "I'm so sorry. I really am. I just wanted to increase business and, well, I didn't realize it would get so out of hand."

I bring her to my chest and gently stroke her hair. Our connection has been undeniable since the first day we met. "It's okay, hon. We'll work it out."

"No! It's not okay!" Cosmo puts his hands in his pockets and paces back and forth in front of us. "I left you in charge to keep things exactly as they were!

Not start a riot! Where would you even come up with the money to send someone on a big vacation?"

Piper wipes her eyes with the back of her hand. "My mom had a life insurance policy. A big one. It feels wrong to use her dirty money for myself. I want to make people happy."

Piper's mother, Olivene Moonlight left a trail of destruction before she met an ugly demise on the Fallen Branch property. We're all glad to have that behind us now.

"I think that's admirable, don't you, Cos?"

He shrugs. "Yeah, I guess."

"This is a good time for the two of you to sit down and discuss what's going on with the bakery. It's a real marketing win for her to have created this kind of buzz. You should be happy. Left in weaker hands, your bakery could have gone under while you were sitting at home, feeling sorry for yourself."

I wait for his thunderous explosion, but there isn't one. He stares at the ground quietly.

"We should go in. There are tons of customers and those two high school girls I hired seem pretty overwhelmed." Piper opens the door and stands expectantly. "You guys coming?"

"In a minute, hon. I need to talk to Cosmo."

When she closes the door, Cosmo turns to me and pulls his hands out of his pockets. "I suppose you're gonna tell me I had this coming."

I fold my arms across my chest, staring at him angrily. "You need to snap out of this. You have a business to run, we have a wedding to plan, life goes on. I love you, Cosmo Hill, for better or for worse. Let's get to the better part now, okay?"

Chapter Three

Pookie
1946

Pookie continued walking until she reached her father's car, looking around at Saturday shoppers walking up and down Flanagan Avenue. Were they staring at her? Did they know she was in trouble, too? No one seemed concerned. It was silly to think anyone would concern themselves with a twelve-year-old girl, especially one who didn't attend public school or have more than one friend in the entire world.

Welcome, along with Raymond trailing behind him, laughed boisterously as he came out of the bakery with his arms full of different varieties of bread. His face broke into a wide grin when he saw her standing there. He placed the bread in the back seat. "Anything exciting from your afternoon, Pookie?" He patted her head and then stood with his hands on his hips, waiting for her reply.

She looked at her father's round face. His brown

eyes danced behind his wire spectacles. His bushy mustache resembled the ones that men sported in those Hollywood magazines she'd read to learn the name of Tulip Sloan's latest paramour. She always thought Welcome Naybor was the most handsome man she'd ever seen. "Nothing out of the ordinary." She looked away quickly. "It's hot, Daddy." Pookie ran up and opened the door. "We'll use the air conditioning, right?"

Raymond scratched the back of his neck. "I've heard of a such a thing, but never seen it for myself. Like a refrigerator? Just what kind of newfangled contraption is this?"

"1941 Packard Darrin. The finest automobile of the modern world," Naybor announced proudly. "The top rolls down, too. My daughter deserved to experience something nice." He tugged playfully on Pookie's braids. "How was the movie? Did everything come out okay with Miss Sloan?"

"Oh, Daddy." She smiled. "You know they did. Shall we get in, Mister...?" Pookie opened the back door and motioned for him to enter.

"It's Dockley, ma'am." He gently placed his worn suitcase on the floor. "I s'pect you can call me Ray, Dock, or whatever suits you."

After they got in, Pookie turned a knob, forcing cool air out of the vents. As they reached the city limits, the air reached the back seat. "Oh my, but that's nice. Never felt so comfortable in a vehicle before," he commented.

"You shall work hard in our fields, so you deserve this treat. Our farm grows produce from February to October each year. We do blueberries, potatoes, beets, broccoli, cabbage, beans, carrots, cauliflower, celery, cucumber, eggplant, rhubarb, spinach, and in the fall, pumpkins and squash of all sizes."

"That's enough now, Pookie," Welcome admonished. "He hasn't agreed to our terms yet. All gentlemen settle their deals with a firm handshake and a good cup of tea."

Pookie sat on her knees and looked into the backseat. "Isn't it dreamy back there?"

Raymond stroked the smooth, camel-colored seat and nodded.

"Daddy makes a special grown-up tea. He'll serve it to you with some corncakes and blackberry preserves. The best you've ever had, I'd imagine."

"I'd imagine you're right." Raymond stared out the window at the endless, tall, pine trees dotting the side of the highway.

"What's it like in Oklahoma? Does it look different?"

Welcome laughed a jolly, belly laugh, belying his diminutive stature. "Don't mind my daughter. She got an inquisitive mind. If you don't want to answer, feel free to rest your weary bones for the duration of our ride."

"Things is dry as a bone. Went through quite a time of drought and still haven't quite recovered. That's at least according to my ma."

"Oh? Do you keep in touch with your family then? Where's your wife?" Pookie rested her chin on the seat, staring into his wide, empty face.

"Every week I send them a letter. They get concerned if I don't. They like to know how things are out here, close to the ocean. They never seen an ocean in their lives, and the lake where we used to go fishing dried up before I left. It's a hard life everywhere, but especially for my ma and son. The boy's ma died in childbirth so we've lived with mine for his full eight years. She does a fine job raising him."

Welcome cleared his throat. "We can talk about care packages to send when you're better settled. I've done that for several of my employees."

"Bless you, sir. That's terribly kind."

"My daddy is the kindest–"

"Now, Pookie, let's not bore our new guest. We're almost home and I expect Mr. Dockley is tired of conversation. Let's give him a few minutes of peace."

"Aw, heck. I don't mind. Miss Pookie can join us for tea if she wants. Seems a girl should get some practice before she becomes a proper adult." He winked at Pookie, who was still on her knees, staring at him. She winked back.

"I'm afraid I must insist our meeting is for gentlemen only."

"Daddy's afraid I'll sneak some of his special tea," Pookie giggled. "Then I'll become Tulip Sloan and start tawking like this, dahling."

Raymond chuckled softly. "I ain't much for tea, but I'd join you for the company, sir."

Welcome reached over and tickled Pookie. "You can see the Hollywood dialect used by Tulip Sloan has already infected my daughter. We don't want to give her any encouragement."

"I heard of her. My ma seen one of her movies on her birthday. Something about an orphan on the street."

"*My Orphan Fannie*! Tulip wrote that one herself. I read it in a magazine. I go to her movies every Saturday. Someday, I will meet her. When I'm an adult. I have lots of plans for myself, though I haven't quite figured out how they're all going to work just yet. Daddy says brilliant plans start as seeds and it takes time for them to reach their full height."

Pookie watched the faces as they drove down the last block of Flanagan Avenue. The man she'd seen in the theatre stood on the corner, waiting to cross. She gasped as the car slowed. He walked halfway across and paused directly in front of them, tipping his hat before moving on.

Welcome looked over when she made such a dramatic sound. "You look as white as a ghost, daughter! Did you have too many of your sour candies?"

"Something like that," she mumbled.

CHAPTER FOUR

Lanie
Piney Falls

"COSMO HILL, YOU'RE getting doughy. Yes, I said it. Doughy. If your behind gets any larger, removing it from this bed will take two sessions." She presses firmly on the middle of his back, checking for abnormalities or foreign substances.

November Bean, my incredibly fit neighbor, straddles Cosmo's body. He has sunken back into his shell, just as I'd feared. He's lying on his side with a pillow pulled up around his ears as she bounces on top of him. If it were anyone else, the sight of a woman perching atop my boyfriend in that precarious position might offend me. But it is November, whose actions make sense only to her. It is just another day in her strange world, and we are lucky to share it.

"I'm afraid you will hurt him, Vem. Just get off for now."

She leans down and sniffs his neck and shrugs before artfully dismounting onto the floor with a sturdy one-foot landing.

"What's with the sniffing? Or shouldn't I ask?"

November puts her hands on her tiny, firm hips. "I've just started teaching a class called Smell Tells. If you've got a sensitive schnoz, you can pick up many things about a person just by getting a good whiff of their being. Your Cosmo stinks of despair."

I take her arm and move her with me into the hallway. I don't know if he's listening, and I don't want to take the chance that we'll send him further into his shell. "I think that's more a matter of clothing he refuses to let me wash, but whatever new things you're learning, I'll always support you."

November looks at me with skepticism. "Could also be a trance. I've got a meditation to pull people out of trances, but I'll need some turtle dung and peppermint oil. It might take a day or so."

"No," I shake my head. "That's thoughtful, but I doubt turtle dung will put him in the mood to visit the Sassy Lasses Winery with me. I scheduled a trip out there today for the two of us to do some investigative work, but he doesn't seem to be ready. His mood is up and down like a Ferris wheel, and seeing his business thriving without him has put him back in a funk. Now I don't know what to–"

"Of course I'll go! I always keep a pre-packed

lunch on hand and I've got two hours of my favorite bird squawk meditation sounds downloaded. Your car or mine?"

"Well, it was kind of a special day I'd planned for Cosmo and me…" I glance through the doorway at the immobile lump on my bed. "They asked for my help and I'm going to give it to them. So, yes, we should go."

"Perfect! I'll go gather my effects and meet you back at your car in fifteen minutes." She pivots and marches out of my house, her wiry hair bouncing as she moves.

"Cos," I say softly, "Piper needs you today. You promised. I need you, too." I lean down close to his ear and kiss him gently. "At least check in with her."

He doesn't move. This kind of heartbreaking behavior has become the norm, but that doesn't make it any easier. Lately, I've been stuffing my feelings deep inside, telling myself I can feel them later when I don't have to be the strong one in the relationship. Vem is already in the car when I make my way down to the driveway. She is bouncing up and down to something I can only imagine is playing only in her head.

"You really should contact Cedar. She could bring him right out of this funk," Vem insists after we've listened to forty-six of the most irritating bird sounds I've ever heard as she hums and whistles along.

"No, I don't want her to know just how bad he is." I look at Vem with anticipation, hoping she's ready to put on something with a melody. She doesn't seem to notice. "His sister would quit her job and come back in a heartbeat. This is her opportunity to do what she wants with her life and Cosmo wouldn't want to ruin that for her. When she calls, he tells her he's been extra tired. Sometimes he just gives up and hands the phone to me."

We reach a four-way stop in the middle of nowhere. There is a sign with large, red letters proclaiming, *Naybor Way, Home of the Sassy Lasses* to guide us. As we progress, there are ornate lights on either side of the oiled road, along with billboards of two women wearing brightly-colored earrings and holding glasses of wine up to their mouths. Each billboard features a different type of wine sold at the Sassy Lasses Winery. *Try a glass of Rebel Riesling today and release the rebel in you!*

"Ugh. They need someone to help with their advertising, not research their history."

"You certainly don't have time for both, Lanie." Vem closes her eyes, leans her head back and begins to imitate one of loudest bird squawks. Suddenly, she jerks her head upright and her eyes pop open. "Your enviably delicate hands are full. How are things coming at the Fallen Branch motel? Will it be ready in time for your wedding?"

"The Inn and Spa at Fallen Branch Resort," I correct, "is way behind schedule. They've run into problems with the contractor and it won't be ready for at least another year. That's why we're looking at the Sassy Lasses Winery. They offered to host our wedding and reception."

Vem turns to me and gasps. "You're thinking you'll have your wedding outside of Piney Falls? In the middle of nowhere? People won't come to a place known to be cursed. They won't stand for it."

"You've heard about this place before?"

"Everyone has. There are more stories swirling around about Naybor Manor than the town of Piney Falls. And you know what kind of stories swirl around Piney Falls. No amount of cleansing can rid our community of our past."

We pull into a long drive with uniformly-trimmed fruit trees lining either side, and continue up to the large, white house with a wrap-around porch. It looks like it would be more fitting on a southern plantation than in the Pacific Northwest.

Two familiar women, the faces from the bill-board, are smiling and waving from the porch. Both women sport short, grey hair; one is messy and curly, while the other is neatly styled with a brown barrette on one side. The shorter of the two, wearing jeans and a ripped t-shirt skips off the porch and comes down to greet us.

"She seems very–"

Vem jumps out of the car before I can finish, slinging the huge backpack she's taken to carrying over one shoulder. She takes the woman's hand and shaking it ferociously. It's not often there is someone we meet who shares Vem's energy level. I get out of the car and stand awkwardly, waiting for them to finish this contest in intensity.

"Mandy Pherson. You spoke with my sister on the phone. I'm so gosh-darned happy to see you." Her voice is one that sounds perpetually hoarse but excited. She has a dimple in the middle of her chin and sparkling blue eyes.

"I can see how you might confuse us. My best friend Lanie and I share similar energy." Vem shakes her hand vigorously. "November Bean, number one confidant, maid-of-honor, and happy wine-taster."

I go over and offer my hand. "I'm Lanie Anders. Thanks for hosting us!"

The taller, more serious-looking woman approaches us calmly. Her flowing yellow caftan lifts slightly in the gentle breeze. "Marveline Pherson. My sister and I are looking forward to your help with our unfortunate circumstances." Unlike her sister, she is wearing full makeup. She has an oval face accentuated by small, dark eyes, and a splash of deep, berry-colored lipstick. She shares the family dimple in the middle of her chin.

"We've got some wine samples waiting for you to enjoy while we visit." Marveline gestures towards the imposing porch. "After you." There is a small, round table covered in a blue-and-white checkered cloth that has been prepared for our arrival. On it is a wicker basket containing crackers, a plate with a variety of cheeses, and several wine glasses. Two buckets filled with ice and bottles of wine sit adjacent to the table.

"I'll have to insist upon red before white. I possess a very particular palette," Vem announces.

Mandy looks at her sister who rolls her eyes and then shrugs.

"We'll begin with Mandeline Merlot, named after the two of us. The grapes were developed especially for this region, and we're the first winery to use them." Mandy pours a small amount in each glass. November sticks her entire nose – and with it, some of her cheeks – into the glass and whiffs until her glasses are fogged over.

"You'll want to pace yourself," Mandy warns.

I take a small sip and raise my eyebrows with surprise. "Very nice."

Vem removes her face, which is sealed inside the glass, with a smacking sound. "November Bean can hold her liquor like no other," she retorts, downing the sample in one gulp and shoving it to the other side of the table expectantly.

Marveline picks up a different bottle and pours a generous amount in Vem's glass. "Sassy Saucy Syrah."

"Please tell me about your winery. What brought you here?" I ask.

"We moved here from Denver about four years ago," Marveline answers. "We had a little inheritance money and always wanted to start our own winery. This place has so much history to be learned. My sister here has always been a history buff."

Mandy chuckles nervously. "Not just any history. I studied my own family history extensively. We have some prestigious relatives and it makes me proud to carry on their–"

"These ladies aren't interested in a Pherson family history lesson." Marveline glares at her sister before turning to us. "We hired the caretakers to stay on and make sure things run smoothly. Unfortunately, our time here has been anything but." Marveline sighs. "The neighbors didn't seem to mind us until we made it known we would open our property to guests. Then they threw a fit. The legends of the property, complete nonsense by the way, scare them to the point they want to find a way to kick us off."

Mandy fidgets with her glass. "They have threatened us more than once. People have thrown bricks through our windows and pulled our vines out of the ground. We've even heard gunshots. It got so bad we had to hire security."

November puckers up her face so tightly I wonder if she has an extra hinge in her jaw. "That's so sour my taste buds may be inside out." She gulps down the last swallow and makes a similar face. "Can I have more?"

"Let's go on to the next wine." I put my arm on hers, hoping she'll get the hint.

"Oh, that's my cue. Sorry." Mandy jumps up and pulls a bottle from the ice, pouring the next round. "Sumptuously Sassy Chardonnay. It has a little peach kick at the end."

"Who did you buy the property from? Did they tell you any of the history?"

"It had been sitting empty for decades," Marveline continues. "After Welcome Naybor, a local philanthropist, died upstairs in 1947. There are lots of rumors as to what happened and why, but no one really knows for sure. He had all kinds of people working for him, but somehow they didn't know he was dead for quite some time."

"And those are what's scaring everyone away? Seems silly." Vem begins her sniffing ritual again, sticking her face into the glass and sniffing hard. "I smell dirty socks, not peaches."

Mandy giggles, glancing at her sister.

Marveline responds with a stern look and a shake

of her head. "There were all sorts of rumors. Many of his employees died in mysterious ways. There were no records kept of those employed here, so no one can verify one way or another."

"I might have to speak to the neighbors just to see what stories they can tell me. Did you find anything on the property when you moved in?"

Marveline nods. "Go get it for her. And don't slam the–"

Mandy jumps up and runs inside, slamming the screen door as she goes.

"You know we just had the hinges fixed!" Marveline rolls her eyes. "There were so many repairs needed, I didn't think we'd ever finish."

November takes Mandy's wine and pours it into her own glass as I purposely look away.

"The legend is that whoever owns this property is cursed. As long as they live here quietly and don't draw attention to themselves, they'll be fine. But as soon as they start to make a fuss, attract attention, or invite visitors, the deaths will start again. It wasn't just Naybor who died. There were a multitude of employees who worked for him. He found down-on-their-luck men who had come to town and invited them to work his farm. Most of them were never seen or heard from again."

Mandy returns, letting the door bang shut again. "Sorry." She sets a hardcover book on the table, its blue cover stained by liquid and faded by the passage of time.

"What's this?" November asks, slamming the cover open. On the inside there is a handwritten title page, *Pookie A. Naybor, Flanagan Oregon 1946.* "Hmmm, written before Flanagan changed its name to Piney Falls. You know our pal Lanie here solved that mystery."

"Careful! That's delicate!" Marveline slides the old book away from November and in front of me. "We found this in one of the upstairs bedrooms on our first walk through. It appears to be a diary. I don't know if these are someone's vivid imaginings or actual events that took place here. It is a place to start your investigation."

I stare at the cover, not wanting to touch it in front of Marveline for fear of being reprimanded. "I'll take this home with me and study it carefully."

"Shall we begin our tour?" Mandy asks, shifting her weight from one foot to the other.

Marveline looks at me skeptically. "You'll bring the book back soon? I don't want it out of my possession for long."

I nod. "I'm a speed reader." Speed reading is a skill I developed as a stab at being an individual; something to set me apart from the 1940s movie actress, Tulip Sloan, whom I deeply resemble and have always been compared to. "I can get through it in less than an hour, but I'd like a few days to digest it."

"We only tried three wines!" November complains.

"I'll pour you some Rebel Riesling to sip while we walk." Mandy offers.

"My fiancé loves a superb wine." At least the normal Cosmo does. "Can I get a bottle of Mandeline Merlot to go?"

"We found a pair of brothers in California who grew those grapes in their vineyard. Much like the two of us, they came from a family with a history of successful businessmen. It's important to continue the family legacy of–"

A series of gunshots breaks the serenity of the rolling, green hills.

"Down on the ground!" Mandy commands.

I drop obediently to my knees, hiding under the table as I try and shield my face.

Chapter Five

Pookie
November 18, 1946

Dearest Ophelia,

You have been so named because Tulip Sloan played a character named Ophelia in her film "What We Lost." After losing her solider husband in World War I, Ophelia Montrose came to the small town of Newman to help care for her mother. While working as a maid for the society people who were her friends before the war, she befriends the other maid. The brave women have both lost husbands and bond over their losses. As always, "Ophelia" triumphs over tragedy.

Someday, I'm going to meet Tulip Sloan in person. I shall tell her how much I admire her and we'll chat about serious matters, like what colors are in fashion and whether I should go to college. As Daddy says, I must make a plan for this to come about. I think I may become an actress.

In NEWS OF THE DAY, Raymond Dockley has developed large muscles. Farm work is difficult and, over the years, I've witnessed many a hired man change his physique. Raymond's face has filled out along with his chest. He could pass for Dag Standard, the hero who saved Tulip Sloan in Storms Over Mississippi. Even though his body has become hardened and fierce, he has a gentle way about him and when he looks at me with those soulful eyes, I feel like there is much more he'd like to tell me but fears I'm too young to understand. He doesn't yet know of my maturity. Daddy says there isn't a twelve-year-old who can match my intellect, in part due to the tenacity of my tutor, Miss Dandridge, but also because I soak up knowledge like a sponge.

Pumpkin season is done and we've still got a few more potatoes in the field to harvest. I would like to follow Raymond to the farthest field from the house, but Daddy forbids it. "Only for grown-ups, Pookie," he says. One day I'll sneak over when Daddy is otherwise occupied and view its magnificence. Maybe with Raymond by my side.

Yours in Delicious Deviousness,
Pookie A. Naybor

"Tell me stories about what it's like to drift around," Pookie probed, using the weight of her petite body to swing the white gate back and forth.

"Interestin', I suppose. You sees all sorts. Don't make no attempt to get to know them, so it's like bein' a bird on a fence. Watching what happens before you fly off." Raymond was digging up the flower beds lining the walkway to the front door of Naybor Manor. He stood up and scratched the top of his head. "Never seen such a fine place as this before, though. Such a waste of colorful flora."

Pookie giggled. "I like how you talk. Like a simple man, and then you throw in big words. As for the flowers, Daddy likes to change the theme every three years. Our minds need that stimulation. Too much of the same thing makes a person dull."

Raymond nodded as he put a handful of brightly-colored petunias on top of a pile.

"The Wormly family built this house in 1904. They made their fortune in shipping and wanted a mansion to look like their plantation home in Georgia. By the time it was finished, they lost everything they owned in the crash of '29. The place sat empty and neglected until Daddy decided to start his own shipping business in 1933. At least that's Daddy's version." Pookie sighed. "My friend, Freddie says that's not what happened at all. He says the Wormley family was cursed and they all died horrible deaths on the property. Much like the murky circumstances surrounding my birth, it's hard to know what's true."

Raymond scratched his scruffy chin. "Y'don't say."

Pookie watched him for a moment, hoping he would inquire further. "Have you been to Georgia, Raymond?"

"Can't say as I have. Been to Canada, up and down this coast, but never that far t'other side of the country."

"My Daddy used to live in the Midwest. There wasn't much money to be made in crops, so he and his brother moved west. His brother died a terribly tragic death shortly after their arrival." Pookie hopped off the fence and began helping Raymond pick up weeds and doomed flowers. She put some to her nose, trying to drink in the last few scents of summer.

"What happened to him, then? The brother?"

"Daddy says a refined young lady shouldn't trouble herself with those details." She clicked her tongue in disapproval. "Any time I ask Freddie about it, he tells me it's just another tale of Naybor Manor. Those are stories, you know. Everybody in town has a tale of–"

"How'd you get your name? I've heard that young girls have that name down South, but up here, they tend to be a Sally or June."

Pookie stood up straight, dropping the refuse on her scuffed, yard shoes. "My mother was a tortured soul with no other options. She didn't want to care for a child, but had heard of the kind nature of Welcome Naybor. While I was still just an infant, she brought me to this house one cold, fall evening. At the last minute, she decided she couldn't possibly face him and admit she was abandoning me, so she left me over there, beside that big white pillar." Pookie pointed to the front corner of Naybor Manor, where an old whiskey barrel of petunias sat, waiting for their makeover. "I would've frozen to death, had Daddy not been overseeing curtain repair and heard her."

"Oh? That is a sad tale. And she named you Pookie? Short for what?"

Pookie motioned for him to lean over so she could whisper in his ear. He stood back up straight and nodded.

"That's my given name, never to be spoken out loud. Daddy said he'd never use a name given me by a loathsome wretch who left me to perish. He called his younger sister Pookie growing up. They were the best of friends, so he gave me her name. When I grow into myself, I can change it to whatever I want."

Raymond smiled, bits of spinach from his meager

lunch still stuck in his teeth. "Now that's a fine way to live. All good families should give their young'uns that chance to name themselves."

They did the rest of their work in silence, working side by side until Naybor arrived from his trip to visit the next-door neighbor. He removed his white hat and rubbed his mostly bald head with the hand missing two fingers.

"Pookie, its quite charitable of you to help Raymond with his chores. It's nearly time for dinner though. You should go wash up now."

"Yes, Daddy. Can I help Raymond tomorrow?"

Raymond cleared his throat. "I asked your pa if I could have the day off tomorrow. Peter from down in the stables is going into town to buy supplies and I want to go with him and mail a letter."

Welcome frowned briefly and then smiled. "You've certainly earned a day of rest. It seems you'd be better suited to enjoy a day of restoration than spending it helping load heavy bags into the farm truck. I've offered to mail your letters too, Raymond."

"Thank you, sir. I've got my superstitions about mailing my own letters. Done it no matter how much snow I had to fight, rain in my boots or tired in my body. Shows my mother and son I care, even if I can't see them."

Welcome bowed. "As you wish, Raymond. And

now, Pookie, we'll retire for the evening."

The following Thursday, after finishing a rigorous exam on the history of Greece, Pookie put on her jean overalls and raincoat.

"You've taken a liking to this one, Pookie?" Welcome peeked his spectacles over the top of his newspaper.

"Yes, Daddy. He's interesting. I like hearing about people from other places."

"Mind you don't get in his way. He's cleaning equipment in Barn Three today." Welcome returned to his newspaper. "And Pookie, remember: these are drifters. They are meant to drift. Don't get too attached."

Pookie ran over and kissed her father on the cheek. "Thank you, Daddy. I'll remember. A man has to be free to do what his heart desires."

He chuckled heartily. "I remember that line distinctly from a Tulip Sloan movie."

"*Wasted Man*," Pookie called as she slammed the large front door.

She pulled her coat around tight as the cool, fall, sea air enveloped her. It was a half-mile to Barn Three, past Barn One and Two and left over a small hill. On the other side of Barn Three she could just barely glimpse the forbidden fields if she let herself.

"Pookie?" Raymond looked up, surprised to see her. "Don't you have your studies to tend to?"

"Finished for today." She found a rusty bucket, turned it upside down and sat down gently, taking care not to rest her feet in mud or her Daddy would make her spend the evening cleaning all of their shoes. "Your stories are more educational. I'm almost a young lady and I've seen none of the world."

Raymond smiled as he turned the tire of a tractor. He wiped the grease from his hands on an already-greasy rag he pulled out of his back pocket. "What stories can I tell you today then, Miss?"

"Tell me about the ocean. You said you were on a ship."

The smile that always graced his face when she was around left his blue eyes. "What would you want to know? It was a ship. Back and forth, here and there. I sailed to Canada and back more times than I want to remember."

"What kind of cargo did you carry? Were your shipmates kind? Was the captain cruel?"

"Oh, Pookie," Raymond chuckled, once again merry. "You always bring a smile to this sorry face. We carried special cargo. We wasn't to tell a soul what was there and we always loaded and unloaded under the cover of darkness." He wiped his hands again, placing a wrench on the ground beside him. "Now, as to shipmates, they was nice, mostly. Earnin' a good wage tends to make a man more of the pleasant sort. We kept to ourselves since there weren't much to argue over."

"And?" Pookie tapped her foot impatiently.

"Oh, the captain? Well, he had a temper. More'n likely due to the pressure put on him by the owner of the ship. Threw a man overboard for calling him a horse's backside. Forgive my bold words, Miss."

"I've heard worse from our help."

"You know our deal now, Miss Pookie. I tell you one story, then you tell me one."

Pookie put her elbows on her knees and rested her chin on her hands. "I suppose. But my stories aren't nearly as interesting as yours."

"Why d'you s'pose you go through so many workers on this farm? It's hard work but it's a fair wage."

Pookie stood and walked to the door, pulling it shut. "We're cursed. We don't tell our hired hands until we're sure they'll stay."

"What d'you mean, 'cursed'?"

"The Wormly family, remember? When they lost everything, they couldn't bear the thought of anyone else taking their land, their plantation-style house, or their dreams. They found a witch and put a curse on this place."

"Don't believe in witches, Miss Pookie. There's got to be a better story."

Pookie nodded vigorously. "This is true. I have proof."

CHAPTER SIX

The Wormley Curse
Courtesy of the Piney Falls Public Library Information Booth

THE WORMLY FAMILY purchased the land, more recently known as Naybor Farm and Naybor Manor in 1904. Captain Wormly was a ship captain for all of his career, making his money by forming his own company, Wormly Shipping, before his retirement in 1903. He brought his wife, Mamie, to the coast upon his disengagement from captaining a ship. Her ill health kept her confined mostly to their home.

Mamie could never have children but adopted several over the years, gracing them with the good name of Wormly and, thereby, removing any reminder of their lower station in life. By the time they built their home on the Oregon coast, all their adopted children had grown and gone. Mamie insisted, despite her age and infirmary, that they adopt one more child, a boy, to help around the farm. They received a sturdy boy of fourteen, named Filmont from the Mother Fyfe Orphanage in Seattle.

A homely boy with dark hair and indistinct features, the orphanage considered him difficult to place because of his stubborn nature. He left behind two siblings at the orphanage who were much more docile. No matter how much training he was given, he couldn't seem to learn the basics of refinement required of someone of Wormly stature. Too tired to instruct him further, Mamie insisted he spend all of his time out of her sight.

Filmont began to work under the instruction of his elderly father, overseeing the planting of strawberries, cabbages, beans and onions. His father promised that when he reached the age of sixteen they would allow him to leave like his older siblings and, depending on his abilities, start his own business or go to a good university.

The first year there was very little sun and continuous rain, even through the normally dry summer months. The strawberries produced few berries, and the onion bulbs rotted in the ground. Filmont thought himself a failure at farming, just as he had failed to keep his biological family together during the depression and after.

Mrs. Wormly assured Filmont it had nothing to do with his skills but privately, she confided to her husband that he must be poisoning their crops in order to get himself out from under their thumb and sent away. Mrs. Wormly was quite superstitious; she once had an older adopted child sent to a work house for displaying signs of possession.

Mr. Wormly was a no-nonsense man who knew how unpredictable weather affected what may or may not happen at sea. He found his wife's words foolish and decided they would plant different crops the following year. They were wealthy enough that one year's failure wouldn't affect their lives.

During the long winter, Filmont spent much of his time in his bedroom, refusing meals and barely speaking to his parents. They invited neighbors over to meet him, but even when he agreed to sit with people his own age, he still refused to speak.

Mrs. Wormly consulted with her astrologer, also a folk healer with many potions, who agreed to travel from Portland to meet the boy. In her notes she remarked, "The boy sat as a rag doll while his limbs were lifted and poked."

The astrologist said Filmont's malady was not enough moon in his cycle. She strongly suggested Mrs. Wormly make a broth consisting of a large yellow onion, seven cloves of minced garlic, salt, two tablespoons honey, one tablespoon of apple cider vinegar and eight ounces of milk. To this she was to add one-half teaspoon of a special powder. It was imperative he sit beside a window while consuming the concoction at least once per day.

When Filmont refused the soup, his mother was instructed to cut off all other nourishment, much to the consternation of his father. Eventually the boy became hungry enough to swallow the wild concoction while sitting in front of the picture window overlooking the empty fields.

As the winter rains raged on, Filmont's dark mood lifted. Besides consuming his daily soup ration, he came down to join his delighted parents for breakfast and dinner. He conversed with them on topics he found in the many books in his room. Growing up in an orphanage with few books, it was a feast of information. He eagerly told them about life in Italy, the greenery of the English Countryside and the wilds of Africa. Filmont also spun a tale of a glorious life with his siblings, one his parents were quite sure he never experienced.

When it came time to plant spring crops, Filmont was eager to join his father. This year in addition to strawberries, onions, and beans, they planted potatoes. The sun shone and enthusiastic green sprouts reached from the ground for the light.

Filmont worked from dawn till dusk, pulling weeds and humming to himself; they were tunes he said his first mother sang when they were cold and hungry.

Mrs. Wormly contacted her astrologer to report

her success. "Don't be fooled, he'll have another dark period before this ends. Continue feeding him the mixture and watch him carefully." Mrs. Wormly told her husband of this recent development and expressed her pride that she had cured their son of his illness. Mr. Wormly shook his head but dared not disagree with his wife.

As the summer progressed, the crops looked as if they would produce nicely. Mr. Wormly hired two extra men to help with harvest and transporting the produce to town for sale. Filmont worked happily by their sides, telling them about his books and his plans to visit these foreign lands before proceeding to a university.

The harvest was bountiful. Two weeks of back-breaking work while Mr. and Mrs. Wormly watched from the porch. At the end of first harvest, Mr. Wormly offered to take the men and his son to a creek he'd found on the far end of the property, where you could hear the roar of the ocean next to the babbling serenity of a brook he named Spoon-back Creek, because its gentle winding nature reminded him of a spoon. He thought the fishing to be exceptionally good, and he couldn't wait to teach his son.

Mrs. Wormly packed a picnic basket full of her husband's favorites, including fresh strawberries and peaches from a neighbor's orchard. It wouldn't work to put Filmont's soup in the basket, so instead, she sprinkled some of the astrologist's special powder on an apple wrapped in Filmont's clean handkerchief.

"Don't worry about me, boys, take your time!" she said, happily waving them off for the day. She valued her time alone and was pleased to be able to write her sister in Boston a long letter about the events that had transpired in the last year, and how grand things had ended for the little family. She told her sister that Filmont would soon be off on his own adventures and it would be time for them to look for another foundling to take in, maybe a girl this time.

The hours passed by and Mrs. Wormly began to worry about her family. Her husband was known to lose track of time while bird watching, but he wasn't terribly fond of small talk, and spending this much time with people he barely knew wasn't like him.

She wasn't one to venture out on her own, so instead she took the horse and wagon to the next farm to ask the men there to search. She stayed with the neighbor, drinking tea and eating leftover rabbit stew, while the search stretched on long into the night.

The next morning, she was informed, sadly, that the men were nowhere to be found.

Mamie, sensing something deeply wrong, sent for the sheriff and all the men in town they could find who wanted to make a shiny nickel for a day's work.

Eight hours later, there was still no trace of the men, their wagon, or their goods.

Months went by with no sign of the men. Mrs. Wormly sent for two more foundlings from the orphanage in Seattle, the siblings of Filmont, she was told, who were old enough to help her. They spent a winter in the large house, waiting for the return of Mr. Wormly and their brother.

She wrote to her sister several times, telling her that she had the sense that something evil happened. The sheriff insisted an Indian tribe was at fault, and though they hadn't attacked the locals in recent years, they were still around the area and looking for men to scalp for their offerings, according to him.

Mrs. Wormly doubted this explanation, as she had at times encountered the Indians and found them unusual but friendly. Mr. Wormly had given them food from the harvest just the week prior to his disappearance, and they appeared grateful.

Locals speculated as to just what happened to the men. The Wormlys were outsiders who brought strange ways with them. Mr. Wormly came into town trying to make friends and instead pushed them away with his stories of faraway lands where bare-breasted women walked about in broad daylight. He ate uncommon green things and sometimes left his shoes in his carriage as he wandered about town.

One prominent rumor was that the Wormlys

conjured magic on their farm, using some of those mysterious greens Mr. Wormly ate so brazenly. They used their concoction to place a curse on the neighboring farms that first year, causing the failure of crops that touched the Wormly property. Their curse backfired when their own farm also failed to produce much of anything.

A search of weather records for the year 1904 shows an exceptionally long rainy period where the sun didn't shine for a record 92 days. The locals insisted this wasn't the cause of their troubles and continued to place the blame for their troubles squarely on the shoulders of the Wormly family.

Three years after the men went missing, the children from the foundling home left Wormly Manor for reasons unknown. Mrs. Wormly, without her old family or new, went to bed in grief. A neighbor who frequently checked on her well-being found her dead, clutching a letter to her sister.

In the letter, she professed her sorrow and loneliness. She had drawn a detailed map with the location her astrologer felt the missing men's bodies rested. Poor Mrs. Wormly mentioned it was hard to breathe. She knew it wouldn't be long until she joined her beloved family and she wanted to make sure someone found them.

The neighbor organized a search crew and traveled out to the area described on the map. A creek bed that ran strong in years of excess water, lay full of logs, pushed into shore by the strong ocean currents.

After several days of hard labor, the logs were removed, revealing three decayed corpses. They figured one of the poor souls was reclaimed by the earth or eaten by bears. It was reported that Filmont's body was so distorted his identification was only assured because of the proximity to his father's body. Mr. Wormly was then positively identified by a former employee, recognizing the pieces of blue-plaid shirt, one of two Mrs. Wormly had lovingly sewn father and son.

Upon Mrs. Wormly's eventual death, investigators reportedly found an open container with a small amount of powder, labeled "Filmont's medicine," in her cabinet; it was later determined to be ground salvia. This herb can cause psychosis and hallucinations. Mrs. Wormly's sister confirmed the container was the substance used to medicate her nephew and Mrs. Wormly wrote to her sister that it often left him in a "glorious, mind-changing stupor" that altered his perception of those around him. He thought Mrs. Wormly to be a pet dog at one point, something she found delightful. This same poison was used to destroy the neighbor's crops, rumor had it.

Mrs. Wormly's sister said Mrs. Wormly had been suspicious that Filmont may not always be consuming his medication; she'd found uneaten food under his bed that had been sprinkled with the substance. Since Filmont was behaving himself, she didn't worry about it any further.

The astrologer, while conferring with law enforcement, determined that on this particular day, Filmont attempted to throw his medicated apple into the creek so he wouldn't have to ingest it any longer but instead, lost his balance and fell in. Brave Mr. Wormly jumped in to help his son, only to be overcome by the energetic, fast-moving water just like his unfortunate son. His hired men, both of them, jumped in to save the Wormly men only to lose their own lives.

Later investigation of Mrs. Wormly's astrologer found this woman to have given her potions to many who later became ill and died. Salvia was common to use for a short-lived "high" but could also cause psychosis. There was no thought to the long term use of this concoction, as Mrs. Wormly was instructed to do with Filmont.

Mrs. Wormly and her astrologer had been quite close, some speculating they were lovers and the potions were meant to kill those who spoke ill of their relationship.

While this may explain the deaths of the Wormly party, to this day we can find no credible explanation for the deaths that have occurred in the decades since. The Legend of Spoonback Creek maintains that the scenic creek has been cursed ever since, and the souls of those men still wander to this day.

CHAPTER SEVEN

Lanie
Sassy Lasses

MARVELINE AND MANDY cover their heads with their hands, even though that part of their bodies is safely under the tiny table. I can see the rest of their torsos openly exposed to the shooter. What I don't see is November.

"Vem? Are you all right? Where are you?" I half-whisper.

"It's coming from behind the big barn over there. I can smell their fear." The voice emanates from behind me, where my friend is standing tall and prideful in front of my crouched body. "Come and get me, punks! I'm not going anywhere!"

"Vem!" I hiss. "Get under the table. Now!"

She takes a long whiff. "They're gone. Both of them. Can't smell them anymore."

Marveline stands up, smoothing her flowing gown and looking at November with judgement. "That was a stupid thing you did. You don't know our neighbors. They're crazed."

I have to admit; there is a sense of calm. Vem's feelings aren't off-base. I take a few deep breaths and center myself before standing and smoothing my clothing. "Are we safe to do the tour now? I'd like to learn more about the property and you can tell us about your neighbors."

Mandy, now standing, looks to her sister for approval. "Can we? They never shoot twice."

Marveline shrugs. "Suit yourself. Sassy Lasses Winery is not responsible for any personal damage to self or property that may occur."

Mandy moves to the edge of the porch and gestures toward the lawn. "Follow me, please."

I grab onto Vem's arm, openly admitting to myself that I'm afraid.

"Not to worry, Lanie. These are bullies. They just want to huff and puff. They don't have the courage to put action behind their bullets in the air." She pats my arm. "Let's enjoy this." She turns to Mandy. "Will there be wine refills at some point?"

Mandy beams. "As much as you want. It's my sister who pinches the pennies. I'm just glad to have someone here who isn't easily scared. She leads us to a wood-sided building with a freshly refinished porch. The smell of pine hits my nostrils and I'm immediately taken back to my first overnight trip to the woods with Cosmo. The old Cosmo. He showed me how to bait a fishing hook and start a fire, where we roasted homemade marshmallows. We sat on that porch for hours, discussing the exciting life we had ahead as Mr. and Mrs. Hill.

"This was the bunkhouse. For all of his faults, Mr. Naybor was an exceptionally generous man. He came to town every weekend, looking for men down on their luck and needing work. Those men would stay here." She opens the door and we walk into a cozy room with a wood-burning stove and a small kitchen on one end. On the other are two couches.

"There are two bedrooms where we found six bunk beds each. They provided three hot meals a day, though they were told to fix their own on Sundays. When we bought this building, it was in the best condition of all the buildings on the property. Despite the rumors, Mr. Naybor kept this place immaculate."

"What rumors? Let's get into it!" November rubs her thin hands together.

I nudge Vem, though I'm wondering too.

Mandy clears her throat. "Well, the rumors that he killed employees when they were of no further use to him. Most of them had no family and no one to report them missing. It is curious that Mr. Naybor constantly needed new people. But we've found no evidence there are any bodies buried here on the property."

November sniffs again. I'm afraid of what I know comes next. She lets out a loud howl, startling Mandy so badly she jumps backward and falls against the wooden kitchen table. I offer my hand to pull her upright. "Sorry, she does that sometimes. She's a cult survivor and it's kind of her coping mechanism."

"I can sense turmoil here. No murder in this building, though." November moves to one bedroom. "Maybe this one, but I can't be sure. It's odd. Wait – the signals I'm getting are mixed. Like the cause of death wasn't obvious."

Mandy stares at her briefly before continuing. "This is the perfect place for the bride and her bridal party to prepare for the ceremony. There is plenty of room. Shall we move on to the next building?"

We step outside and walk down a freshly-oiled pathway, lined with giant, orange begonia bushes. The barn is similar in appearance to the barn where Cosmo, Cedar, and I had a violent confrontation with other cult members. I push away the ugly memories, trying to stay focused on what's in front of me now. And November.

"You'll notice we've refinished the floors here in Barn One." Mandy points to the beautifully weathered wood floor as we enter the barn. "It would make a perfect dance hall space. Naybor had cows, goats, pigs and one horse. Fortunately, when he was discovered dead, one neighbor came and took the animals."

"What happened exactly? We've never known."

Mandy puts her hands on her hips. "The rumors run the gamut. We've heard everything from harvesting organs to poisoning the neighbors so he could buy their land. It doesn't matter what I think. These neighbors decided he was planning to take over all of their properties. Even though most of the original owners are long dead and gone, there are still bad feelings. They were happy when this place was overgrown with weeds. Now that someone wants to come in and make a business, they don't trust that we won't do the same thing. It's absurd."

"Just Mr. Naybor and his daughter lived here? Was there a Mrs. Naybor who disappeared, too?"

Mandy shrugs. "No record of a missus. Pookie's disappearance is part of the legend, too. She's the author of the diary you're going to read. People think he killed her the way he killed everyone else on the property, and then ended his own life."

Vem snorts. "What an awful name for a kid. Why would you torture a child in that way?"

"Do you feel like doing some walking?" Mandy continues. "We can go to the stream. On a good day, you can see Mount Hood from there."

We follow her down the path for three-quarters of a mile until we hear the pleasant sounds of a babbling brook through tall grass. When we reach the edge, Mandy turns to face us.

"Spoonback Creek. This is the site of another story. It goes that the Wormlys drowned there, forever cursing those who came after them to suffer the same fate. Their ghosts stand on the banks and laugh maniacally as poor unsuspecting victims take their last breaths. Many alleged deaths, but no bodies were discovered over the decades."

"That's not quite true. One for sure. Maybe more."

We turn around in unison to see a stocky, kind-faced elderly man with a short, white beard. Behind him stands a tall, thin woman who looks as stern as he does welcoming.

"I'm glad you're here. Lanie and November, these are the caretakers. They sort of came with the place." She chuckles. "Delbert and Esmay Mission."

Delbert moves forward and sticks his hand out while his wife stands firm. "Nice to see some fresh faces here. Not that the beautiful Pherson sisters aren't a welcome sight each day."

I shake his hand while November circles his wife. "Something about you seems familiar to me. Have you attended one of my Morning Moan classes? Perhaps a stretch session?"

The auburn-haired woman shakes her head and looks away. "I don't get out much. We're country folk and that suits us just fine."

Studying her weathered face, I can tell she is much younger than her husband, though she is hardened for her years. In the Figuring Faces seminar I once took for my old job as the marketing manager for Work Ahead Office Supplies – The Most Profitable Office Supply Chain in the World, I was taught to study wrinkles around the eyes and mouth as a tool for determining age and product interest. I slept with Jansen Dome, the seminar leader whom I determined to be forty-two with the wrinkles of a fifty-seven-year-old smoker.

"How long have you lived here, Esmay? And how did you come to be here?"

She shrugs. "We've been here – what – is it going on ten years now, Delbert?" She stares at her husband lovingly. "The bank hired us to live on the property and keep people out. There's a tiny house on the other side of Spoonback Creek and up about a mile, right on the edge of Naybor land. Luckily these ladies invited us to stay on and help clean up the place." She looks at Mandy and gives her a quick, forced smile.

"Delbert, you were saying there was a body found here?"

He clears his throat. "Yes ma'am. Late fifties, I believe. It was long after Mr. Naybor's life ended. Some kids were out here trying to have a party. One of them started digging up dirt, looking for buried treasures. That was a rumor; that Mr. Naybor buried treasures on the property." He scratches his head and looks off in the distance. "Anyhoo, this kid got all excited when he hit on something hard in the soil. His friends helped him dig until they unearthed a body."

"Who was it? We've had more than our share of those in Piney Falls." Vem finally moves away from Esmay. "Heads, no heads, over the falls, on the land, we've got them everywhere."

"Vem!" I caution.

"Those times was different." Delbert crosses his arms over his large stomach. "No way to tell for certain. It'd been there for several years. The police thought it was one of Mr. Naybor's employees who vanished. Buried the poor man in the Piney Falls cemetery without a headstone. Course the kids insisted they saw Mr. Wormly's ghost standing on the other side of the creek, laughing."

Mandy sighs. "That's another one of those rumors. Maybe when you do your research for us, you can determine if that's true or not."

Delbert looks at her with disgust. "It's true, ma'am. The body, that is. The ghost is nothing but wild-eyed kids. Rumors of more deaths too. These locals lived it. They all know Mr. Naybor stole everything from these poor souls, taking advantage of the downtrodden and–"

"Delbert and Esmay will be happy to help you with anything you need while you're here for your wedding," Mandy continues, looking at me pointedly. "I was hoping your fiancé would come today. Delbert would gladly show him around and make him feel welcome."

"Cosmo's been really depressed for months. His sister moved to San Diego and he doesn't know how to go on. He doesn't even go into his own bakery unless we force him," Vem reports, with no prompting from me.

"What's the name?" Delbert asks, limping slightly as he moves forward. His rounded stoop makes me wonder how much caretaking he can actually accomplish.

"Cosmo Hill. He grew up in a cult. Most everyone had a strange name there." I don't want to tell this story today. You can never tell how people will react to the sad saga of the Fallen Branch cult, or if they'll be receptive to those who were a part of it, whether or not it was against their will.

"Hey!" November protests. "Year of the N was an excellent year for names."

Delbert displays no emotion, usually a sign to the contrary; they DO know about Cosmo's history as a wrongly-convicted murderer.

I wait to see if an explanation is necessary: that

everyone in the cult was named for the year and corresponding letter assigned to that year. Delbert appears done with the conversation and looks away.

"Shall we continue?" Mandy asks.

We circle back towards Naybor Manor with Delbert and Esmay trailing behind us.

"Have you thought about a bridal shower? We could host up to 200 people here, if we can round up enough chairs."

Getting married later in life doesn't mean I don't want everything a twenty-something bride would have. I would like a non-traditional shower, with both of us present. I wonder if Cosmo will come around enough. "I'd like that very much. I'm a little concerned about your neighbors, but I'll bring Cos out here next week and see if I can get him behind this. That will give me enough time to read through the diary and get it back to your sister."

"We'll hire security." Mandy pleads. "We'll do whatever it takes. You can have a huge discount. We just need to host some events to show people it's not a dangerous place. Sassy Lasses Winery will be a relaxing destination." She stares at me with tears in her eyes. "My sister needs this. We sunk everything we had into this place and if we don't start seeing a profit, I...fear for her sanity."

If I can't solve their mystery, I least I can give them this gift. "I know what it's like to be an outsider in this community." I touch her shoulder. "I'll do whatever I can to help you."

"Lanie, stop."

I look at Vem with annoyance but continue walking. "There's so much history here, you can work that to your advantage. The stories, whether true or not will give people a reason to visit. I do marketing for the Inn and Spa at Fallen Branch–"

"Lanie, STOP!"

I snap my head around. "November Bean, you're just being rude! We're trying to work things out with our hosts! What could possibly be so important?"

November puts her arm up slowly and points to the tall grass off to our right. "The body lying over there."

CHAPTER EIGHT

Pookie
January, 1947

Dearest Ophelia,

When I showed Raymond the old piece of clothing, a lonely arm from a shirt found in Barn Two, he said it could belong to anyone. But when I showed him the matching blue-plaid arm found in my bedroom, he thought that peculiar. He believed me, that it was left behind by the ghost of Mr. Wormly or Filmont.

Now I'm quite sure: I'm in love with Raymond! I realize he is far too old for me and being a man of the world, he would never lower his standards and fall in love with a girl who has barely left Naybor Manor.

A man with such dreamy, blue eyes and muscular arms could find a place beside Tulip Sloan in her latest picture. He would rescue her from certain peril, grasping her from the arms of an evil man trying to throw her off a building. "Git yer darned hands off her!" Then he'd pull her in close and kiss her hard. Roll credits.

Daddy always assures me in the end that there will always be men down on their luck needing a place to be, and that we'll always have a place for them here. He's just trying to make sure I understand gratitude for those around us. And humility. I love Daddy even more for saying those things to me.

I shall never tell him how much I've fallen for Raymond though. He wouldn't understand my experiencing such deep feelings for someone who wasn't properly educated. Raymond didn't even graduate high school, but finished the tenth grade, unlike his brothers.

Recently, I've come to wonder if Raymond doesn't have some secrets. He never responds when I ask him about where he was before landing here at Naybor Manor. I know he worked in shipping, but that was many years ago. There are many unaccounted for years in between. Sometimes I feel like he's speaking to me in riddles, like I'm a silly child who will never solve them.

Yours in Burgeoning Love and Affection, Pookie A. Naybor

"I didn't like him," Freddie stuck his hand in the popcorn sack, taking the last bit mixed with Tart Chewies even though it was Pookie's turn.

"Why not? He's a fine, sturdy man."

Freddie laughed. "That don't sound right. My dad called our neighbor's horse 'sturdy.' You don't say that about a man."

Pookie looked at him seriously. "You're right. I've never had a boy...a friend of his stature before. How should I describe him?"

Freddie scratched his freckled cheek. "He's your hired man. That's how you should describe him. He won't be around long anyway. Your hired hands always leave mysteriously."

"Don't be silly. They are gone because they're drifters. They drift."

Freddie looked at her incredulously. "Don't you know 'bout the ones who go crazy and run off into the woods?"

"Of course I do. It's not true."

"Well, I bet you didn't hear this one," Freddie turned his skinny, little body around to face her. "Might not get the entire story in before the news reel, but this was right before your daddy bought the place. There was a bunch of women who lived in the house you live in now. They were prostitutes. Some big ship captain came in and killed them all. Their ghosts run around on your property now. Every night, they roam around and the workers who are still out and about are so scared they run and jump in the creek. Kills 'em or they go crazy."

"What's a prostitute?"

"Shhh...it's starting."

After Tulip Sloan overcame her misery and lived the life of a wealthy heiress, Pookie pulled on Freddie's arm. "Tell me about this man who killed the prostitutes. Why did he kill them? Why were they working as prostitutes?"

"Oh geez," Freddie snorted. "Your daddy don't teach you nothin'. There weren't jobs here for women back when. My ma's lucky because she knows how to iron and takes in washing. But other'n the cannery, there ain't nowhere that'll hire a decent woman. So women had to be indecent to get work. Least that's what Ma says happened."

The two of them walked out of the building, Pookie holding tightly to Freddie's hand just in case the stranger came back.

"He's gone, whoever he was. Prolly another drifter heard about your property and wanted to scare you a little." Freddie patted her shoulder reassuringly. "I won't run off if we see him again, I promise."

"Freddie, am I naïve?"

"I don't know that word, Pook."

"It means ignorant. Having no idea about what is

going on around you."

"Oh. I s'pose. Ain't all women?"

Pookie slugged him in the shoulder. "No, they are certainly not. It's just that Raymond sometimes treats me like I'm a simpleton, or at least he doesn't trust me that I can be told things in confidence."

Freddie studied her face. "You're gonna hit me again if I say this."

"No, I won't. Promise."

"You haven't seen anything of the world, like I have. You just keep to yourself on that farm while the rest of us go about our business. There's only sunlight and rainbows for Mistress Pookie. You've never seen ol' Captain Dan when he gets so liquored up he relieves himself in the alley. You don't understand what happens when a feller goes to school and has to fight his way home afterward, just cause he don't have the nice clothes folks think he should."

Pookie's cheeks turned crimson. "Then I shall make it my mission to learn these things. I'll learn about everything there is to know about rain clouds and storms in Flanagan. That will be my goal for my thirteenth year."

Freddie laughed. "Pookie, you are a strange one."

CHAPTER NINE

Lanie
Piney Falls

"I'M JUST BEING honest with you, Lanie. I've been having premonitions that something bad will happen. We should have the party right here, in my backyard. I can make my famous chocolate guacamole dip and Vem's Vodka Vitality. It'll be less classy but just as fun."

November Bean is dressed from headband to toe in charcoal brown, her color of the day. Her cat-eye-shaped glasses match her usual monochrome look.

"You're being ridiculous, Vem. You found the body of the Pherson's hired hand, killed and placed in that particular spot by the Pherson's next-door neighbors to cause problems. They've all but admitted to it. It's tragic, especially for the family of Bill Bogus, but there's nothing further to worry about. The police will sort it out."

"And what about the di-a-ry?" she asks in a sing-song fashion. "Could that hold the key to this mystery with some deep, dark meaning?"

"Pssht." I've had a hard time concentrating on the musings of a silly young girl when Cosmo is here in front of me, living with the actual issue of depression. Barely made it six pages in. "This handwritten book is nothing more than a young girl's fantasies and quite frankly, it's a little repetitious and tiresome."

November and I are supposed to be putting together Piper's birthday plans, but so far, we've had to stop twice for a moaning session and now her worries about the party's location will consume the next hour at the very least.

"Look!" I point to the hummingbird feeder where two, bright blue birds are inhaling sugar water with a fury. "Don't hummingbirds mean good luck?" I stare at her hopefully. "We're looking at things all wrong."

Vem rolls her eyes. "Lanie, I've told you a hundred times. Hummingbird luck only comes on Mondays. We're well into Wednesday. You're just trying to distract me." She pushes her frizzy brown hair out of her face. "If you won't listen, I suppose I have no option but to go along with this party idea. I can't let you go out there by yourself. Should I make more calls?"

I nod. "Cosmo will be there too. We'll be fine."

"Will he?" She cocks her head to the side.

"You're not able to get him out of bed regularly."

My phone buzzes, rattling the glass table top. When I pick it up, I'm pleasantly surprised by the caller ID. "Cedar! I'm so glad you called. How are things in San Diego?"

A familiar high-pitched voice giggles on the other end. "Oh, so wonderful, Lanie. I never knew a job could be so fulfilling." She sighs. "I only wish Cosmo's life was going as well."

Her enthusiasm is infectious. I wish I could bottle it and release it into Cosmo's nostrils. "I'm glad you called. I know we agreed on once a month, but he's been so hard to get moving. Nothing I say or do seems to help." I walk carefully into the bedroom, not sure how I'll be received today. He will stay in bed until noon most days and if I try to roust him any earlier, he grumbles and won't talk to me for the rest of the day.

"Cos? It's Cedar. She wants to tell you all about her job."

He is in his usual side lump position, immobile. When he hears his sister's name, he rolls slowly onto the other side and extends his hand. "I'll talk."

I start to hand him the phone but then bring it back to my ear. "Oh, and Cedar? I would like some information on the Pherson family of Denver, the people I told you about? Prominent people who owned a pharmaceutical company."

"I have resources at my disposal. Things I can't tell you but they are mind-blowing. Leave it to me."

Reaching down to kiss his forehead gently, I place the phone in Cosmo's warm hand and walk out of the bedroom, closing the door.

When I reach the patio, Vem has a sour expression on her face. "What's wrong now? Another dark premonition? I can only handle so many in a day."

"I just called Gladys. You know how she has been all over Piper like a bad habit? Well she's adamant she's not going to any party out at that gol-darned curs-ed farm." Vem lowers her voice to Gladys pitch. "Too far for an old woman to travel, anyway."

I stifle a giggle. "She told me that the other day. Piper will probably be relieved to hear it. Gladys won't leave her alone. The only centenarian with enough energy to spy on people. What about everyone else? Are they coming?"

"Yes. Practically the entire town. It will be a real whoopdinger of an afternoon. As long as–"

Cosmo appears behind us. He is wearing his grey sweats, the same ones he's worn religiously for most of the winter. His hair is unusually messy and his eyes squint as though they haven't seen daylight in weeks. He stares blankly at November and then at me. "She wants to talk to you again."

Vem stands up and moves so close to him the

usual Cosmo would have picked her up and threatened to throw her over the side of the porch. "Cosmo Hill, you need to get dressed. I can sense turmoil at your bakery; things are changing without your knowledge. It's your baby! Don't hesitate!"

He reaches around her and hands the phone to me. "Cedar. On the phone for you."

As I take the phone from him, I use my other arm to grab his and pull him in close. "In front of November and the world, kiss me good morning."

November puts her hands over her glasses and hums her favorite meditation tune.

Cosmo leans in and kisses me softly. I take his chin in my hand and stare into his deep blue eyes, searching for some spark of life and see only deadness. "I'm going to shower," he says, moving inside quickly.

"Cedar? How was he today?"

"Oh, Lanie. I wish I could come up and help. Maybe it was a mistake for me to move. I didn't realize it would be so hard on him."

"I was trying to keep it from you for this very reason. You need to be able to grow into the best Cedar you can be. He needs to do the same thing, but he's gotten himself stuck in a rut."

"I told him he has to go to Piper's birthday celebration. He needs to get out as much as she needs him to be there. He said he'd go for me."

But not for me.

"Well, that's something I guess."

"Oh, and I have some information regarding the Naybor farm for you. Tulip Sloan visited Piney Falls, or rather Flanagan, as it was known. They had a big parade for her down Main Street and all of the dignitaries attended. She and the head of the studio stayed as a guest of Welcome Naybor for two nights. She and her boyfriend died less than a year later. The police said there was nothing concerning at her home, but there were rumors."

"What kind of rumors?"

"That she was into something dark. She had several connections in organized crime. They may have killed her."

Tulip Sloan always seemed to me like she was hiding something from the public. While other actresses of the time had a waxy onscreen presence, Tulip's was like she was present in the room with you. She was emotional yet there was something behind her eyes that made me feel connected. Like she must've had a distant mother too, or now, maybe mob connections.

"Thanks, Cedar. I'll be in touch with more info I need you to track down."

Chapter Ten

Story of Daisy Devine – 1924 Courtesy of the Piney Falls Public Library Information Booth

AFTER THE WORMLY family died off, there was a long period of decay before Welcome Naybor moved in. That doesn't mean the house remained empty, however. It was common knowledge to the folks in neighboring Flanagan that a big estate was sitting unoccupied. To some, apparently, it was an opportunity simply waiting for the right opportunist to take advantage of the situation.

One such soul was Daisy Devine, as she was known. A beautiful woman with large, expressive eyes and the figure of a calendar girl, she showed up one day on the train from Portland. She was dressed in a fashion foreign to the area, a long-sleeved black dress belted to a low waist with an ornate gold belt. Her hair was daringly short. She displayed dark red lipstick on her pouty lips. She looked like she'd just landed from another planet, according to the locals.

When asked by several townsfolk if she needed assistance, she replied, "I am quite assured of my destination, thank you."

Daisy brazenly set up shop in the empty Wormly Manor, lighting the porch with many lanterns and claiming the Wormly master bedroom as her own. She hired a few large men to keep others off her claim and soon other equally alluring women began arriving in Flanagan, each as tight-lipped as the last.

They erected a sign at the main road turn off: "Daisy Devine's House of Energy and Chivalry." The flyers they posted around town boasted, "The Latest in Good Health and Enjoyable Entertainment."

Curious Flanagan residents drove down the road to find the women laughing and drinking on the paint-less porch with nefarious locals perched by their sides. The farming community around them was shocked and horrified to learn of such goings-on and demanded the sheriff remove Daisy and her lot at once.

Without a complaint filed by the estate's owner of record, the sheriff was reluctant to remove Daisy. It was also rumored that the sheriff frequented Daisy's parlor on more than one occasion.

This continued for over two years before the Wormly Curse reared its ugly head. Wily Will, a ship captain of ill repute, did not report back to his ship after his temporary leave. After checking all brothels in Flanagan, his shipmates took it upon themselves to search the Wormly property. Wily Will's body was located in Spoonback Creek in approximately the same location as Mr. Wormly and Filmont had been located some years earlier.

Being a man who drugged and kidnapped unsuspecting souls and forcing them into servitude on his ship, no one in the community shed a tear over the demise of Wily Will. A search party was organized and within days, three more bodies were recovered in or near Spoonback Creek. All were the type who caused trouble wherever they went. It looked as though Daisy Devine was doing a great public service to the good people of Flanagan. Public opinion of Daisy and her establishment soon rose to the point she was invited to attend the 4th of July parade as an honored guest.

Daisy herself never addressed the deaths. The sheriff was still a frequent guest of her establishment and seemed to have little concern of his own. Like them or not, Daisy and her group of boisterous women were there to stay.

Word reached Flanagan one day that Daisy's sign on the road had been removed. No lights appeared at night and the stately home was quiet. All outward appearances were that Daisy Devine had disappeared into thin air.

When one of her regular visitors inquired with

the sheriff's office as to her whereabouts, they were shocked to find the sheriff himself had packed up and left without a word. The townspeople were furious and loaded up their wagons with weapons, planning to find the culprits behind this odious act and remove them from the Wormly property once and for all.

The eerie sight that met them shocked even the most hardened soul. All of the young women formerly in her employ had vanished as if spirited away in the middle of the night. The abandoned house looked as though its inhabitants were forced to leave within minutes. Dishes sat on the table and cups were half-full of coffee. Flies buzzed around a buttered piece of toast and the local newspaper, a month ago Monday's, lay open to the help wanted section. The only trace of the living was Daisy's fine black dress, the gold belt hanging precariously off the shoulder.

As they crept through the house, they saw drops of blood on every hard surface. After assuring themselves no injured persons needed their help inside, they removed to the outlying buildings, dividing up to search each one.

One unlucky soul searching the bunkhouse found the remains of Daisy. It wasn't clear if she had been shot, strangled or both because of the decomposed state of her body. In the next room, the sheriff's body was found in much the same manner.

When pressed, the sheriff's brother, Reverend Arlow, admitted he felt Daisy and her women had used some kind of evil magic to hypnotize normally fine, church-going men. He himself had only visited the establishment once, just to satisfy his curiosity about the goings-on therein. He found everyone to be under some sort of spell, with the bleary eyes and slurred speech that caused them to speak in riddles.

Disgusted by what he'd seen, Reverend Arlow insisted he had never returned and didn't have any idea of the tragedy that had befallen his brother and Daisy Devine. When asked about any weapons he might own, he said he'd misplaced his rifle after last hunting season and didn't remember where he put it. Reverend Arlow was never questioned further.

The rest of the women were never found and assumed escaped or dead in Spoonback Creek. To this day, there is no explanation for the death of Daisy Devine or why she ended up on the Wormly property in the first place.

CHAPTER ELEVEN

Lanie
Sassy Lasses Winery

E ARLY ON SATURDAY, Piper, November, Cosmo and I head to the winery. Marveline and Mandy are on the large porch when we arrive, stringing together purple and pink balloons.

There are sixteen tables set up on the lawn, each covered in a yellow-checkered tablecloth with deep purple daisies adorning the center. There is a band setting up on a makeshift stage, just to the right of the area where the body was discovered on our last visit. On the perimeter of the property, private security officers are patrolling back and forth. It seems in direct contrast to the joyous nature of the day, but most likely necessary.

I clasp my hands together. "This is wonderful! You two did a marvelous job here!"

Mandy beams. "Thank you! And this," she turns her attention to Piper, "must be our birthday girl. We're so honored you chose our winery for your celebration!" She pulls her in and hugs her tightly, patting her back.

Tiny sobbing sounds are coming from Piper. Ever since her mother's death – the mother who forced her to hold her emotions inside – Piper has been prone to sudden bouts of joy or sadness. We've all come to embrace them as her battle scars, just as Vem has her moaning and Cosmo has his fits of anger and now depression.

"They never allowed me to have a party growing up. Ordering a birthday cake might have alerted someone we were in their town and we didn't want anyone to know where we were hiding out. We just pretended like it was any other day."

I hug her shoulder. "It's okay. You can cry. You can do one of Vem's moans. It's your day. There are no rules. Let's make this the best party you've ever had."

"And the handsome fellow next to you has to be the groom." Marveline wipes her hands on her cherry-print apron and extends one to Cosmo.

I tighten up on the inside, hoping he will respond.

"Cosmo Hill. Nice to meet you," his voice booms. He offers his hand and even half-smiles, the look that stole my heart and still makes me weak.

"We'd like to show you around later, so you can get a feel for the place as your wedding venue."

Cosmo shrugs. "I'm leaving most of that up to

Lanie."

There is honking in the yard and a car pulls in, carrying Urica Jolloby, the owner of a local art gallery. She gets out along with her passengers, blond-haired twins Faythe and Finnegan Lane, who are co-managing Cheese with Your Burger since Emma Thompson's arrest for trying to force Piper to join the Broken Branch cult. I'm a little disappointed Urica hasn't brought her best friend, Gladys, despite Gladys's insistence she wouldn't come.

Piper waves excitedly to them before running over to hug them. It fills my soul to hear her giggle with people her own age. Finnegan, a tall, thin boy with a full head of curly blond hair and bright green eyes, towers over Piper. He picks up her small body and swings her around, her feet flopping behind her. She laughs as his similarly curly-headed sister protests, "Put her down, Finn!"

The door slams behind me, and Esmay appears at the tables, arranging napkins and pouring water. It's obvious that along with being a caretaker for the property, she also helps with events. She is wearing makeup and actually looks much younger than she did on our last visit.

"Esmay, what a lovely brooch. May I see it?"

She blushes. "Oh, this thing? I've had it for years. Found it at a thrift store."

On her chest is a large, square emerald on the

bottom, acting as a flower box and three daisy-flowers made from pink, auburn and yellow stones shooting out of the emerald. "It's exquisite. Whoever left it at the thrift store did not understand how valuable it was."

Marveline rings a bell from the porch. "Can you all please find your name cards at the tables? We'd like to serve lunch."

At my table is Urica, Cos and Mandy. Urica, dressed in a rainbow tunic with her long, grey hair braided down her back, pulls out the chair next to Cosmo and sits down, scooching in as close to him as she can. "Haven't seen you at the bakery in weeks. Word 'round town is that you're a lost puppy without that sister of yours."

Cosmo leans back and crosses his arms. "Is that a fact? Well, I'm here now, aren't I?"

"You sure are. Lanie needs a man who can pull his weight." She pats his leg. "And you showed up for her at the right time. This place is nothing but dreadful stories."

"What stories can you tell us, Urica?" I ask a little too eagerly.

"The one that sticks out to me is the legend of the Brown-Eyed Beauties."

"Sounds more like a magazine I found in a convenience store bathroom. You sure you didn't mix things up?" Cosmo winks at her, displaying his familiar humor.

I want to tell him that's inappropriate, but really, anything coming out of his mouth today is a positive. "Go ahead, Urica."

"Well, there is a story that at one time, there were a couple of pretty ladies who lived here." Urica crosses one leg over the other and leans back in her seat. "They'd come to town all dressed up, wearing the finest clothes available for the day. They'd go to the theater and then to the pharmacy for a sarsaparilla. Never talking to anyone. When they finished, a fancy car came and picked them up and took them away. One good ole' boy followed them all the way back here." Urica points downward. "To Naybor Manor. He said Mr. Naybor threatened his life if he didn't turn around and leave. One day, those ladies just stopped showing up. Since none of the townies knew their names or where they came from, nobody knew where to look. They were all in awe of Welcome Naybor, you know. If he didn't want you on his property, you turned around and left and felt bad about it for the rest of your days."

"And what did the townspeople think happened to them?"

Urica reaches back and flips her long braid from the back of her head to the side. "Drowned. In that cursed Spoonback Creek, of course."

Mandy clears her throat loudly. "Those are just

tall tales. We've found no evidence of anyone drowning in that stream, at least after the initial deaths of the Wormly family. Just an unpreventable tragedy."

"That's certainly not what my folks–" Urica begins.

Mandy taps on my arm. "Lanie? Can we talk?" I nod, gesturing to Cosmo as I get up. I think he'll be fine, but then again, I don't know for sure.

Mandy and I walk away from the group, where it is quieter. "Have you been reading the diary?"

"Yes," I nod, maybe a little too enthusiastically. "She sounds like a normal, teenaged girl." I'm only on page ten. So far, she's expressed a deep infatuation with someone named Raymond and complained about her homework. So much for speed reading. "She's got the usual worries, but nothing remarkable. Have you heard any more about the man who died?"

"Bill Bogus. Poor man. We haven't found any next of kin. The autopsy was inconclusive." She rubs her forehead with one hand. "I was wondering if you would feel brave enough to pay a visit to our neighbor, Truman Coolidge. His family has been on the land for three generations, so the police are hesitant to upset him. Since they can't find definitive proof of foul play in Bill's death, they don't want to cause any unnecessary hard feelings."

"Is he the one you think possibly murdered Bill?"

Marveline taps on my shoulder. "I'm going to take your Cosmo to meet Esmay's husband, Delbert, so he can get a tour of the place. Cosmo said to tell you not to 'freak out' that he's doing something functional." She shakes her head disapprovingly. "Mandy, please take Lanie to see our flower field." She turns to me and smiles broadly. "It's quite breathtaking."

"Good idea!" I look over at Cosmo, who is giving me the thumbs up sign and a weak smile. "Tell me more about Bill," I say as we begin walking. "Had he been here long?"

"No. Two months was all. He was a loner; a drifter I guess you could say. He asked if he could work for the summer and we said yes, with an unspoken contract that he would move on at some point."

"Does it worry you that this was the same scenario as the rumored deaths that occurred in the forties?"

Mandy smiles. "Lanie, we're in a different era," she says in a condescending voice. "People are accounted for now. They can't just disappear without an explanation." We walk around behind the bunkhouse, where a rainbow of flowers greets our eyes. The daisies stand tall, pointing their faces toward the summer sun.

"Oh my! These are stunning!"

"We decided to grow a field of flowers to sell to the local vendors. Anything to supplement our income. I want my sister to be happy and she wants this place to succeed." I make a mental note to plan my wedding around these happy blooms. Maybe that will pique Gladys' interest.

There is an abrupt tap on my shoulder. "Hey, there's my handsome–"

"We're leaving now. And I'm not getting married here."

Cosmo, for all of his faults, is never openly rude to people (outside of November), especially those he doesn't know.

"Cos, did you look around? Delbert's been here many years. He has some delightful stories to tell." Marveline is standing behind him, arms folded. She looks as if she'd like to take him over her knee and give him a sound spanking.

"This isn't up for discussion. I'm ready to go home."

I gaze at Mandy awkwardly. "We may have to make alternative arrangements for November and Piper."

She nods sympathetically. "Understood."

"At least let me say goodbye to everyone. Can you tell Piper–"

"I'll wait for you in the car." He snaps.

There is a rage building up inside of me. I've been

so patient with him all of these months. I'm trying to let it release naturally, but today it doesn't want to budge. In a marketing seminar I took in my previous life, called Blow It Out Your Ears, Not Your Mouth, we learned to release our anger through internal dialogue instead of openly displaying it with our clients. I slept with the seminar organizer, Fleck McMasters. Outside of his seminar, he was an angry man. None of his words are doing anything for me today.

"I'm so sorry, Mandy. This just isn't like him. Cosmo isn't usually this rude. I'll be in touch." As I turn to walk away, I hear a bloodcurdling scream.

Over in a field of lavender, far to my right, Faythe is holding onto her brother. Cosmo, Marveline, and I all run to the scene. In the middle of the aromatic purple field swarming with bees there is another body; another man.

"That's Gene Yardley," Marveline says without emotion. "Another employee down."

Chapter Twelve

Pookie
February 1947

Dearest Ophelia,

While I find myself with a deep and endearing love of Raymond, part of me doesn't trust him. I love that he asks me questions about my life and about Daddy. But then I have to ask myself, why? What is his need for this information?

He is not like our other workers. He has read many books and has a deep interest in those he works with. He's traveled all over the world, sailing the high seas and finding adventure in faraway lands. He's like a character in one of my books, but he's real.

Why, though, can't he see Daddy is just as magnificent? "Miss Pookie, your daddy ain't the gentleman you think he is. Your eyes is clouded by affection and you're missing what's going on around you."

I said nothing in argument. Maybe he's been hurt by a former employer, or his family back in Oklahoma. He doesn't know Daddy as I do.

I can say the same of Daddy and his mistrust of Raymond. Just last week, while Daddy was doing his crossword puzzle, I asked him if Raymond could join us for dinner.

"Don't get yourself endeared to the hired hands, Pookie darling. You know they never stay around long. Raymond may give you attention the others don't, but he's no different from the rest." He scratched his balding head with his pencil and looked up at the ceiling. "A five-letter word for defeat or surrender?"

I wished he could see Raymond the way I do. Yield. The word was yield.

Troublingly Yours,
Pookie A. Naybor

"Did you know Paulo is gone? Two days ago, he came in from feeding the chickens and said he didn't feel so well. Your daddy called down here and asked me to burn the trash. I only do that once a month and that day ain't till next Thursday. He asked a week early. I came back an hour later and Paulo's bunk was empty. Picture of his mama and his pa's watch was gone too. Don't you find that right peculiar?"

Pookie twisted her braids and giggled. "I like how you say that. 'Raht' peculiar. I've heard no one talk like you before."

Raymond shook his head. "You're frustratin', Pookie. My family moved round a lot. I mix up my country boy words. That ain't the point. Did'ja hear what I was saying? Paulo just up and disappeared? That don't sit funny with you?"

She used her toe to draw a heart in the barn's dirt floor, staring at Raymond hopefully. When he didn't respond, she huffed and flopped down on top of her drawing. "That's how things work here. Men don't stay here longer than a season, sometimes not even that long. Didn't Daddy tell you that when you started? That's why they're called drifters. They drift."

Raymond grabbed her arm and pulled her up, causing her head to flop back and her eyes to widen.

"You don't get the seriousness of this situation, girlie!" He spat. "We are folks too. Good folks. Paulo was my friend. He wouldn't leave without saying goodbye. Least leavin' a note."

"Maybe he didn't learn how to write." She swallowed hard. "Maybe he didn't have the words to tell you how he felt. Those can be hard to offer to a person you've grown very fond of."

Raymond lowered her back to the ground and gently wiped his spit off her sleeve. "Sorry, Miss. Didn't mean to get upset. You're just a kid and don't have no idea what happens with adults."

She stared at him with curiosity and excitement, "I'm not a child. My thirteenth birthday is coming up in four months. I know quite a lot about the adult world."

"Oh?" Raymond smiled, returning to his work. "What's your understandin' of the matter?"

"Well," she began pacing around him in a circle. "I know that you leave at night. I've watched you out my window when I'm writing in my diary. You wait till Daddy's light is out and then you leave. One of these times, I will follow you."

Raymond stopped sweeping and looked at her with his serious face. "A lady don't need to be out at night. Bad things happen after dark."

Pookie shrugged. "I might not be as inclined to follow if you'd tell me where you're going."

"This ain't no game, Pookie. I mean it." His face was somber. "Stay in your room and write your stories. This is for adults."

"Like Daddy's secret field?" she persisted. "I've snuck over in the spring and seen the bright red flowers. I know beyond the field is Spoonback Creek. Someday I'll go there too. I'm not afraid of those stories."

Raymond shook his head and laid his rake on the ground. "Come sit with me for a spell." He motioned to a hay bale, and they went there together.

She placed her hand on his leg daringly.

"It's true, you're gonna be a grown-up real soon. And grown-ups know there are things to talk about and things to keep to themselves. If I tell you something, would you keep it to yourself?"

Pookie nodded solemnly. "Of course, Raymond. You're my confidante. I wouldn't betray your trust." She thought about how she'd wished for a friend who treated her like an equal. Miss Dandridge pretended to show interest in what she said, but Daddy paid her well and she would do the same with the refrigerator if he told her to.

Raymond got up and walked outside, looking around to make sure no one else was close by before he came back and sat beside her. He took her small hands in his. "Pookie, your daddy's been doing some things he shouldn't. I'm worried these men aren't disappearing by their own free will."

Pookie gasped. "Not Daddy. He's the kindest, most generous person there is. He helps the poor and the degenerate…"

"That's his cover, Pookie. He pretends to be a good man so he can get away with other things. He might even hurt me one day. Just remember I'd never leave here on my own free will without saying a proper goodbye."

Pookie reached one hand up to his face and rubbed the rough surface. "You don't have to worry, Raymond. I would never let anything happen to you. If you think someone is harming these men, then I shall help you find the truth. But I can assure you it isn't Daddy."

Raymond pulled her hand away from his face and stood. "We'll see about that, Miss." He rubbed his chin. "For now, you keep your eyes open and let me know if you see anything peculiar. Can you do that?"

Pookie nodded.

"And you just keep to yourself. That means letting a man do what he needs to do under the cover of darkness. Spend your time writing in your – what'd you call it?"

"Diary. I call her Ophelia."

"Writing in Miss Ophelia. Tell her everything, even if it seems like nothing. You and me, we'll meet up once a week and discuss what you've found. Does that sound like something grown-up to you?"

Pookie struggled to contain her excitement. "Yes, I promise. I won't say a word, Raymond. Next Friday, we can meet in this barn after I finish my studies. Daddy is always busy with his book work on Fridays, so he won't pay any attention." She pulled on his shoulder and then kissed him on the cheek when he reached her level.

"Thank you for trusting me." She turned and ran so he wouldn't see her blushing.

The following Saturday, Pookie and Freddie sat in the theatre, waiting for *Our Miss Darling* to begin.

"Do you promise you won't tell anyone?" Pookie asked Freddie, after confessing her secret conversation with Raymond.

Freddie shrugged. "Ain't no secret there are strange things happening out at your place. I've been telling you; the entire town knows."

"What else do you know, Freddie? What could I tell Raymond?"

Freddie scratched his red-stained cheek. "Well, I heard tell of one of your drifters showing up in town. His eyes were wild and my mom said he was crazy on drugs. He was swaying this way and that, hollerin' about murder and how he wouldn't go back to that place." He paused, watching her face for a reaction.

"That's silly, Freddie. I would know if one of our employees was acting strange. I've not seen anyone do–" she paused, remembering what she promised Raymond. "Did he say anything else?"

"Well, my ma says one of your pa's friends whispered in the sheriff's ear. He hauled that crazy-eyed man off and no one ever saw him again. Not my uncle Buffus, who was sobering up in the jail and knows everybody who comes and goes. Nobody."

"Do you know who it was? What was his name?"

The curtains began to rise.

"I think it started with a P. Phil, I think. But there's more, Pookie, I promise you. That's just the latest one I heard about. Last summer, your daddy brought vegetables to the poor and the next week, they all came down with a horrible sickness. Some of 'em died."

"That was just a stomach flu passing through town. I wasn't well myself," Pookie replied dismissively. "Was it Paulo? Is that who you're talking about?"

"Shhh!" The man in the seat behind them leaned forward and tapped them on the shoulder. "You kids be quiet now, the newsreel is starting. I want to know what's happening with the new manufacturing plant."

"Probably." Freddie whispered. "Or something close. I'm tellin' you, Pookie; there's strange things happening all around your daddy, if you'd only open your eyes and look."

The next evening, a Sunday, Pookie dutifully said her prayers and waited to hear the comforting purr of her father's snoring. She crept out of bed slowly and put on her overalls, stuffing her nightgown down the side holes.

Daddy had a special flashlight he used to scare the raccoons at night, kept on the mantel of the library. She tucked that into the pocket of her heavy winter coat and pulled on her boots before carefully opening the front door.

Once she was outside, she ran as quickly as possible. If Daddy were to wake up for a midnight corn biscuit and blackberry jam as he often did, he might check her bed to make sure she was sleeping soundly. She didn't want to give him time to discover she was missing before she had accomplished her mission.

Pookie hid behind the giant oak tree, just to the right of the bunkhouse. Just as he did every Tuesday and Sunday, Raymond appeared, pulling the door closed behind him. Pookie held her breath, waiting for him to pass her before taking up behind him at a safe distance. He trudged through the fields, pausing a few times as if he sensed someone behind him before continuing on.

He finally came to a stop at a wooded area far back in the hills. Another man appeared with a large burlap bag. Pookie settled down in the tall grass, straining herself to hear the conversation.

"You did it then?" Raymond asked. "I think it's the decent thing to do."

"All taken care of. Just like I promised."

In the darkness, it was hard to determine which voice belonged to which man, especially when she wasn't close enough to hear exact conversation.

There was more mumbling before the other man handed Raymond a shovel and left. Raymond took the bag and dragged it over a small hill. Pookie crept on her hands and knees, slowly, until she reached the top of the hill. She shined her flashlight away from Raymond, but she could make out his silhouette, digging.

He rolled the bag into the hole and covered it up, before standing quietly. He looked around as if he sensed her presence before taking his shovel and heading back toward the bunkhouse.

Pookie laid back down quickly, hoping he wouldn't head in her direction. There was no need to worry as his footsteps became softer until they couldn't be heard at all. She wasn't sure if she should get up to follow, risking her exposure, so she stayed silent instead. The next thing she knew, the sun was nudging her eyes persistently. She had to think for a moment why she wasn't in her comfortable bed, but when the realization hit, she got up and ran over the hill, to the spot with freshly upturned dirt, fell to her knees and began digging. When she uncovered the bag, she poked at it, something firm. There was a hole in the bag where she could see human flesh.

CHAPTER THIRTEEN

Lanie
Truman Coolidge's Farm

"WHAT'S THIS GUY'S name again? If he does something funny, I'm going to shout it and we're running in the other direction." November rolls her window down and lets out a howl.

With two recent deaths now at the Sassy Lasses Winery, I am skeptical that anyone will want to hold events there. It may be easier to wait and get married at the Inn and Spa at Fallen Branch Resort when it's finished.

Vem insisted on driving back out here with me today to visit the neighbor of Marveline and Mandy. She sensed something evil, as per usual. I'm beginning to wonder if it isn't an easy way to avoid cleaning her house.

"Truman Coolidge. His family has been on the property for three generations, all equally disagreeable according to the gossip Mandy heard." I turn down at the gravel road, the one with a red-lettered sign marked, PRESIDENTIAL LANE. Underneath, there is a wooden sign with the words "NOT FRIENDLY. SELL YOUR NONESENSE ELSEWHERE" painted in red, white and blue.

We roll up in front of a modest, two-story, brick home with large hedges towering over each window. In stark contrast, there are small concrete busts of each United States president lining the neat, green lawn. Beside each statue stands a small American flag.

A large, grey dog comes barreling towards the car as I open the door. "Treasure your fingers!" Vem warns, leaning across me and slamming the door shut.

I stare at her with disgust. "What are we supposed to do now? He knows we're coming!" The dog is barking and jumping on our windows, smearing drool and whatever else he's accumulated under his paws all over my freshly washed vehicle.

"Well, we're not risking our lives for your investigation. I can sense that dog is out of balance. He would benefit from my Fido Friendly Yoga Hour." Vem wraps her arms around the middle of her peach jumpsuit. "Maybe you should call this Truman person and let him know we're here. Or maybe this is his way of making us his next victims." She shivers. "It would be a gruesome way to go."

Before we can make any decisions, a portly over-all-clad man with short, grey hair and a bushy mustache steps out the front door. "Grover! Inside now!" He commands. The dog obediently runs for the house, pausing only to lift his leg over the statue of Chester A. Arthur, 21st President of the United States.

The man comes to my door and raps harshly on the window.

Vem puts her arm on mine. "Proceed with caution, Lanie. Remember, I know martial arts and have a killer instinct."

As I stand up beside him, he sticks a chubby hand in mine. "Truman Coolidge, ma'am. Assuming you're Lanie Anders?"

"Yes, thank you so much for allowing us to visit." I turn around, motioning through the window for Vem to get out of the car. "My associate, November Bean, and I have some questions we're hoping you can answer."

Truman scratches the arm of his red, white and blue t-shirt. He appears to be chewing on a long-stemmed piece of grass. "I set up a table 'round the back there, with some of my grandma's sweet tea and White House Molasses Cookies from the official recipe. Several president's favorites, you know." He guides us toward the backyard. Vem reaches my side and grasps my arm tightly. Neither of us are ready for more canine surprises.

"Yes, I noticed you have quite a display of presidents. Is it a hobby of yours?"

He stops and hooks his thumbs around the straps of his overalls. "First and last names are presidential. Don't take that responsibility lightly, ma'am. You're welcome to view my collection of presidential statues round the yard when you please. Got a museum-quality display and a ten-minute film inside. Don't trust that to strangers until visit three."

We reach his backyard, a pleasant covered patio with four bright red chairs and a blue metal table set up with drinks and cookies. "Please, sit." Truman pours us each a glass of tea and passes a plate heaped with sugared molasses cookies to November.

Vem picks up a cookie and sniffs it carefully before putting it back on the plate.

"I've had several conversations with your neighbors, the Phersons. They are lovely women."

Truman leans forward, moving his face uncomfortably close to mine. "Don't trust 'em. They came out here with their fancy cars and acted like they were too good for the likes of an old farm boy like me. One of my namesakes, Calvin Coolidge, never believed in the power of silence. I don't bother 'em, but I won't help 'em neither."

"Is it them, or is the property in general? Marveline mentioned that your family had a feud with the previous owner, Welcome Naybor."

The old man blessedly leans back, clasping his hands over his enormous belly. "Well now, that's a different story entirely."

"Did you have him killed?" Vem asks, impulsively grabbing a cookie and stuffing it in her mouth.

"Vem!"

"My family didn't like him, that's true. My grandpa wanted that land. As the story goes, he was on his way into town to sign the papers when his horse spooked and overturned. Killed him instantly."

"The Wormly family bought it instead. I read about their tragic deaths."

He scratches his head and puts a beefy arm on the table. "That's right. After the Wormly family's untimely deaths, my dad tried buying the land to let the evil rest. Saved up for years to make that purchase. Instead, Welcome and Larry Naybor offered twice as much for the land. 'Nother outsider comin' in just to cause trouble."

"And now there are deaths, just like during Mr. Naybor's time on the property." I hold my breath, hoping this won't make him come unglued.

"We don't know a Larry, do we Lanie?" Vem says through a mouth full of molasses cookies.

"We only know of Welcome and his daughter, Pookie, living in the home. You're saying there was someone else?" I ask, ignoring Vem.

"Yes'm. Originally, Welcome and his brother

bought the property. Larry was the nice one. Poor Larry died and then it was just Welcome, 'til he had his daughter. Cursed place."

Truman pulls the grass from his mouth. "It's a dang shame 'bout those two men. But those women are making the same mistakes Mr. Naybor did – they're hirin' drifters and that's a bad element. My mother used to say, 'If you hitch your wagon to a turd, you're always gonna smell bad.'"

I study his face, trying to find any clues that might lead me to his dark inner thoughts. I could actually use November's smelling instincts right about now.

"Mr. Truman," Vem stands, putting a hand on each hip, "if you keep killing people, you'll never rid yourself of this curse."

I smile at this tactic that I taught her. We had a lengthy discussion about the seminar I attended where I learned that making yourself look bigger can be intimidating to the person you're speaking with: Body Wow. I got food poisoning and left early before I slept with anyone.

"No killing. I do my woodwork and, besides the farming, that's enough to keep me busy. One day I'd like to build my own all-presidential library, but for now, I'm–"

"I know a little something about curses, sir. Been studying them for six months, just in case I need a few extra tricks in my bag. You have the power to rid yourself of this now, and I can help."

Truman cocks his head to the side. "Is this one missin' a light in the attic?" He jabs a thumb in November's direction.

"Mr. Coolidge, I think what November is trying ever-so-awkwardly to say is that there are concerns that the neighbors will do whatever it takes to rid themselves of the Phersons."

"Now lookee here," his face pinches up small. "I already told the police I don't have any reason to kill nobody. Would I rather the place was empty? Sure. But I'm a president-loving man. Wouldn't dishonor either Mr. Coolidge or Mr. Truman's name by killing. Now, that Mr. Naybor...he's another story."

Vem eases her posture and I motion for her to sit again. "Another cookie?" I shove the plate in front of her.

"You've never shot your gun in the air to scare the women?"

Truman sighs. "One time. When they first pulled in with their moving van. It was foolish on my part, thinkin' I could scare city folk away. Never done it since. Well, maybe twice. Yeah, let's go with twice."

"Please, do tell me more about Mr. Naybor. I've just begun my research on him."

"My dad always said he was slicker'n goobers on a doorknob. That man dressed fancy and drove an expensive car. Dad said when he came into town on Saturdays, everybody stopped what they was doing just to stare at his shiny car. He'd throw pennies to the kids and wave to the grown-ups."

"He was kind of a showman?" I ask.

"Like all showmen, it was a front. In his case, he brought in food for the poor but expected something in return." Truman takes a toothpick from his pocket and sticks it in his mouth, moving it around on his tongue.

"What could they give him?"

"Favors. Rumor was he was into all sorts of illegal activities. During prohibition, he had commercial ships going back and forth from the United States to Canada, where he brought back bottles marked as maple syrup. Nothing sweet inside. Those were full of whiskey."

I shrug my shoulders. "I'm sure there were a lot of enterprising folks who sold alcohol during the depression. That doesn't make him–"

"Man had a temper on him. But like I said, he was slick. If he felt you done him wrong, and he got that feeling a lot, he'd make sure you had no customers willing to buy your crop, or worse."

A chill goes up my spine. Vem must be rubbing off. "What 'worse' do you mean?"

"Lots of his employees disappeared. It was a well-known occurrence. One man worked for us for a summer. Pleasant fella and hard worker. He told Dad he needed extra money since he had a baby coming soon. He worked on the Naybor property for a month. One day he comes to Dad and says he's made a mistake and Mr. Naybor would probably be coming soon to get him fired here. Dad says, now don't you worry, your job is safe here. The next weekend, he goes to work at Naybor Manor and he doesn't come back."

"Didn't your dad go searching for him?"

Truman shakes his head. "Naybor didn't like Dad either. Anybody he couldn't control was his enemy. Thought Dad looked at him funny one day. Dad – Millard Fillmore Coolidge, that is – was smart enough to steer clear of him after that. Men with that kind of power don't need a proper reason to do a farmer in."

On our drive home, Vem tips her seat back and tries to sleep. The phone rings and I answer it quickly – she can be scary when she's woken suddenly. It is the coroner, Nate Cadbury. In his spare time, he does plumbing as a side business, so I'd contacted him about working on our new home; that was before Cosmo fell into darkness. He promised to call me when he found a cause of death for the two employees at Sassy Lasses.

"Miz Anders? Just wanted you to know, we've got an idea, but not an exact one. Opium from the poppy flower mixed with black plum-flower root. A quick high followed by a prolonged, agonizing death. We've seen it gaining popularity around here. The amount in those bodies was enough to kill a good-sized moose."

"Thanks, Nate."

"One more thing: I've seen this once before, back about ten years. It was a drifter we'd assumed had gotten some bad drugs from somewhere else."

My mind races. I think about the strange concoction of salvia that Fillmont Wormly was forced to take. These are different plants, but more deaths on the property make me wonder if they are somehow connected. It's no curse, but it may not be a coincidence either.

"Miz Anders? Are you still there?"

"Yes, Nate, just trying to put a puzzle together in my head that may not be a puzzle at all. Let's get together soon and talk plumbing. Cosmo will be ready to start work on our place any day now." That is an outright lie. I can't see a time in the near future when we'll be working on anything. I push those dark thoughts away.

"I don't think Truman did it," I say to myself after hanging up. "It just doesn't sit right with me. He's strange, but he's no chemist." I look over at my friend who is resting peacefully. "There must be someone else angry enough with the women to–"

"Marveline." Vem snaps her seat to an upright position. "I think it's Marveline. She's hiding something."

"Maybe."

We pull up in my driveway and I see Cosmo looking through the window, drinking his coffee. My heart leaps. "Look who's up!" I say gleefully. Without waiting for Vem to get out of the car, I leap up the stairs and open the door, running toward him so hard I knock him off balance. His coffee spills on our newly-stained wood floor but I don't care.

"You're feeling better then?"

He kisses my head. "A little. I felt bad about what happened the other day."

Luckily for Piper, we could create enough of a diversion she didn't know we had found a body. Cosmo agreed to stay until she blew out her candles. She didn't suspect a thing.

I can't seem to let him out of my embrace. "Cos, it's okay. I know you're having a hard time. There have been big changes in your life. Cedar was your rock and now she's hundreds of miles away. But I'm here. I'll be your rock, if you'll let me."

He pulls me in tight. "I'm sorry I've been such a jerk, Lanie."

After I wipe up the coffee spill, we move to the couch. On the way by the big picture window, I see Vem skipping up to her house. I'll call her later and apologize for my abrupt departure.

"During Piper's birthday party, Marveline introduced me to the caretaker."

I stroke his neck, relieved he isn't jumping from my touch. "Delbert? He upset you? He and his wife, Esmay, are a little odd, but we're used to odd."

"Delbert is an old acquaintance of mine from way back."

"From Fallen Branch?" I frown. "Strange that November didn't say anything."

"No, it was after Fallen Branch." Cosmo pauses, his long thinking pause that always means something important will follow. "I met him when I was in prison. He was there, too. Served at least thirty years. We were like oil and water, scuffling in the yard every time we were given the chance. We made a promise that if we ever saw each other on the outside, we would walk the other way."

I try to imagine my gentle giant scrapping in the prison yard with another man. "What was he in prison for?"

"Murder."

Chapter Fourteen

Pookie
1947

Dearest Ophelia,

I fear I've fallen in love with a man far more dangerous than I imagined. After running home and pretending I'd just awoken, I asked permission to see Raymond before my lessons began. Daddy said I could, just for a few minutes if I promised I would not keep Miss Dandridge waiting.

My dear, sweet, Raymond. I wanted him to explain to me what happened the night before. The man I see is a gentle soul who wouldn't hurt anyone. I planned it out in my mind, how I would gaze at him adoringly and he would crumble under my powerful feminine wiles. He would confess to running over Paulo with the tractor by accident and the stranger, his shipmate he thought was missing, offered to help bury him so he wouldn't get in trouble. Raymond would kiss me passionately after his confession. I would promise never to share his secret.

Instead, as I ran out the front door, he was standing just outside of the yard, cool as a cucumber. He opened the little white gate and tipped his hat. "You're looking fine this day, Miss Pookie," he said with his endearing half-smile. It was as if nothing happened at all. He didn't feel like he could trust me.

My heart sank. Could Daddy be right, that these drifters are all the same, incapable of living respectable lives so they have to move on when their game is discovered? My Raymond covers up a murder and pretends like its nothing. I don't know whether I should tell Daddy. He would most likely call the sheriff and have my poor Raymond arrested. Then I would never understand what drove him to such madness.

This weekend, I shall demand we invite him over for dinner so I may study him. Maybe he will exhibit a characteristic familiar from one of Tulip Sloan's movies. Then I will fully understand him and perhaps even pity the circumstances he found himself in.

Miss Dandridge says I'm a girl with too many emotions. She thinks these emotions need to come out before I burst in the most *unladylike way. Being the thoughtful sort, she has provided me with materials to paint. She says I needn't share my work with Daddy if it is something I prefer to keep to myself and perfect. My teacher is such a wise woman.*

Yours in Thoughtfulness,
Pookie A. Naybor

"Daddy? You promised you would be civil. Please remember he is our guest and we must treat him with respect."

Welcome looked over his spectacles and folded his paper. "Why would you even say such a thing? Don't I help the poor? Employ those in need? Pookie, how can you think your father would be unkind?"

Pookie came over to his chair and hugged him from behind. "I'm sorry, Daddy. You're right. I just sense you don't like Raymond so much. I want him to enjoy his time with us. Maybe he'll stay longer than a season. Maybe he'll…"

"Hold on, Little Miss," Welcome chuckled. "You remember drifters aren't the type to stick around. We will be grateful for the time he's given us, and happily welcome new employees into our Naybor Manor family when his run is over. It's fine to entertain him for an evening, but let's not decide he's anything other than what he is."

Pookie tilted her head to the side and looked at

her father. He thought of drifters as less than him. It was the first time she'd had that realization and it made her insides feel funny.

When Raymond knocked on the door at precisely five-fifteen, Pookie was pulling her signature peach pie from the oven. She'd made a roast with Naybor Farm potatoes, pickled beans canned by their next-door-neighbor, who snuck out to visit Pookie when her husband was busy, and rolls she made the night before, while she sat up thinking about questions to ask Raymond.

"Evenin', Miss Pookie."

Raymond gave off the scent of the licorice-root soap placed in the bunkhouse. Welcome imported the bars from Canada and insisted all of his employees use it nightly. If they didn't exhibit that distinct scent each morning, he would fire them on the spot. Pookie was never allowed to use such a "manly" scent on her delicate body.

"Please, come in," Pookie made a sweeping motion with her arm as she opened the door, just as she'd seen Welcome do a hundred times with his guests.

Raymond's eyes grew large as they reached the table covered in Naybor finery. She pulled out the chair she'd placed slightly closer to hers before seating herself in the next chair over.

"Pookie," Welcome nodded encouragingly, "it's

only right you say the blessing, since you prepared this lovely meal."

"Oh, no, Daddy. I would like Raymond to say the blessing. He's got a gift for words that I don't. And he's certainly much more to say today."

Raymond looked at Pookie and frowned. "I don't know 'bout that. But I'll be happy to." He took Pookie's hand and looked at Welcome expectantly. Welcome kept both of his hands pressed firmly into his lap.

"Dearest Almighty," Raymond began. "We give thanks for those 'round us here at the table and all this deliciousness Miss Pookie prepared." He dropped Pookie's hand, causing her face to drop as well.

"That's it?" Welcome asked.

"It was lovely," Pookie remarked, staring at him adoringly. She'd heard his stomach rumble when he walked in the door, so as soon as he finished, she stood and brought all the steaming dishes to his side of the table.

"The rest of the boys at the bunkhouse will be hankerin' for details on this special feast. Thank you for inviting me, Miss Pookie," Raymond took a giant spoon of potatoes and put them on his plate.

"Are you still writing letters to your family, Raymond? I'm happy to transport them to the post office in town whenever you'd like." Welcome took one of Pookie's rolls and passed the plate to Raymond without looking up.

Raymond smiled. "I enjoy my time driving into town for supplies. I'm fine mailing my letters on my day off. My ma likes hearin' about things out here. She's never been away from Oklahoma, in all of her forty-eight years."

"Raymond goes for long walks in the evenings," Pookie announced daringly. "He must have incredible energy after his long day of work on the farm."

Raymond and Welcome looked at Pookie sharply.

"Helps me to clear my mind after a day of labor." He stared so hard she thought he might bore a hole into her.

"But shouldn't one have a destination when they travel? Isn't it important to know just where you want to turn around so that you've reached your goal?"

Welcome sighed, setting his fork down with a bang. "Pookie, I'm finding your tone a bit impertinent. Apologize to Raymond, please. Let's have polite conversation at the table and nothing more."

She tried remembering a scene from one of Tulip Sloan's movies. One where Tulip acted as the sleuth solving a mystery. Daddy couldn't possibly understand how important these questions were. "I'm sorry, Raymond. I was just curious about your walks. And I was wondering if I might accompany you on one."

Raymond's eyes grew wide. "A feller can't clear his head if he's got company. You're welcome to help me with my chores, but I'd like my time alone to remain so."

"He's right, daughter. He's entitled to his privacy without being concerned a nattering girl will disturb him."

Pookie put her head down and said no more.

They ate the rest of their dinner exchanging only small pleasantries, especially when it came to Pookie's peach pie. "This has to be the best I've et. Honestly, Miss Pookie."

Welcome got up from the table and returned a short time later with two cups and saucers. Raymond shook his head. "No, thank you. Body don't take kindly to tea."

"That's a shame. My tea is known for its relaxing tendencies. Those who drink it always beg for more." Welcome took a small sip and then another.

As they said their goodbyes, Pookie wanted to run to Raymond and hug him tightly, promising she would never be impertinent again. He refused to look her in the eye as he removed his hat from the rack and took his leave. Instead of understanding her code for important information, he found her irritating and girlish.

The following weekend, Pookie went to the theatre unsure if she would share her information with Freddie or not. She realized she was now working as a double agent, sharing secret information with two different people. It was just like Tulip Sloan's character Delora in *My Favorite Spy*.

Freddie wasn't exactly trustworthy when it came to secrets these days. He found out about the brassiere Daddy purchased for her from a fancy store in Portland and told every kid in town, causing them to stop her on the street and snap it.

"You're awful quiet today, Pookie. Don't like that much," he remarked as he munched on his popcorn.

"Well, I have some information that might not surprise you, Freddie," she began carefully, wishing she could stop herself from talking. "But you have to swear you won't tell a soul. At least until I can make sure I know exactly what happened."

Freddie put the popcorn down and took his friend's face in his greasy hands. "You've gotta tell me, Pook. This sounds serious. You gonna be in trouble for something?"

Pookie shook her head. "It's Raymond. You know I told you he's been leaving at night, twice a week. I followed him last week."

"He's got a woman. I knew it! That's what Ma said when I told her."

Pookie was slightly disturbed that Frankie confessed all of her stories to his mother. "It's not a woman. I followed him to a remote part of Naybor Farm. He met someone there and they had a serious conversation. The other man left something with Raymond that he buried–"

Freddie's eyes were as round as saucers. "A body! Your hired man buried a body!"

"Shhh!" She clapped her hand over his mouth. "You swore you wouldn't say anything, remember?" She leaned over and whispered in his ear. "I think he's helping a killer. I just have to find out why." Pookie waited a few minutes before removing her hand from his mouth.

"You've got to go to the gosh-darned sheriff! I told you he was no good. I told you!"

"I'm not going to the sheriff until I understand fully what's going on. You don't know Raymond the way I do. He's a kind soul. He wouldn't hurt anyone without a good reason."

"Can I help?"

Pookie's face was serious. "If you PROMISE you won't tell anyone. Not even your mother. Otherwise, you can't be a part of my inner circle."

Freddie made an "x" over his chest. "I promise. At least I won't tell nobody until we find out the truth."

"Remember when you told me about stealing

your mother's cigarettes and selling them to all of your friends for a penny each?"

Freddie looked at her guardedly. "Yeah, so what of it?"

"Well, if you tell your mother or anyone else about Raymond, I'll make sure she finds out what happened to her cigarettes. I bet you'll be doing extra chores for a long time to pay for all of those."

"Aw, geez. You know I won't say anything. Really, Pook."

"Good." Pookie smiled, though she had no doubt he would run home to his mother and blab everything anyway. He was her only friend, other than Raymond, and she needed him. "Now, I just have to figure out what to do next. We had him over for dinner and he wouldn't say anything in front of Daddy."

"Keep following him. Every time he goes out, you go out with your notebook. You love to write, so write all the tiny bits about where he's going and what he's wearing. That's what Tulip Sloan would do."

Just as she had been keeping detailed notes for Raymond, she would begin doing the same for Freddie. There was nothing wrong with that. In *Woman of Detail*, Tulip followed her husband for weeks before discovering he was cheating on her with a spy from Germany.

"I'll start tomorrow night. Every Sunday evening, I watch from my window while he leaves the bunkhouse. Instead of being so lazy, falling to sleep like a princess upon my throne, I shall follow him again and again."

"Then you'll bring your notebook back and we'll figure out what to do next, right, Pook?"

CHAPTER FIFTEEN

Lanie
Sassy Lasses Winery

I GULP. "COS, was Delbert convicted the way you were, easily framed because you couldn't hire a good attorney?"

Cosmo shakes his head. "He really killed someone. Like me, he was a kid – an angry one. Bad things tend to happen when that attitude goes unchecked."

He slides his hand behind my neck, tickling me gently with his rough fingers. It feels like old times. I want to grab him and hold him tight in case this is some kind of a dream. But I don't. He's too fragile right now.

"It's a sad story." Cosmo breathes out slowly. "Delbert came here from down South. He had a hard life. His parents abandoned him so he grew up with his elderly grandma and when she died, he was on his own. He stole to eat. When that didn't work anymore, he started collecting debts for the local mobsters. They scared the hell out of him, and when they wanted to step him up to hit man, he took off."

"Why did he end up here?"

"Heard about the northwest all of his life. Thought the coast sounded pretty. When he got to Portland, being a young guy, he thought he could start over with a new identity. He was wrong. His buddies found him and made him do a hit in exchange for his own life."

I shake my head. "That's so sad. He never had a chance. Poor Delbert."

"Of course, he got caught; and of course, they all abandoned him. He pretty much gave up on life at that point. He agreed to plead guilty, hoping to get a lighter sentence. Here's the rub: at the sentencing he found out it wasn't just anyone he'd killed; it was the judge's brother. Ended up getting a thirty-year sentence. Buck Rogers Time, they called it. A release date so far away that it's difficult to imagine."

"So, Delbert spent most of his adult life in prison?"

"He sure did. By the time I'd arrived, he'd been there for over twenty years. He owned the place. I was too young and cocky to understand it was his playground."

I get up and pour myself some Sassy Lasses Rebel Riesling, bringing back a beer for Cosmo when I sit. "Cos, what happened?"

"I'd spent my entire life being told what to do and when to do it. You'd think I would be the perfect inmate." He chuckles. "Instead, I was mad. I resented that there was an order to things in prison, just the same as there was in the cult. Delbert and me, we ended up on opposite sides. I challenged him day after day. Finally, he had to put a young punk in his place."

"Did he hurt you?" I touch his face, thinking about the horror Cosmo experienced before our connection. It's easy to forget he lived another life; a harsh one.

He pulls my hand to his face and kisses it. "There's a code. We're not supposed to talk about what happened behind bars to the outside world. But I know that you and I made a pact, too, and it's more important than those promises."

"If you can't tell me, I respect that." *But it would kill me to have another secret between us.*

Cosmo sighs. "Lanie, Delbert didn't touch me. He didn't have to. He was king of the yard by then and all he did was give the nod and everyone else took their turn."

"Oh, Cos!"

"After that day, he became my celly. He was there, watching my every move. It was worse than anything they did to me in that prison yard. If I got out of line, said anything wrong, he was physically inches from and put me in my place. Hellish first year."

"Are you still scared of him? Is that why you didn't want to have the wedding at Sassy Lasses Vineyard?"

"When his release date came, he told me the sight of me made him sick. Made me promise to walk on the other side of the street if I ever saw him again. He didn't need any reminders of his time inside. There'd be no contact. I agreed to that. I'm going to hold up my end of the deal. There's something buried deep in that man, something festering that I want no part of."

I try and picture the kindly old caretaker we met torturing my poor Cosmo. The picture just won't form in my head. "Couldn't he leave during our wedding?" I can't bear the thought of telling Mandy and Marveline that we won't have our wedding there. They need us as much as we, well I, need them.

"Delbert may not have been a seasoned criminal when he went to prison. But I can tell you, the years behind bars really honed his skills. I don't want to cross him."

"Is he still capable of...murder?"

Cosmo shrugs. "Anything is possible. He whispered with his crew late at night about a lot of things. You know how I hate to give credence to any of November Bean's crazy feelings. But I always had a sense there was more to that guy."

That night I fall into an uneasy sleep, wondering if Marveline and Mandy understand Delbert's past. The next morning my phone rings insistently until I pick it up.

"Lanie? Are you coming?"

I look over at the clock. 7:15. I normally only get up this early for meetings about the resort with the Sleepy Sounds Corporate team.

"Gladys? What am I supposed to be doing? Are you even at work yet?"

There is a snort on the other end of the line. "Course I am, silly. Up with the sun most days. Don't see any point in sitting at home staring at the wallpaper when I could be doing something useful."

"Tell me again why I should be suffering there with you?"

"You asked for information on those gaddy women. The Pherman sisters."

"The Phersons? I asked you? Last I recall, you didn't want to be involved in this. You were too busy mentoring Piper."

"That immature girl hasn't been answering my calls. I tell you, if I were her mother–"

"Her mother is dead, remember?" I run my fingers through my knotted hair. "If you have some information to help me, I could be down there soon. I'll need coffee first."

"You can get coffee when you stop to get my scone, toots. Pluto Peach."

"I remember, thanks."

I brush my lips lightly across Cosmo's forehead before heading to the shower. Gladys has a rhythm like no one else. I guess I shouldn't question it.

When I arrive, she is pacing back and forth, exhibiting more energy than should be legal for a woman of nearly a century.

"'Bout time. I was ready to call Boysie." Boysie Lumquest, her son-in-law, is the police chief at the station and subject to her every beck and call, as apparently I am as well.

"I doubt the two patrolmen on duty have time to search for a missing scone delivery person. Piper sends her regards, by the way. She says she's been busy and will call you once Cosmo comes back in to help her at work."

"Lanie, would you please make something up so that busybody will leave me alone? I'm trying to get to know people my age and she's cramping my style."

"Humph. Doubtful she'd think twice about me." Gladys waves the thought away like a day-old scone placed under her nose. "More importantly, we need to discuss your life. We all know that boyfriend of yours isn't going to pull himself out of his slump until you two set a date and get married."

"He's doing much better!" I protest. "Last night, he was like his old self. I'm sure it won't be long until he's back to his regular schedule."

I set a vase on the desk, a peace offering from Piper. The owner of the gas station insisted upon leaving them for Piper even after she politely declined. "A gift for you."

"Blech. Get rid of 'em. Roses make my stomach queasy." Gladys pulls the sack from my hand while simultaneously pushing the vase away from her. "When you've lived ten decades like I have, you get to recognize the ups and downs in a life," she continues. "That boy's been mostly in the downs. You are his only up. You'd better make sure you marry him before he ends up in that down spot permanently." She plops down into her chair with a thud and points to the chair closest to me. "Sit down while I eat," she commands.

Gladys is known for her voracious and messy eating. Actually, most people in Piney Falls have a similar style. I'd like to know if there was some kind of mandate in the early years where every family had to eat with gusto. I position myself strategically in the folding chair, far enough away that I won't get crumbs but close enough that she can hear me.

"So, remind me when I asked you to help find information on these women?"

"Lanie," she says with crumbs spewing forward.

"You said, 'I need help researching that winery. When my friends need help, I come a'runnin' if I can. Friendships are everything to a woman. I found myself with extra time on my hands and searched the dark web for you."

I decide not to waste time pointing out that she refused to help me before. "And? What did you find?"

Gladys shoves her mess aside and puts her feet on the desk. "Two sisters from a wealthy family. Pherson Pharmaceuticals in Denver. Parents died, causes of death, drug overdose. Morphine, to be exact. They thought, wrongly, that their company was in the throes of bankruptcy. The wife had a leg injury and she treated the pain with morphine. Those rich folks can get access to any medication–"

"Are there any other children besides Marveline and Mandy?" I'm trying to decide if I'm more irritated that she obtained this information without my asking, or that she's telling me through a fountain of food.

Gladys shakes her head, causing crumbs to tumble from her mouth, coating the floor with golden-yellow bits of scone.

"They certainly benefitted from their parents' deaths then. That's curious. I wonder how they chose Piney Falls for their destination?"

"Folks come here for strange reasons. Look at

you, toots. Came to write a book and now we can't get rid of you." Gladys winks.

"I suppose you're right. I'll need to talk to them again and see if anything is amiss."

"Now can you tell them to leave? Let that property go back to nature, as it should?"

I shake my head. "No, Gladys. I'm afraid they're here to stay. I wish I understood why you and others are so set on their failure. They just want to run a business. That's good for everyone."

Gladys walks around her desk and puts her frail, sticky hands on my shoulders. "Lanie, that place has caused us all more pain that you can imagine. Ever since the Wormlys. Did you hear about them? And everyone on the land ever since? Nothing but misery and death."

I start to correct her, but change my mind. "Yes, I've gotten information from the state historical society. One big mystery. Anything else?"

"Isn't that enough? I guess we could talk about your wedding. Now that you're going to rid yourself of that winery place, we can find a nice place in town. When will the hotel and spa be finished?"

"The Inn and Spa at Fallen Branch Resort? It may be a few more months than we anticipated. They've run into some zoning issues, among other things." The last time we had our conference call, Derrick Williams told me it may be closer to a year.

Good things take time, Lanie. You know how the business world works. Gladys would pop her cork if I told her the truth.

The old woman points her finger at my face. "You promised us town folk that place would be up and running long ago. We wouldn't have agreed to putting it on the cult land if you'da told us it would take years. How much longer do you think I have on this earth? Nobody lives too many years past their hundredth birthday."

I sigh. It would be very sad to cut the ribbon on the property without Gladys front and center. "I have no control over that. I do the marketing. They are taking their time and making it nice for you. Remember, you wanted a fancy pool to soak your pathetically pooped parts? Your words, not mine. They're digging that right now."

Gladys's face softens. There isn't much in her small world that gets her as excited as the thought of her own personal pool time.

I smile encouragingly and search my mind for a diversion. "Someone should throw you a big party. It's a genuine achievement to reach your age and remain in such good health."

Gladys brushes crumbs off her desk. "Used to. Every year. It was Gentry Phillips' doing. He died. Then it was Curtis David's turn. He up and moved away. I'm only up to last decade. Do you want me to go on?"

"No, I get it." I chuckle. "Thanks for your information. Maybe I can plan a birthday party for you. It's a shame you missed Piper's party."

"Heard enough from Urica. Found a body. 'Nother one. Does that seem like a party an old woman should attend? Gracious, girl."

I shake my head. She's finally making sense. "No, you're right about that."

I get up to leave, wondering what I should do to fill the rest of my morning, at least until Cosmo is ready to join the world. Eight-fifty-eight. "Maybe I'll attend one of Vem's classes this morning. I forgot to look at my schedule, but I think today is Mental Mountain Moaning. You should try one, Gladys. There are for people of all ages."

"Oh? I'm afraid something might just fall off if I did that. You never know. I heard of a man in Tellum who pushed himself out of his chair to answer the door and his arm came clean out of the socket. Had to amputate, 'cause there was no fixing it at his age."

I struggle to keep a straight face. "Maybe you could pull up a chair and watch a class. You might get a kick out of Vem's teaching style." *Bawdily Bodacious. That's my style, Lanie. Tell everyone you know.*

"Oh, and Lanie? There's one more thing."

"Yes?"

"If you won't tell those women to leave, at least tell them they're sitting on a piece of history."

"They know that. They've done an incredible job restoring the place to its old glory."

"That house has all sorts of hidden rooms and passageways. It used to be the talk of the town back in the day. Maybe something in there for the museum. Rumor has it, there's proof that something horrible happened in them."

CHAPTER SIXTEEN

Pookie
1947

Dearest Ophelia,

I can barely keep my eyes open. In the glamour magazines I read, it says a woman must be sure she sleeps for nine hours every evening or her eyes will become permanently baggy. Tulip Sloan herself sleeps ten hours every night. She tapes the top of her eyelid to her brow, to prevent saggage. It's evident she doesn't have to worry about bags anyway. She's the model of perfection.

It quite shocked Miss Dandridge the other day when I fell asleep while writing an essay entitled, "The Great War Between the States." She knew of my admiration of President Lincoln and wondered if I might be ill. She thought I might be upset about my impending womanhood and suggested I write my hopes and dreams on a paper and put

*them somewhere secret. I did just that, choos-
ing the ornately-carved oak table in the
hallway. My secrets, hidden so well out in the
open. Someday I shall read my note with
triumph, knowing I've accomplished everything I wished for.*

*For now, my thoughts lie elsewhere. I've
been so troubled by my darling Raymond's
deceit. One morning as Daddy and I sat eating breakfast, he commented on the fine work
Raymond did for us. He would be sad when
this drifter took his leave.*

*Well, Ophelia, right then and there I al-
most told him of Raymond's transgressions.
That he had buried a body on our property –
who's body I was too weak to determine.
Then I looked upon the innocence of Daddy,
his soft-as-a-peach face freshly shaven and his
neatly-trimmed, dark mustache moving back
and forth as he silently mouthed the words on
the paper. Dear, sweet, Daddy. I couldn't
bear to break his heart. He's worked so hard
to keep our Naybor Manor the finest home
on the coast, giving jobs to countless down-
on-their-luck men.*

*Instead, I kissed the top of his balding
head and went about my day. That night, I
snuck out again, following Raymond at a
distance as he met his mystery man at the*

designated location once more. On Naybor property, we have lighted roads. Daddy thought it necessary so that his employees could work late into the night to harvest crops right up until the end of the growing season. We have six primary thoroughfares on the property and each one has rows of lights on either side, illuminating the road. Raymond and his friend met near Naybor Lane East, just off the gravel, where their faces were barely visible. They stood watching warily for the unlikely occasion of a truck driving up and encroaching upon them.

I strained my ears to hear what was being said, but very few words drifted to my location on top of the hill where I lie in the tall grass. My ever-present flashlight and notebook rested beside me in the bag Daddy bought for me to use while we planted seeds. After several mentions of "the target" and "a count of evidence" the two men parted. I was flat to the ground, daring only to breathe in shallow breaths until I knew Raymond was long past me. I am getting good at this sleuth business.

You, Ophelia, are the only recipient of this information now. Freddie's eager ears will have to wait until I've been able to determine much more. Maybe next week I'll *creep a little closer and I'll be able to hear at least a full a sentence.*

Yours in Concern and Love,
Pookie A. Naybor

She was feeling a chill from the prior evening. Pookie put on her rain boots and found an umbrella in the stand by the front door. Raymond would surely share with her if he were going to do something terrible.

She sloshed down to the bunkhouse, slipping and sliding and almost losing her footing as she went. When she reached her destination, the door opened.

"Well hello there, Miss Pookie." Raymond pulled his hood up. "Didn't expect to see your bright face at this tender hour. I was on my way to milk the cows."

"Can I walk with you for a few minutes?"

Raymond shrugged. "Suit yourself."

As they walked along the road, Raymond swung the bucket by his side. "Glorious mornin'. Be glad we're above ground to witness it."

Pookie stared at him, wondering if he was making some kind of sick joke about Paulo. "Daddy says I should apologize for the other night. It wasn't right of me to be impertinent while you were our dinner guest."

"Well," he cleared his throat. "I s'pect your daddy is right. You weren't the friendly young lady I've come to know. I wasn't sure what was going on with you, if it was a bad day or—"

"It was a bad day. I have those sometimes. I'm sure you do as well."

They reached the barn and he sat down on the little milking stool beside Dahlia, the rust-colored one of their two milking cows, and patted her broad, brown side.

"Try not to have the bad days, Miss Pookie. You have to feel thankfulness for each and every one."

"Oh, yes indeed." She paced around him, trying to form the words in just the right order. "When you have bad days, what do you do about it? Do you pound your fists on the table? Or do you, maybe, go on long walks to figure things out?"

Raymond looked up and studied her face. "What'r you askin', Miss Pookie?"

She shrugged, looking at her feet. "I just wondered what you did. We all have our vices. You don't have anything to be ashamed of, Raymond, really."

He went back to milking. "I'm not ashamed of nothing, Miss Pookie. I learned when I was travelin' the world and we were in close quarters. You don't let others see your bad day. It's like you're sharing a private part of you with a stranger, and once they get ahold of that, they chew on it like a piece of juicy meat."

I sat down beside him on the hay covering the

barn floor. "Someone used your anger against you? On the ship?"

"One man. He thought he was smarter'n everyone else on board. In some ways, he was. Just like a cat, he waited and watched for you to make a mistake. Then he'd pounce. You were never the same after that."

"So, he hurt you?"

Raymond nodded. "Me and several other crew. Some worse'n others. If they didn't do exactly what he said or breathed a word of his misdeeds to anyone else, he'd torture them, some until they took their last breath."

I put my arm on his shoulder. "Oh, Raymond. I'm sorry you had to live that way. It's a good thing we're not like that here."

He stopped milking and looked at her muddy boots. "Where you been in them things, Miss? Looks like you've been on an adventure of yer own."

"Huh?" She looked down at the boots she'd worn the night before, following him through the rain. They were covered in mud, not unlike everything else in the barn. "I wasn't paying attention when I came down here this morning. I slipped."

He leaned in close and pulled off a long piece of grass. "This ain't from the drive. This is from a field. Have you been a 'wandering where you're not supposed to go? Out in the forbidden field?"

She pulled her boot back and crossed her arms. "No! Of course not. I would never disobey Daddy like that."

"You been somewhere, Miss Pookie. I ain't no dummy. You gonna tell me, or make me guess? Don't want me tellin' your daddy you was out and about where you shouldn't be."

She gasped. "You'd betray me?" She couldn't let him know she'd been following him, not until she had more information. "You're right. I tried to see the forbidden field. I just peeked at it and then ran back. I promise, I didn't see a thing."

"And what kinds of things did you see there? What crop is there?"

Pookie's eyes flashed. "The most glorious purple yams. I dug one up, there were only a few left from the harvest—"

Raymond clenched his jaw. "This ain't a time for games, Miss Pookie. If you done something wrong, you need to confess to me now. I don't want to be caught in a lie and havin' to explain things to your daddy. I'm just a hired hand here, not your nursemaid."

His words stung like an angry hive's wrath after a humid, mid-summer, honey dive. "I don't need a nursemaid. And I certainly wouldn't ask you to be one for me." She turned and tried to storm out, flipping her hair in an effort to make a Tulip Sloan-style dramatic exit. Her boots, however, remained stuck in the thick mud as she tried to twist her body, causing her to land with a thud on the ground.

Raymond began to laugh. He laughed so hard he himself lost his balance and fell off his little stool. "I'm sorry, Miss. Don't mean to laugh at your troubles." He stood and tried in vain to wipe all of the mud off on his pants. "Let me help you up," he said, offering her a muddy hand.

Her face was dark and she stared at his hand for a moment before taking it. When he pulled, she pulled as well causing her body to be propelled into his. Her breath quickened.

She leaned her head against him for a minute. "I know you do things you shouldn't, Raymond." Pookie sputtered. "I know."

CHAPTER SEVENTEEN

Lanie
Sassy Lasses Winery

MARVELINE, DRESSED IN an orange sherbet-colored flowing chiffon gown that seems out of place in this country setting, looks at me with skepticism. "Even though we moved here intending to serve the public, my sister and I still value our privacy. We are planning to host all of our events outside, or at least in the refurbished barn. I don't feel so comfortable inviting you in."

Make your hook their living room couch. It was the funniest seminar I ever attended. The seminar leader, Hanz Lassiter, gave the entire speech atop a green velvet couch. That was where we made love later. "This isn't about being snoopy. I can understand your reluctance to let us into your personal world. I'm just looking for clues, something that might explain the Naybors better. We'd only be inside a few minutes." I look at Vem, who has already pulled out the information she downloaded from the internet regarding cleansing a space filled with evil energy. I can also see her nose is twitching as it goes into high gear, searching for olfactory clues.

"No, I'm afraid we can't allow it. The police continue rummaging around enough to leave us feeling quite violated." Marveline crosses her arms and leans against the doorway. "I would happily entertain you on the porch though. I'd like to hear what else you've uncovered in your investigation."

Mandy appears behind us, her hands dirty with rich, brown soil. "I didn't know you girls were coming today. Are we ready to plan your wedding?" My cheeks turn crimson. I have to find a polite way to tell them I'm backing out. The only person who agreed to give them a chance.

"Mandy, please bring our guests some lemonade. Or would you prefer some Chardonnay?"

November, who has been blessedly quiet up to this point, opens her mouth to speak just as I'm stepping on her foot.

"We'll just have lemonade, thanks."

November scowls but follows me to the outdoor table where recently we were shot at while engaging in innocent conversation. Marveline is close behind us, as if she is afraid we'll try and sneak by her and get inside.

"So, what can you tell me, Lanie? Who is trying

to get rid of us?"

"I have some thoughts, but first I'd like to ask you a few personal questions. Please feel free not to answer if they make you uncomfortable."

Marveline purses her lips and leans back in her chair. "What would you like to know?"

"Well, for starters—"

"We were wondering if you killed your parents. Lanie is, anyway. I just wanted to take the day off from Medieval Moaning prep. I'm starting a new class next week. I will require everyone to eat a roasted turkey leg while they stretch. It's the latest in next-level stretch classes."

I step on November's foot once more, this time making certain the heel of my shoe digs into the center of her foot.

"Ouch! I'm trying to cut to the chase, Lanie! If we're not going to have wine, then at least give me time to make lesson plans when we get home."

I shake my head in Vem's general direction before turning to our host. "Marveline, you've realized by now that my friend can be a bit abrasive," I say apologetically. "We just came across some information about your parents and wanted to confirm some of the circumstances surrounding their passing."

The screen door bangs shut as Mandy appears with a tray. On it are four glasses of lemonade and some pink-frosted, sugar cookies. "Did I overhear you asking about our parents? What does that have to do with this case?" She sets the tray down in front of Vem, taking care to remove her fingers quickly away from the cookies.

"It sounds like a genuine tragedy, their passing. I'm just wondering if someone heard about their deaths and wanted to capitalize on them. Did they have enemies?" I'm slightly fearful of Marveline. She may lunge at me. Even with her blunders, I'm grateful to enjoy the always-fierce protection of November beside me.

Instead, she nods supportively. "I understand why you're asking. Covering all the bases. Our parents were very complicated people. Mandy and I were, shall I say, relieved when they were gone?"

That is not at all what I expected her to say. "Really? How so?"

"Let me," Mandy puts her hand in front of her sister. "Mom was very mean to us. Verbally abusive. She called Marveline the broom and me the dustpan. Only good for cleaning up their messes. When she had her accident and was constantly in pain, her behavior became even worse. One time, she shoved me down a staircase when I refused to get her more morphine."

Marveline crosses her legs. "After a lifetime of humiliating us for being weak, our mother became a drug addict. It was embarrassing for all of us. Our only sanity was planning our escape. We both learned all we could about the wine business. We loved our father very much and couldn't bear the thought of leaving him, so we were biding our time."

"Did your father suffer from a morphine addiction as well? The police report says he also died of a morphine overdose."

"We initially thought that was the case. Mandy found information that changed our minds."

Mandy clears her throat and fans furiously at her face. "Sorry. This gets me emotional every time I tell it. Mom found scraps of paper where we'd written information about long-term care facilities. We wanted to give our dad options for her medical care. She mistakenly assumed he would lock her away. That's when she crushed up her pills and put them in his drink. We were out for the evening and when we returned—" She dissolves into tears. "They were both dead in the living room."

I reach over and rub Mandy's back. "I'm so sorry. That must've been awful."

Marveline taps her red, acrylic nails on the table. "As you can understand, we couldn't spend another minute in that place. We went through with our plans to buy this property and start our winery."

"After our relatives worked so hard to leave their proud legacy to us. Mom goes and spoils it, making a mockery of the Pherson name."

Vem hands Mandy a crumpled tissue from her purse.

"I think we've spent enough time on that ugly topic." Marveline announces. "I'm eager to hear what you found out about our neighbor. Has he agreed to leave us alone?"

"He's not the one shooting at your place. At least not now." I look over at November who has finished off the entire plate of cookies and is now staring impatiently at the car. I try to catch her gaze, but she refuses to look at me.

"I think it's someone else who's been shooting at you. Maybe there is another neighbor who doesn't want you here? Can you think of others who might have threatened you?"

Marveline lets out a hearty chuckle. "Haven't you learned by now that the list of people who don't want us here is much longer than the list of those who will support us?"

"Maybe you could give me those names? I'll be happy to talk to all of them. Oh, another area where I have had little success is in finding out what happened to Pookie Naybor. I have a friend who is good at these types of searches, but she has a short attention span and a long nap time, and she's apparently done." I press my lips together to suppress a giggle thinking about my last conversation with Gladys. *Tired of helping you, Lanie. Do your own nosing around on this one. I don't have nothin' to do with that evil place and I'm on borrowed time as it is. But you keep plannin' that party for me.*

"Did you find anything from the diary?" Mandy asks.

"Nothing that makes sense. She was in love with a hired hand. She had great aspirations. Maybe she went to Hollywood and became a famous actress. She could be living openly as someone else and we'd never know."

CHAPTER EIGHTEEN

Pookie

1947

Dearest Ophelia,

I've been following Raymond for weeks now. He's getting suspicious of me, that I can tell. The other day he asked why my eyes had dark circles all the time. I told him it wasn't polite to comment on a lady's appearance if he didn't have something positive to say. That shut him right up.

All of this time, I've been afraid of the truth, but I fear it's time to be the grown-up I'm always saying I am and face it. I am the mouse to Raymond's virile cat who has been playing with me, watching my reactions. It's time to see who or what is buried in the field. As my closest confidant, you will be the first to hear my findings.

I've made such glorious paintings of my thoughts. Miss Dandridge said we should close our eyes and commit every detail of our special people to memory. That's how they can be recalled and painted with care.

I showed one of my paintings to Miss Dandridge. At first, she was shocked but upon reflection, thought it quite grand. "You've such a wonderful eye for detail, Pookie. Keep those thoughts stored in your mind so that you may paint them all with perfection."

I have the perfect place to hide my work. One day I shall show Daddy, once I have achieved the skills of Mr. Monet. He will be so proud of me.

With Affection and Determination,
Pookie A. Naybor

"Daddy? I'm going on an adventure today. The weather is pleasant and it shouldn't rain. My chores are finished and homework completed. You have no reason to keep me inside!"

Naybor guffawed. "Oh, Pookie. You are a treasure. Have Mrs. Wilson make you a sandwich with some of that fine roast from last night's meal to take with you. And be back before dark. You know the sun sets quite early these days."

Pookie bent down and kissed his smooth face. "Thank you so much, Daddy."

He looked at her with surprise. "For what?"

"For being the wonderfully kind person I know you to be. Not the monster from Freddie's tales."

Welcome picked up his paper. "Freddie is a boy with a large imagination. Perhaps if he spent his Saturdays learning a trade instead of filling your head with nonsense, he would get further in the world."

Pookie took her satchel, filled with dried plums and a roast beef sandwich, along with her notebook and headed out. She meandered across the fields, stopping to eat her lunch, and lie against the grass to study the clouds. As was her usual routine, instead of searching for a body, she allowed herself to drift off to sleep. She dreamt of her future in Hollywood, attending movie premiers with the dapperly dressed Raymond on her arm.

When she awoke, the sun was almost resting on the horizon. She got up and started running, knowing from past errors that if she arrived too late someone would notice her absence. Today, though, she stopped herself. There was a reason she'd come out here. It wasn't to pretend she was somewhere else; it was to uncover Raymond's secrets.

She opened her notebook to her last entry:

It makes little sense that during the day, Raymond is the most dedicated employee at Naybor Manor. He does twice the work of the other hired hands and never complains a lick of aches or pains. On his days off, he rides into town to mail his letter and comes home to a supper of whatever leftovers the cook brings to the bunkhouse from our weekly meals.

How does someone so normal lead a double life as a murderous letch?

Pookie went to the spot she thought Raymond had buried someone. There was no disturbed ground, so she continued on until she came across an upturned piece of soil that make her stomach lurch.

"It's probably something harmless. Maybe he stole a coat from the general store in town on his Sunday visit," she reasoned. "Or it may be someone's animal he accidentally hit with the farm truck. I don't need to know everything." Pookie turned to leave, but again stopped herself. "No, I'm a grown woman who solves problems. Just like Tulip Sloan, I can fix anything if I put my mind to it."

She dropped her satchel and began digging with her hands, the moist dirt moving away easily. When she got to something solid, she paused only for a moment. An undeniable stench came from the ground, something she had smelled before but she couldn't place it. Her stomach lurched from the powerful scent. She reached into her satchel and removed Miss Dandridge's large scissors used only for holiday sewing projects. She took a deep breath through her nose and cut the burlap quickly. Now she remembered where she remembered the horrible smell from: the time she found her pet kitty, Larchmont behind the barn, torn to bits by a wild animal.

Blank eyes stared up at the sky, boring a hole through her skull. The face she saw was bloated and blue in color. It almost didn't seem like an actual person. For a moment, she tried to convince herself it wasn't. Then she looked again, this time at the mouth. There was a single gold tooth on the top. Just like Paulo.

Write it all down, Pookie. Then we'll discuss it. She pulled out her little notebook and began scribbling details that would make sense when she discussed them with Freddie.

Blue skin. Brown shirt, torn. Hair is a mess, not combed the way Paulo always did. The poor soul's last few minutes must have been torturous.

Pookie started thinking about interactions between Raymond and Paulo. Raymond was kind to everyone. Paulo was quiet but never mean. The only time she'd seen them together was the day she'd come to Barn Two while they were stacking hay bales. Raymond was telling Paulo to be careful, that he didn't hurt himself. *Stacking hay?*

She wrote those last details in her notebook before pushing the dirt back over Paulo's face. "When this is all done, I'll make sure you are buried in the

Flanagan Cemetery. After I've made sure Raymond won't get in trouble."

As she walked toward Naybor Manor, she thought about what a responsible adult, someone of thirteen years of age, would do. The answers weren't coming.

CHAPTER NINETEEN

Lanie
Piney Falls

"I'VE MISSED OUR talks. I'm so glad you could come over tonight." I pull the lasagna from the oven, perfectly browned and filling the room with a cheesy, garlicky aroma. Cooking is a skill I've just recently improved upon, thanks to Piper's tutelage.

"Lanie, that's the best one yet!" Piper squeals enthusiastically. "Next, I want to teach you how to make desserts. Then maybe you can help me at the bakery when–"

"When I can't drag my sorry behind out of bed?" Cosmo has showered and is dressed in jeans and a dark blue polo shirt. I bought both of those for his birthday. There is just a hint of grey chest hair peeking over his top button. He looks and smells magnificent.

"I didn't mean that." Piper looks at me helplessly. "Just that we possess all the supplies there to bake any kind of creation that suits us."

"She wants to make sure I don't burn this place down. You have much better insurance on the bakery, Cos." I wink, hopeful he won't be offended.

Cosmo reaches into the refrigerator and pulls out a beer, offering it to Piper, squeezing my shoulder as he passes by.

She shakes her head at the proffered beer. "I'm more of a wine drinker. Do you have any more Sassy Lasses Rebel Riesling, Lanie?"

"I sure do, hon. Sit at the table and I'll bring everything over."

As we all settle in for dinner, a warm feeling surrounds me. The three of us feel like a self-made family. We all came from different places, but together, we're really something special.

"Let's get rid of the elephant in the room, first thing," Cosmo remarks, scooping three heaping servings onto his plate.

"Elephant? There are many possibilies, Cos. Please explain."

He looks at me with the half-smile that makes me quiver. "You know. Or...maybe you don't. Piper's got herself a boyfriend. They were swapping spit out in the alley the other day."

Piper smiles shyly before playfully punching Cosmo in the arm. "I didn't realize you saw us." She turns to me. "You know I've been hanging out with

Faythe and Finnegan Lane. Well, he asked me out last week. We went to a movie and then I made him dessert. Chocolate flan. I think he likes me." She giggles and puts her hand to her mouth.

"Of course he does, sweetie. You're a gorgeous, successful young woman. He is powerless to your charms."

"We men are putty in the hands of those types," Cosmo winks at me. "Just glad you're not waiting until you're over forty to figure that out."

Piper puts a helping of lasagna on her plate and I hand her the salad. "Well, he wants me to meet his parents. I guess that's a big step when you're dating? He said they normally like to meet his girlfriend along with her parents. But, well, you know where I stand there."

"You were cheated when it came to parents." I remark.

"I try not to dwell on that." She points to the garlic bread and Cosmo slides it to her side of the table. "There was one idea I had," she begins. "Maybe you two could go with me to meet his parents. Sort of...stand-in parents." She glances nervously, first at me and then at Cos. "If that would be okay and everything."

I smile at Cosmo and he raises his eyebrows to keep from being emotional.

"We would be so honored, hon," I squeeze her

shoulder. "Just let us know when."

Cosmo turns away from the table, trying and failing to wipe his eyes out of sight. When he turns back around, those beautiful pools of blue are lined with red. "I've been meaning to talk to you about something, too. Leaving you in charge of the shop, with no help. It's a pretty crappy deal and I'm sorry. Some days my brain won't kick into gear. There's just a thick fog and nothing beyond it. Wish I could explain it better."

I pat his hand. "You explained it perfectly."

"Thought maybe you deserved a raise. I think that's the way those things work. Doris says if I don't, you'll run off and find someone who pays you what you're worth."

Piper gasps. "As much as I've complained about it, running that place on my own has been a great experience. I've learned so much. Thanks for trusting me." She gets up and throws her arms around both of us. "You two. I love you more than I could ever express."

After our hug, we eat together in a cocoon of comfort, the three of us relishing each other's company as we discuss our lives. When we finish, Piper stands and smiles broadly at both of us. "You're like the parents I never had. It makes me emotional to think about it, but you needed to know. And that's all I'll say on that matter. Should I cut up the blackberry pie?"

And she is like the daughter I never thought I desired. "I'll help you."

"No, that's okay. I'll do it." Piper disappears into the kitchen, returning with plates and slices the sugar-crusted, juicy, purple perfection. "So, tell me about your detective work, Lanie. What have you discovered about the murders at Sassy Lasses?"

"Well, I'm afraid I've not found much yet. The neighbor of the Pherson ladies is definitely a character, but he's adamant he hasn't shot at anyone. And the caretaker, he's..." I look at Cosmo, waiting to see if he'll chime in. He shakes his head. "The caretaker and his wife seem like agreeable people, but they've got some rough edges. I'd like to investigate them more. What troubles me the most are the owners themselves. They won't let me into their house."

"Didn't you say they decided they wanted to start a winery and for some reason were dead set on this place?"

"Yes on both counts."

Piper sets three picture-perfect pieces in front of us, each with a scoop of vanilla ice cream on top. "Well, don't you find that strange?" she asks. "It's an awfully specific location to land, especially one where they had to start from scratch."

Cosmo leans forward, dipping his fork into the

gooey filling and lifting it to his mouth. "Mmmm. Better'n anything I've made."

"What did you say brought them to Naybor Manor? Was it a tragedy of some sort?" Piper takes a giant forkful of pie and stuffs it in her mouth. "The only way to eat good pie is in big bites," she proclaims.

"Yes, their mother had a morphine addiction. Murder-suicide." I follow her lead and stuff a big bite in my own mouth. "This is magnificent, Piper!" I exclaim.

"Lots of stories of drugs around this place. Didn't you discover Mr. Naybor also trafficked in morphine?" Cosmo adds. "That's a little too coincidental, don't you think?"

CHAPTER TWENTY

Pookie
1947

Dearest Ophelia,

The time has come. I'm making Daddy his favorite standing rib roast tonight, with new potatoes and creamed corn. For dessert, he'll enjoy my secret recipe vanilla cake with sinfully rich chocolate frosting. When his belly is full and his face relaxed and content, I shall ask that he prepare his tea before I tell him the story of Raymond and the body he buried.

My heart is heavy, feeling as though I'm betraying the only person in the world who truly understands me. What would my heroine Tulip Sloan do in such a situation? Just last week, Freddie and I watched "Mission to Farraway Island." Babette Walters was forced to choose between saving the life of the only man she'd ever loved and saving the residents of the island from foreign invaders. After

*much deliberation, Babette decided she had to
let her true love perish in order to get to the
town in time and warn them. She chose duty
over heart. Now it is my turn to do the same.*

Yours in Sorrow,
Pookie A. Naybor

Pookie stood anxiously behind Welcome.
"Would you like more cake, Daddy? There's so
much I doubt we'll finish it before it turns."

"No, daughter, there isn't space for one more
delicious morsel in my generously sized body. You've
outdone yourself. Tomorrow, I will tell Mrs. Wilson
how much I appreciate her tutoring you in this
important skill. Come sit with me while I digest!" He
patted his hand on the table expectantly.

"I'm waiting for the kettle to boil. For your
grown-up tea." Pookie returned to the kitchen
quickly, whispering as she went. "Daddy, I must tell
you something of some urgency. No, Daddy, I must
inform you of something, no matter how much it
hurts my heart."

"The grown-up tea is in a locked cabinet. Just
bring me the green tea from the dish cupboard," he
instructed.

She returned a short time later with a hand-
painted teacup, filled with steamy, golden-colored
tea. She set it down in front of her father and stood

beside him.

"Sit down, Pookie. Gracious! This is not a time for seriousness. Though we need to discuss your birthday."

Reluctantly, she moved back to her seat. "There is something I need to talk over with you, Daddy. Something I fear is of grave importance."

Welcome studied her face before bursting out in laughter. "You say that every year. I've never left you disappointed on your special day before, have I?"

"No, Daddy. Last year's traveling circus was spectacular. The bear riding the unicycle was a real highlight." She pulled one side of her mouth in an upward position.

"And the year before, the Shakespearean troupe performing for all of us. Your birthday is always my finest achievement. This is a special year for you, Pookie. Although I've always considered you mature for your age, when a young lady turns thirteen, it's a time of great joy and celebration."

Pookie forced a full smile. "I'm very excited. Whatever you plan will be perfect."

"And who should we invite to this celebration? Can I take a guess?"

Pookie nodded. The evening wasn't going at all as she had meticulously planned.

"Let's see, you'll want Miss Dandridge as usual. And Freddie. It would only be polite to invite his mother. Now who did I leave out." Welcome looked upward, as if he were thinking hard. "Oh, I know. Your dear friend, Mr. Dockley. The night wouldn't be complete unless you could include your favorite farm hand to enjoy your special day. Doesn't that sound sublime?" He looked at her expectantly.

"Yes, I do want Raymond. It's just that I–"

"You don't want a party this year? That doesn't sound like my girl."

"Oh, Daddy. The world is in such turmoil. The war is over, but people still suffer."

Welcome wrinkled his brow. "I'm not following you, my dear."

"Paulo has disappeared. Our Paulo, who has faithfully attended to our grounds for over a year now. I can find him nowhere. And when I went to the bunkhouse, all of his things were gone."

Welcome's face tightened. "You know how these drifters are. They are gone with the breeze. That's never bothered you before."

"Yes, but this time–"

"This time what?" Welcome snapped. "You've got to stop feeling things so deeply, Pookie. The world is a harsh place. I've kept you sheltered here. Maybe it wasn't always wise, but you've never had to see the ugliness that exists. Not all are able to live a life of stability."

Pookie thought back to the bloated face she saw,

the last few minutes of terror Paulo must've felt. At that moment, she realized Raymond wasn't at all the type of person who would cause that kind of pain. Someone else did this to him, and Raymond was only getting rid of the evidence. She was certain.

She dipped her chin and batted her eyes, as she'd seen Tulip Sloan do a million times. "You're right, Daddy. I haven't seen anything. I don't know why I'm so sensitive today. I'll be so happy when you plan my party."

CHAPTER TWENTY-ONE

Lanie
Sassy Lasses Winery

"DID YOU EVER learn anything from the diary?" November is picking her teeth with her lime green fingernail. Today she has matched not only her clothing, shoes and frames of her glasses but also her fingernails. Her level of commitment is impressive.

"To be honest, I quit reading about halfway through. This girl was full of herself and pretty wrapped up in Tulip Sloan movies. Who's to say she didn't invent things she saw in these movies and this diary isn't about her life at all?" I stare intently at the road in front of us, not daring to glance in her direction. "I know most everything about Tulip and half of her references don't make sense to me."

"Hmm. That doesn't sound like you, Lanie. You're always dedicated to getting to the bottom of things." November stops the car in the driveway of the Sassy Lasses Winery. We made an appointment today to tell them I can go no further in my investigation.

"Vem, Cosmo's depression has worn me out. None of these people will tell me what is going on and frankly, I'm just tired."

Vem rolls down her window and lets out a howl. A rooster from another farm crows in unison. I can't help myself. I let out a loud howl, too.

"Lanie, this may sound harsh, but you need to hear it. Cosmo's pain isn't yours. You weren't in the cult or in prison for a murder you didn't commit, and you didn't lose a sister who was like your right arm. You have to let his pain be his alone. Love him without falling in."

Somehow, she always seems to understand me, even when I think her brain is lost in a field of tie-dyed daisies. "Oh, Vem. I have fallen in. Way in. Now that he's able to come out of the bedroom some days, I feel like I'm carrying that pain for him. It's almost harder to function with his dark cloud in every room instead of just the bedroom."

Vem reaches over and begins massaging my neck. "There's a place back here that, if I find it, will bring you clarity. If only I'd brought my ground mustard and pine bark paste. You'd really experience a moment."

I've grown so used to her strange ways that I lean back and just enjoy the ride. Just as she predicted, my mind opens. "Wait. What you said earlier, about Cosmo's pain not being mine, I think I may know of a way for us to get inside Naybor Manor."

"But I need to do this for at least an hour. Otherwise, it's doubtful you'll get the full effect. And I need to start a chant using only the letter B."

I sigh. "Later. I promise. For now, I need you to come with me and follow my lead. No going off on your own tangent." I open up my door and start to get out of the car, but lean back in. "Thank you, November Bean. You are truly a wise and wondrous goddess." November nods solemnly in response.

She hops out of the car, slings her backpack over one shoulder and follows quickly behind me. "When you said no improvising, did you mean you don't want me to–"

"Nothing. Just stand pleasantly by my side until I ask for your help."

Vem shrugs. "Okay, but I can be very convincing. When something dark comes into my head, you never know where it might lead."

We ring the bell of the Pherson's fortress. Eventually, Marveline opens the door; her flowing, lavender gown is accented by a chunky, gold-chain necklace. She looks radiant.

She stares awkwardly for a moment. "Ladies! We weren't expecting you. I've not prepared lemonade or any pastry. Shall we sit on the porch?" She motions toward our usual chairs.

I clear my throat. "No, we really need to come inside today, Marveline. I spoke with Mandy earlier and she said it was fine if we came by. I've reached a point in the investigation where I need to see Pookie's world. I need to study her room and everywhere she spent time."

Marveline makes a chirping sound and crosses her arms. "We don't allow visitors inside. I thought I made that clear."

"I understand you've been hurt terribly. After your parents' death and the subsequent bad press, you are wary of trusting anyone. You felt like your parents' troubles were yours. But you don't need to put them on your shoulders. They aren't your burden."

"Hmmm…" November stands up a little taller.

I put my finger to my lips, cautioning her to keep her ever-bubbling thoughts to herself.

"You asked for my help and I can only give that to you if I'm allowed to fully understand the history of this home. Specifically, the people who lived here. Maybe there is a connection to the murders and those who want you out. Please trust me – us – for now. If we betray your trust, you don't need to pay me and you'll never see us again."

Marveline's eyes scan me and then November. "I suppose you're right." She opens the door wide, allowing us to enter the massive space, where a grand marble staircase stands majestically in front of us. To our left is a formal living room, one Pookie described many times as the scene of happy gatherings. Her young-girl optimism grates on me, especially the days Cosmo won't speak to me or anyone else.

Marveline leads us up the staircase where four tall, wooden doors are in view, two on each side of the hallway. At the end of the hallway sits a wooden table, ornamentally carved, with a vase of flowers on top and adorned by a large mirror.

She opens the first door where a stuffy, stale smell assaults our nostrils. Instinctively, I poke Vem in the ribs before she can make a rude comment.

"Ow! Really, Lanie!"

The room is painted a dour, pale yellow with a wallpaper border of tiny, yellow roses. With some sunlight and a fresh coat of paint, it might be useable. There is a four-poster bed and a small desk beside a window seat covered in magazines. A fireplace sits just to the right of the desk.

"We found this room in almost pristine condition." Marveline is using her tourist guide voice, the one I've heard several times now. She could work for us at the Inn and Spa at Fallen Branch Resort if things fall through here.

"Other than a new mattress, there wasn't much to be done in the order of remodeling. It was almost like a shrine. While the rest of the place fell into shambles, this room somehow remained intact. Over there," she gestures toward the desk, "is where we found the diary. I don't think it was touched in his last days."

"Do you know exactly what happened to Welcome Naybor? You said he died of a drug overdose. But did anyone offer an explanation of what lead up to that day, and what might have happened to his daughter?"

Marveline crosses her arms, a silver bracelet now visible on her thin wrist. "My sister and I only know of his drug dealings in general. He had many well-to-do clients, so more than likely, he destroyed families known for their glitz and glamour."

She looks back and forth between November and me. "There are rumors that Naybor killed his daughter and buried her out here somewhere. We don't have proof. No one has ever found her body."

"What do YOU think happened? Surely you and your sister discussed possible scenarios?"

November approaches Marveline and sniffs her. "Something smells funny."

By now, Marveline has grown used to November's strange outburst and ignores her, bending around to look at me. "We – Mandy and I – believe that a drug cartel took the girl. Welcome owed money to many influential people. Our other idea is that because he sold his drugs to well-known people, one of them got wind of his breakdown and kidnapped the girl in order to keep him quiet. He was so despondent, he ended his own life."

I shake my head. "That's really sad. Pookie seemed like a happy-go-lucky girl."

Sitting down gently on the bed, I run my hands over the rose-print comforter. "If you wouldn't mind giving us a few minutes to look around here, we'd be so grateful. I promise we won't snoop anywhere you don't want us."

Marveline's face is tight. "As I've mentioned, we're not big on guests. But you are doing us a favor. I'll wait at the end of the hall to see you out."

As she leaves the room, November stares at me with wide eyes. "Deccit, Lanie. I've been practicing my smell tells. She's got the distinct odor of someone hiding her true self.

"I don't doubt you Vem. Since I know you also realized this room smells funny, what are you picking up?"

November paces the room, her proboscis held high in the air. She stops when she gets to the closet doors, which are closed with a rubber band around the brass bulb handles.

"We shouldn't. It's private!" I caution.

"Do you want to know or not? Did we waste a trip?"

The old Lanie, the one who saw things in black-and-white, would turn her nose up at this kind of irrational detective work. Piney Falls Lanie understands Vem's unconventional methods always bring results. "Okay." I whisper, remembering Marveline said she'd be just down the hall. "Go ahead. But if we find something too personal, we'll close it immediately and leave."

November removes the rubber band and opens one side of the closet, the door squeaking uncomfortably loudly. We both stand, waiting for Marveline's scolding, but it doesn't come.

"Go ahead, Vem. Step inside and give it a good whiff." I can't believe I'm saying that.

November steps gingerly over the threshold and into the cedar-lined closet. The space is empty and dark. Quickly, she returns, her face ashen.

"What did you see? Was it horrible?

"Something I've never told you before, Lanie. I probably should have mentioned that small spaces make me anxious. The fierce November Bean does have her kryptonite. I'm afraid you've seen it."

"Oh," my voice falls. "So that was all for nothing?"

"Probably." She concedes. "Unless that slight breeze I felt means there is some kind of secret passageway behind the removable panel on the back wall."

Chapter Twenty-Two

Pookie
1947

Dearest Ophelia,

I continue to paint during my lesson time, trying to make every detail of my work stand for something, as Miss Dandridge suggests. I no longer share with her my finished products and she no longer asks. She sits and reads the work of Mr. Henry David Thoreau to me while I paint, and it suits me fine.

Last night I followed Raymond once more. As dedicated as I am to this project, I fear my eyes and brain won't be able to handle it even one more time. It was pouring rain, my boots filling up with water as we crossed the fields. I dared not stop to dump them for fear he would leave me and take this opportunity to meet his friend in a different location.

The same gentleman, Bowler Man, as I've

taken to calling him since he wears a dark
bowler hat and a long coat, met Raymond in
their usual location. As my knees sunk into
the saturated soil, Raymond yelled so that his
voice rose over the fury of nature.

"What do you need this week?"

"We need a location from the target. Get
me a time and date for the drop off. Any other new men involved?"

"None at this time! No more mistakes!"
Raymond screamed.

"Get yourself inside then and out of the
elements. You're doing fine work."

I gasped, thinking of Raymond referring
to Paulo as a "mistake."

The men parted and I heard an automobile in the distance, a warm dry place to sit
that made me jealous of Bowler Man's ability
to leave the scene so easily.

I trudged slowly home, thinking about
what I'd learned. What target was he referring to? Was Raymond sneaking off at other
times to another location, where bad things
were happening?

When I reached the back door, I took my
clothes off and put them in the washing machine, feeling thankful our housekeeper
taught me how to use it last year. I took the
hose and filled the machine, added soap and

turned it on. Even though it was quite noisy, I knew Daddy wouldn't wake up. Thankful that once his midnight snack was taken care of, he slept so soundly and as he says, "Old men sleep like logs without the confines of youth to wake them."

It was hard to keep my eyes open as I watched my muddy clothes swish back and forth before putting the lid on. I decided to sit and rest, just for a minute, wrapping myself in the extra blanket we keep in the laundry room around my frigid body.

The next thing I knew, Mrs. Wilson was shaking my arm. "Miss Pookie, what are you doing down here? Your father will expect you at breakfast in half an hour!" She inspected my matted hair and my dirty body. "Whatever mischief you've been creating, you need to rid yourself of it now. I'll wring your clothes and hang them up to dry. Go wash in the servant's bathroom and I'll bring you something to wear. Hurry now!"

Yours in Exhaustion and Confusion,
Pookie A. Naybor

When she greeted her father at breakfast, her hair was haphazardly twisted into one soggy braid. Luckily, Welcome didn't seem to notice the drips of water on her shirt.

"You don't look as though you slept much last night, my darling. Bad dreams?" He peeked over the top of his morning paper, just for a second.

"Yes, Daddy. About the fairies and the prisoners again. I'd better stop eating fruit before bed."

"Eat your breakfast, Pookie. Miss Dandridge informed me she will teach you about the great Roman Empire today. You don't want to miss those exciting lessons."

"Can I go see Raymond first? I promise I'll be quick and I won't prevent him from doing his duties."

"Quickly. As long as he isn't in the middle of something important."

She jumped up and ran to the back door.

"And Pookie," Welcome called after her, "remember to mind your manners!"

It was raining again, so she pulled on her thickest sweater and red overcoat.

When she reached the bunkhouse, Raymond was nowhere to be found. The building was completely empty. Cautiously, she crept to each bedroom door until she found the one with Raymond's familiar scent. Over the bed was a picture of a lady who looked just like Raymond – same eyes and rugged jaw. She was not smiling, nor was she looking at the camera.

As Pookie stepped into the bedroom, she noticed

his top dresser drawer was slightly askew.

His underthings were folded neatly on top. Glancing around once more to make sure she was alone, she reached in, touching them as excitement coursed through her body. She brought his undershirt to her face, smelling his familiar, clean scent.

She continued digging through the drawer where she found several envelopes addressed to Pearl Dockley in Sulfur, Oklahoma. They were completely empty, to her disappointment. Probing deeper, she found a folded paper, which, when she unfolded, appeared to be a schedule of some kind. It had columns for "customer" "date" and "amount."

"Now what in tarnation would a respectable woman be doing diggin' through the privates of a man?"

Pookie jumped and shoved the schedule into the top of her sweater before turning around. "I'm...uh..."

"You're bein' a snoop is what you are. I'd appreciate it if you stay clear of my things, Miss." Raymond came over and looked down at the drawer before shutting it tightly.

"Please, you won't tell Daddy, will you?" Pookie begged.

"Not if you tell me something first."

Pookie looked at the floor. "Whatever you want."

"Tell me why you're so gosh-darned interested in a hired man? I got nothin' that would please a young girl's mind in here. Only the worries of the world, and them are too much for the likes of you."

"I'm not a young girl. I'm almost a woman." She protested. "My thirteenth birthday is in two weeks!"

"Then you need to go find yourself a fine thirteen-year-old boy and keep out of my private things. Now, one more time, what're you doing in here, Miss Pookie?"

Pookie stared at her boots. "I...love you Raymond. Ever since the first day we met, I've been madly, deeply in love." She lifted her brown eyes, now brimming with tears, to gaze into his. "I know you think I'm a child, but I'm not. I'm a young woman on the cusp of adulthood. Awaiting your return of my affections."

Raymond sighed. "Oh, Miss Pookie. There's danger in the world. You can't be in love with me, now or ever. You've got to keep your eyes and ears open for it and save the romance for later on. Do you understand?"

"I knew you'd say that!" she sputtered. "As far as I can tell, the only danger in my world is you. Slithering around, doing things that an upstanding man should never do. Well I've had just about enough of all of it. I'm telling Daddy to fire you today!" She turned and ran out of the bunkhouse, clutching the front of her shirt and forgetting to put her hood up to protect herself from the now-driving rain.

When she got to Naybor Manor, she went in the kitchen door, slamming it hard.

Mrs. Wilson scowled at her. "It's a good thing I don't have a souffle in the oven!"

"Pookie! Miss Dandridge is here! Don't keep her waiting!" Welcome called.

She stood at the back door, outwardly dripping cold, winter raindrops and inwardly simmering with anger.

"Pookie? Did you hear me?" Welcome moved with purpose into the kitchen, territory he had no familiarity with outside of his midnight snacks. He put his hands on his hips and looked at his daughter with concern. "What's got you in such a terrible snit?"

"I hate Raymond. He is the most foul, awful man. He's—"

"What are you saying, my dear? Did he harm you?" Welcome moved in close and pulled her soggy coat from her body. He took her chin in his hand and lifted her face so he could inspect it.

"No, Daddy. I—" She looked at her father's wrinkled brow. He would do anything to keep her safe from harm. The farmhand who stole her locket, the one with Tulip Sloan's picture on one side and

Pookie's baby picture on the other, was fired on the spot. He begged for one more chance, his wife was pregnant and he hadn't thought things through. Welcome told him there would be no work for him on this farm or any other in the region. No one crossed Welcome Naybor without regret.

"Raymond, he...was just too busy for me right now. I should have waited until later in the day to visit." She swallowed hard. "He did nothing wrong. I just got in the way of his chores and he asked if I'd step aside."

Welcome clicked his tongue. "I've told you before, Pookie. Your curiosity can appear as insolence if you forget your place. Remember, we are grateful for those around us who provide such comfort. Be grateful for Raymond and stay out of his way."

"Yes, Daddy. I'll go prepare for my lessons now."

Pookie's binoculars had almost worn a mark into her forehead, something that would become noticeable soon enough. She looked at her notebook, where she had been noting date and times of Raymond's "meetings."

Tonight, Friday, was not his usual night out. She squinted in the binoculars to make sure it was him. Same easy gait, same winter coat. She sighed as she pulled on her shoes. A trick she learned from Miss Dandridge, who often came in with soaked feet, was to use bread bags to cover her shoes.

This time she didn't have to travel far. Just over the hill from the bunkhouse, Raymond stopped. He rocked back and forth, shifting his weight to one foot and then the other. As Pookie hid behind a large bale of hay, a familiar face emerged.

"I hope this is important. I like to keep myself to a schedule." Welcome Naybor, dressed in his night clothes and winter jacket, crossed his arms.

"Yes sir, Mr. Naybor. Just lettin' you know I'm keen to what happened with Paulo. I'd like to propose a deal."

"Oh? Only my most trusted men may assist me as Paulo did. Are you telling me you are trustworthy, Raymond?"

"Never was one for stickin' my nose in where it don't belong. I'm loyal to those that deserve it and try to leave the others to face their demons without my help."

Welcome laughed. "A drifter taking the moral high ground? Can't say I haven't heard that ruse before. We will need to talk terms. Usually I like to do that over a cup of tea. Would you like to come up to the house?"

"Not much of a tea drinker, Mr. Naybor. I'll agree to whatever you had goin' with Paulo. He was a smart man. I s'pect he negotiated a fair price for himself."

"You make this too easy, Raymond. I'll be out with instructions tomorrow then. Can we shake on this like gentlemen?"

Pookie leaned out, just far enough she could witness her father and the man of her dreams shaking hands, uniting over the death of another.

CHAPTER TWENTY-THREE

Lanie
Sassy Lasses Winery

"THIS CLOSET IS much smaller than it appeared. Child sized. I may have to stop and chant or November Bean will lose her incredibly fascinating mind."

The panel at the back of the closet removes easily. When we carefully pull it aside, there is a passageway, covered in finished wood and reclaimed by time and massive spider webs. Strangely, that part doesn't bother Vem.

When I shine my phone in the space and realize what we are facing, I retrieve the fireplace poker to use to fight our way through the deftly-fashioned barrier.

"Look ahead, Vem, the ceiling appears to get taller. That will be better for you, right?" I shine my light down the corridor so she can see. I continue on while she stands in place, chanting whatever foreign-speak is in her mind today.

"Much better. Ohm-ma-boo-bah-bing-bah-noo."
She lets out a loud sigh. "That's my chant for small
spaces. It usually doesn't work."

After we've walked 700 feet, according to my
phone, there is a pile of papers sitting in the center of
the floor. I bend down to look at them.

"Wait, Lanie! Stop! I smell something evil."

I take a deep breath, trying to center myself before I respond. "November, we are here to gather
information. This is information. I'm going to pick it
up and look at it. Maybe you can smother it in pickle
juice later and ward off the nasty juju."

"Oak brining water. Two different things, Lanie."

There are at least thirty paintings in a stack on
the floor. I pick them up and blow the dust off.
"Shine your phone light on these, Vem."

The first one is a young girl, smiling while she
holds the hand of a stern-looking man with round
glasses. They are standing in a field of red flowers.
"Look at the date. 1947."

There are several more paintings of farm scenes,
this farm. The next page is a detailed ink drawing of
a man with shoulder-length hair and hollow cheeks.
His hands are worn and cracked. He is wearing jean
overalls with holes, a long-sleeved, checked shirt and
carries a knapsack around his neck. His wide-
brimmed hat comes down low on his forehead, but

his eyes look almost lifelike. Hungry for something, though I can't tell what. There is a single, blood-red tear running down his face. It is an exceptional, almost lifelike depiction.

"Raymond Dockley, 1947. She mentions him in her diary. I think she had a crush on him. A major crush."

The next is of a young girl, also in overalls, with long braids and soulful eyes. She is holding Raymond's hand as they walk. There is picture of Raymond with another man whose body is cloaked in a long coat, and a wide-brimmed hat covers his eyes.

Another group of paintings depict a stern-looking man with various other people. The girl with the braids is always off to the side.

There is one final painting of a family – a mother, father, two sons, and a daughter. They are standing by a creek filled with knives.

"There's a lot of sadness...and something else. I feel choked. It's choking." She slaps my arm. "Pookie died in this very passageway! I bet that's what happened, why I'm feeling this heaviness. I didn't come prepared for that. Probably need to run home and grab my ground ivy and nutmeg."

"I hope she didn't die in here." I wonder how we'll be able to take these with us without Marveline's knowledge. As I move forward, I step on one more paper. It's of a drawing of a teenaged girl dressed as a grownup. Her hair is styled high on her head and she's wearing heels. For all of her glamour, her eyes look sad. I lean in close and something on her chest catches my eye. "We have to get out of here. I need to see someone."

Vem stares at me, her hands pressed above her head. "Can't you see I'm in the middle of something important?"

"This can't wait." I tug on her arm. She is firm, but she'll give in, eventually. We are equally stubborn.

"Just in case you were wondering, I can smell the outside from here. I believe if we keep going, we'll end up somewhere on the grounds."

I sigh with irritation as I make an abrupt turn. "Some of your revelations would be better mentioned earlier in the conversation."

"What are we going to tell Marveline if we end up outside? And how are we going to get those paintings out of the house without her noticing?"

"You're right. We're going to have to go back where we came from. I think I can roll these up carefully and put them in your backpack." These are the days I feel some guilt for shaming Vem's use of an industrial-sized pack. "Once we figure out what they mean exactly, I'll return them to the Phersons. About face, Vem."

As we make our way back to the bedroom, I begin to wonder why Marveline has been so hesitant to let us in. Does she have any idea what happened to Pookie? Mandy has seemed more open to conversation, maybe she is the one I need to focus on.

When we are done, we put the panel back and I carefully roll the drawings up to put in Vem's backpack. Vem and I stare at each other, taking a few solid moments to collect our thoughts.

"Ready?" I ask.

"Ready, captain!" she says, saluting me.

Marveline is seated at the end of the hallway in a chair she must've brought from another room. "My goodness, it took you two long enough!" she says exasperatingly. "There must be more visible to the detective's eye than to a commoner like myself."

"It wasn't Lanie's fault." November pushes herself between me and Marveline. "There are many rituals that need to be done, especially to an old space like this. I always insist she spend a full ten minutes clearing her mind and snorting crushed elk dung before we begin any investigation. I'm happy to share some if you'd like."

"Thank you, but no. I'll pass. I'm assuming you're finished looking through our home now?"

I stare at the stylish oak table behind her. "Did you bring this from Denver? It's exquisite."

Marveline's eyes light up and she moves aside.

"This was here when we arrived. Sitting downstairs in the hallway. Take a look!"

I touch the surface, so familiar from Pookie's stories. The hall table Pookie described as the place where she occasionally kept her notes and secret dreams right under her father's nose. I open the drawer and bend down to look inside. "Vem, can I have the light?"

As she hands it to me, I see something taped to the back of the drawer. It is a note, folded twice. Written diagonally in childish scribble are the words "hopes and dreams." I unfold it to read what's written inside: "brave, strong and beautiful."

"I'd like to look this over. Can I take it with me? Oh, before we leave, we need to find Esmay."

Marveline nods. "She's in the barn with my sister. Please let me know what you discover!"

Vem and I walk quickly – a lively scurry – to the barn. As urgent as we are both feeling this situation might be, Lanie Anders does not run. It's been a lifelong point of contention for me, not running in any situation no matter how dire.

When we reach the barn, Mandy is working on the wooden sill, cleaning one spot intensely. She is listening to a recording of an older woman telling stories, stopping her work every few seconds to repeat what she's heard.

"The snow was so high we couldn't see out any

of the windows," she says in slow voice different from the bubbly Mandy we've seen.

Vem speeds ahead of me and to Mandy's side. "Where can we find Esmay?" she asks.

Mandy looks up, shocked to see us, like we have caught her doing something wrong.

I try to smooth things over. "Sorry to interrupt you. Are those family stories?"

"What? Why are you ladies here? My sister didn't mention anything about you visiting today. And yes, my grandmother recorded family stories."

"We're looking for Esmay. Have you seen her?" Vem asks excitedly.

Mandy itches the back of her neck. "I sent her into town. That woman refuses to leave here unless I demand it. I needed more cups for a birthday party we're hosting next week."

"How wonderful that you're preserving your personal history," I add, still feeling tension in the room.

Mandy's face softens. "Yes, I'm going to memorize every word so I can become the family historian. My grandmother did her best after my grandfather died in a plane crash." she sighs.

"You're hosting a party? You've gotten more bookings, then?" Vem inquires.

Mandy shrugs. "Just a few. This is that crazy neighbor's granddaughter. He said after he talked to you, he started feeling guilty about the way he was treating us. Saturday we're doing a presidential-themed party. For an eight-year-old."

"Well, that's good news. Maybe her husband is here?" If I try talking to Delbert for Cosmo, I might be able to soften the freeze between them. Anything is possible.

Mandy turns back to her work and begins scrubbing furiously. "Haven't seen him. He's probably got a project going somewhere today."

I'm used to her sister's dismissive attitude, but this is new for Mandy.

"We'll check back next week then. Thanks, Mandy!"

As Vem and I head back to the car, Vem pulls me close and whispers in my ear. "I could smell her lying."

For once, I don't disagree.

CHAPTER TWENTY-FOUR

Legend of Lisping Larry
Courtesy of the Piney Falls Public
Library Information Booth

AFTER THE DEATHS of Daisy Devine and the sheriff at Wormly Manor, there were people who camped out on the property for brief periods of time, never staying longer than a year. When Welcome Naybor acquired the land, public opinion was equally divided on whether it was a good idea to have people in the house again.

Welcome and his brother, Larry Naybor, were wealthy shipping magnates who came to Flanagan in 1933. In the midst of the depression, the two wealthy brothers seemed like saviors to the down-and-out locals, infusing the community with much-needed cash. Their arrival and enthusiasm reminded many of the Scheddy brothers who brought the canning industry to Flanagan a decade earlier.

Every time they went into town to buy supplies, Larry was friendly to the townsfolk, while Welcome kept his distance. Larry offered to help those who needed a little extra, buying them a sack of flour here, some dried fruit there. Always under the disapproving eye of his brother.

Welcome had a routine each week: the livery stable, the general store, and then the bakery, while Larry wandered the streets finding whatever suited his fancy that day. Larry possessed a lisp that sometimes made him hard to understand, so folks just nodded their heads when he spoke, often ending their conversation with a pocket of coins they hadn't asked for but didn't realize Larry was offering.

As the two men built their business, their personalities continued to diverge. Welcome became more aloof. He told the few people he spoke with that this partnership they'd formed wasn't working out; Larry wanted to throw their money away on frivolities and one day he'd regret it. Friendships and popularity weren't an important part of success. It was clear Larry earned the position of the favorite Naybor brother in the town of Flanagan.

As the harsh winter rains began, Larry came down with an illness. The doctor summoned from town said he'd seen nothing quite like those symptoms: crazy eyes, a fever that came and went, and gibberish so strange he wasn't sure it hadn't come from the devil himself.

The next week, Welcome came into town alone.

After asking to address worried neighbors in the general store, he told the anxious crowd that Larry succumbed to a mystery illness. Welcome Naybor was now a single business entity without a partner, and the locals would call him Welcome Nah BOR. The Ladies League asked if they could bring supper and mourn the passing of one who was unfailingly generous. Welcome refused and insisted his brother's name never be spoken again.

As the winter months turned to spring, there were hushed whispers that Larry Naybor was still alive, banished to a life on the run. Rumors of Larry sightings in Flanagan became commonplace.

One person said he tempted fate by fishing at Spoonback Creek every weekend. One Saturday, he glimpsed a fellow running on the other side of the creek and he feared this person wasn't well. He made his way over, catching up to the man. When he tapped the gentleman on the shoulder, the gaunt face that met him was none other than Larry Naybor. The man asked where he'd been. Larry opened his mouth to talk and his tongue was gone.

That was the last sighting of Larry. To this day, no gravesite has been found, nor has there been any credible explanation for his death.

CHAPTER TWENTY-FIVE

Lanie
Sassy Lasses Winery

"YOU ARE GOING to tell me who or what is so important that you had to drive my car, right Lanie?" Vem is leaning over close to me, practically sitting in my lap. She has no comprehension of personal space.

"When we get to town, I promise. I'm trying to work things out in my mind. And I had to drive because you don't chant and drive well together. I've seen the edge of the road up close and personal one too many times."

November leans back onto her own side of the car and folds her arms across her chest. "You may have a point. I need to finish my chant for found treasures. Don't bother me until we get to town." She closes her eyes and begins spouting words I've not heard before as my phone rings insistently.

"Can you tell them to call back? So rude!" November puts the phone to my face, causing me to swerve momentarily.

"Just answer it. Whatever is so urgent, I can call them back later," I snap.

Instead, she puts the phone on speaker. "Lanie? Are you there? You've got to go talk to her now. I can't take much more."

"Hi, Piper." My voice softens. "We're on our way back to town. Is Gladys bothering you again?"

"Last night I went out on a date with Finnegan. Can you believe it? My third actual date!"

"He smells funny to me," November interjects. "Like soap made of burnt plastic."

"I'm sure he smells lovely. Go ahead, hon. What did she do?"

"We were going to make our own pizzas, so we walked to the grocery store. What a dumb idea. There she was, putting canned peas into her basket. I tried avoiding her, but she was like a dog with a bone once she saw me with a guy."

I imagine Gladys following them around the store, wanting to know their every intended move. How embarrassing. "What did she do?"

"She pushed into line behind us when we were checking out. We grabbed our bag and left quickly, assuming she would get held up talking to the checker who seemed to be a distant family member."

"Her husband's cousin's daughter Melba. She hates her but can't get enough of her." I know way too much about Gladys's life, but I can't help but listen to the overly-loud phone calls she makes in my presence.

"Yeah, whoever it was. We forgot all about her until we got to his place. I was showing Finnegan how to make the dough and his neighbor knocks on the door. He says, 'Do either of you know this old lady sitting in the parking lot? She's got some binoculars out and she's pointing them right at your window.'"

"Oh, Gladys. How could you." I lament. "I don't understand her obsession with you. How long did she stay?"

"Until Finnegan called the cops. Mr. Lumquest showed up and told her she had to go home or he wouldn't give her this week's police reports."

"Those are one of her very favorite things. I guess she hasn't discovered she can access them online. Good for Boysie."

"Lanie, will you talk to her please? I can't take much more. She just doesn't seem to understand the word 'no.'"

"We're on this, Piper," Vem chirps. "We're almost to town. Lanie and I will threaten to remove her standing scone order. Won't we, Lanie?"

"Something like that."

We pull up in front of the Public Records building and November eagerly unfastens her seatbelt.

"Vem, could you go get me a couple of scones? A way to sweeten the pot, shall we say?"

November rolls her eyes. "Oh, you're trying to get rid of me so you can rough her up. I get it."

I suppress a giggle. "No roughing, I promise. I just need a few moments alone with her. She tends to get a little riled up when you're around."

She nods and heads off toward Cosmic Cakes and Antiquery while I brace myself for Hurricane Gladys.

She is taking her usual afternoon nap when I arrive, her orthopedic shoes propped on the desk and a small round pillow supporting her neck. I initially sit patiently waiting for her to wake up, but then I remember I've got other urgent business today.

There is a large, black stapler on the desk, one she told me is considered an antique incapable of destruction and could probably withstand any blow. I push it to the floor.

Gladys stirs and finally opens her eyes. "Goodness, toots. You scared the daylights out of me. What're you doing interrupting me in the afternoon? Did we have an appointment?"

I will have to measure my words carefully. "Gladys, Vem will be here soon with a scone. Maybe they even baked cinnamon rolls today."

She leans forward, narrowing her eyes. "You're tryin' to sugar me up, toots. Why would you do that?

What do you need?"

"I don't need anything. Well, actually I do." I fold my hands in my lap. "While it's so admirable that you want to take on the grandmotherly role for her, Piper is not comfortable with your level of – shall we say – 'interest' in her life. She'd like it if you would back off a bit."

I hold my breath, waiting for whatever comes next.

"You're here to be her goon? Her muscle? Why didn't she just tell me herself when I saw her last night?"

"You were spying on her with binoculars. I think the fact that she called Boysie should tell you she's not appreciative of your level of care."

"Harrumph." She crosses her arms and leans back in her chair. "She told you I followed her? Well, that's a fine how-de-do. I was just trying to make sure she was safe. I don't know anything about this boy, and I figured she has no one looking out for her."

"Finnegan is a fine young man. He's working on his business degree and then he plans to buy Cheese with Your Burger. Piper is an excellent judge of character." There is a heavy silence in the air. "Do you want to know what I think?"

Gladys shakes her head furiously. "I don't. But you're going to tell me anyway, I'd imagine."

"I think Piper reminds you of your daughter, Carlene. You have so many great family members, but they all have each other. You see Carlene in her because she ran off and had nobody. You think Piper has nobody since her family is completely out of the picture." That all just fell out of my mouth, but hearing it out loud, it makes perfect sense. I wait for her to throw me out of the building and tell me never to return for my insolence.

"Lanie," she says, tapping her finger to her chin, "you might be on to something. Never thought about things in that manner."

"Well, if you need some other way to divert your attention, you could always help me in my search for Pookie Naybor's remains. I have some information Vem and I just discovered and you might be able to–"

"Not on your life!" she snaps. "I told you already, I want nothing to do with that place or those women. Evil. Bad news. No. Nope."

"Okay, okay," I put my hand up. "I get it. It was just a thought. Maybe instead, you could try something else?"

Her eyes narrow suspiciously. "And just what would that be?"

"Planning your own birthday party. You said the person who normally does it died. We don't have anyone else your age in this community and you should be celebrated. Give me some ideas and I'll make a huge party for you."

Gladys's face softens. "Yes, that's grand. I can see it," she moves her hands in front of her face, where an imaginary scene is forming. "Gladys Petrie's Centenarian Celebration. We'll get a bright, yellow banner made and maybe find a band with a lead singer in tight dungarees."

"Excellent! You need to be celebrated, Gladys!"

She plops her feet back on top of the desk. "I'll get to work on that tomorrow. Getting too late in the day to start a new project now. I'll message you. You can go now, toots."

As I leave her office, I bump into Vem. She has nothing in her hands. "Out of Pluto Peach for today."

"That's okay. Let's see if we can track down Esmay. Maybe you can put your sniffer to the pavement like a bloodhound and we can find her," I giggle.

Vem rolls her eyes. "Oh Lanie, don't be ridiculous. I don't need my nose to tell me where she is. That woman across the street wearing the dark hood over her head? That's Esmay. She's been watching us ever since we pulled up."

CHAPTER TWENTY-SIX

Pookie
Naybor Manor – 1947

Dearest Ophelia,

I have the most glorious news. First, it is my 13th birthday. Daddy says this means I am a young woman now and I have to accept the responsibilities that come with that. I'm not entirely sure I understand what that means, but I do realize it's always good not to slouch when sitting at the table, and always make sure I smell like a lady.

Daddy brought a tray into my room this morning, with a lovely rose and two sugared pieces of toast. He made me tea, but he said it wasn't the grown-up tea, for I wasn't quite ready for that. It was a lovely tea made from berries, the ones we dried last summer.

He informed me the day would be full of surprises, and that after my chores and daily activities, I should take a bath and find my prettiest dress for dinner.

Ophelia, I am not one to enjoy my dress-es. In fact, the last time I wore a dress we went into town to attend the funeral of one of our neighbors, struck down by malaria while serving in Europe. It was a terrible occasion. His small children whimpered the entire time, not because they were sad (they barely knew him), but because their mother was wailing and carrying on. Her new boyfriend had to hold her arm the entire service.

After that experience, I vowed I would never wear such an uncomfortable frock again to remind me of such a morose situa-tion. Surely, we are not going to a funeral this evening! Knowing Daddy, it will be some-thing so grand my eyes will barely comprehend the vision. You will be the first to be informed.

I must go tell Raymond what lies ahead. Even though our recent meetings have been awkward, I know he has my best interests at heart.

Of late, he has been removing his over-shirt to attend to sweatier tasks. Daddy says I ought not stare when the help remove any of their clothing. It is their right; they work hard and often feel the need for some fresh air on their limbs.

I've tried not to stare at his muscular arms, but they are solid and tanned, unlike Daddy's delicate arms that are very similar in size and appearance to mine.

In Respectful Excitement and Anticipation, Pookie A. Naybor

"Good morning, Miss." Raymond was chopping wood, wearing just his breeches and suspenders.

"Do you know what day it is?" Pookie asked.

Raymond continued to chop. He stopped to wipe his brow on his forearm. "Tuesday, I s'pect."

Pookie searched his face for concern over their last few meetings. He should be angry with her, maybe even frightened that she had taken his schedule from his drawer. Surely, he realized by now. Instead, all she saw was concentration.

"No, silly. It's much better than Tuesday. Today is my thirteenth birthday! I'm officially a woman!"

Raymond stopped chopping and smiled. "I knew that. I was teasin'. A'course it's your birthday. And a happy day to you!" He bent down slightly. "I do have a little surprise for you, but I gotta finish my early chores first."

Pookie blushed. "Oh, that's perfectly fine. You don't have to give me anything. I just wanted you to join me in rejoicing over my entry into the adult world!"

Raymond rubbed the back of his neck. "Now Miss, you're a fer bit from that world. Let's not think about that ugly place today. You think of life as a child for as long as you can. Best to enjoy it where you are and give that other world the space it needs."

Pookie stuck her chin out indignantly. "I am so an adult. Daddy has lots of grown-up surprises for me today. He even made me tea–"

"The grown-up tea? He made that for you?" Raymond came close and took her chin in his hand. "Look at me. I want to see your eyes."

She looked into his tender blue eyes, trying hard not to imagine them even closer right before he kissed her sweetly on the mouth.

"What's wrong with my eyes?" she sputtered.

"Look okay to me." He released her chin and put his hands on his hips. "That tea's not for you. Only real grown-ups. Take me serious now. Don't drink none of that tea, I don't care what yer pa says."

"It was a different tea, Raymond. I'm not ready for the other."

He picked up his axe and began chopping again, his muscular arms bulging with each whack.

"Do you know what big surprise Daddy has for me this evening?"

"Can't say as I do. I'm just the help, not your daddy's confidant."

Pookie thought back to the night she caught him

deep in conversation with her father. How Raymond was trying to negotiate new terms of his employment. If only Daddy knew what she knew; his value to Naybor Manor.

"What time is it?"

Raymond looked up at the sky, trying to place the exact location of the sun under the heavy blanket of clouds. "I'd say two-thirty."

"Oh no! I must finish my lessons. Daddy says I'm to dress up for a big surprise later. You'll come up to the house with your gift?"

"I will, Miss. Soon as I finish my chores and look respectable."

Pookie walked closer, hugging him from behind in between axe swings. "I understand you don't trust me. But I care for you deeply."

Raymond reached around awkwardly and patted her. "I know you do, Miss. You're one of the good ones."

After an easy go at her lessons (Miss Dandridge only had her recite states and capitols, something she could do in her sleep), Pookie took a bubble bath. Her stomach hurt from drinking the berry tea, something her father always seemed to forget, and the warm bath made it feel better. When she returned to her bedroom, a magical surprise awaited her. A crimson dress had been laid out on her pillow. She picked it up gently, reading the note pinned to the sleeve.

This is a Mary O'Donohue original. Miss O'Donohue designs gowns exclusively for Golden Lights Studios and all actresses within.

"Oh, Mrs. Wilson, do you know how frightfully delightful this gift is? Tulip Sloan raves about her creations, wearing them in all of her fashion magazine shoots. 'Her designs are incredibly flattering with a focus on strong shoulders and a slim hip – using clever draping techniques to enhance and accentuate the female figure.' That's what it said in *Hollywood Gal* magazine."

Pookie held it up, admiringly. As she did, another piece of paper slipped to the floor.

Dear Miss Naybor,

This dress was designed especially for you. With a modern square neckline, the long sleeves have shaped darts on the inside elbow and the back zip for ease in getting the dress on. The calf-length skirt contains a full faux wrap. You will notice the self-covered belt is the latest in Hollywood fashion. Miss Sloan recently wore a similar pattern in her upcoming film, Goddess of Penimen Lane.

Please enjoy with my compliments!

Sincerely,
Mary O'Donohue

Pookie stepped into the dress and gazed at herself in the full-length mirror.

"If I hadn't been standing here, I wouldn't have understood the transformation. You've turned yourself into a lady of means! Not the girl who got into the bathtub!" Mrs. Wilson touched her sleeve admiringly. "Like a princess going to a ball."

There was a knock at the door and the house-keeper's daughter entered, carrying a curling iron, hair spray and several brushes.

"Miss Pookie, your daddy asked me to fix up your hair real nice. For your important dinner guest. I work at a hair salon in Flanagan. I've got some ideas if you aren't opposed."

Pookie grabbed both of her hands excitedly. "Oh yes, please! I have no idea about hair styles, other than keeping my braids even. Oh, wait!" Pookie knelt down, reached underneath her bed, and pulled out a stack of magazines. She turned to a page with a photo of a Hollywood starlet, glancing demurely over her shoulder through a pile of fur.

"Can you make it look like this? I know I'll never be as impossibly beautiful as Scarlett Naveno, but maybe just a hint of her style?"

Mrs. Wilson laughed. "Now Miss Pookie, you are a handsome young woman. You just give that picture to my daughter here and she'll have you looking like you're attending one of those premieres in no time!"

She walked toward the door and then stopped to turn around. "Make sure you finish her up in an hour. The master of the house has some big plans for her and she can't be late."

"I can give you big rolls on either side of your head. During the war, they called it a Victory Roll. Now we call it an 'updo.' Is that to your liking, Miss?"

"Oh yes, please!" Pookie nodded excitedly.

Mrs. Wilson's daughter spent over an hour carefully pinning, and then spraying, Pookie's long, unruly hair.

"Are you sure you don't know who our dinner guests are this evening?" Pookie asked several times. "Someone must've spilled a hint!"

The woman smiled. "No Miss, nothing at all."

After what seemed like hours, she led Pookie once more in front of her mirror. The young woman who stood, dressed in a bonafide, crimson, Hollywood dress with an elegant updo wasn't Pookie Naybor. She was a glamorous starlet.

"You like it, Miss?"

"I... I don't know." Pookie touched the stiff, foreign-feeling, high pile of hair.

"It's part of being a grown woman," she chuckled. "A little discomfort for beauty. You'll get used to it. Your daddy wants you downstairs as soon as you are ready."

Pookie slipped on her good shoes, a half-size too small. The last time she wore dress-up shoes, they were to attend a wedding in Flanagan. The bride decided to leave town with her second cousin just thirty minutes before the ceremony, causing Welcome to pronounce it "a waste of expensive clothing." As she crossed over to the grand staircase, Mrs. Wilson, tapped her on the back.

"Guess these didn't make it into your bedroom." She held up a pair of shiny, black high heels with lace on each side and a bow on the top.

"I'll help you into these. It's not like those clunky kid shoes."

Pookie rose three inches above Mrs. Wilson. "These are fancy!" she remarked, as she pranced in a circle with one hand on her hip. In only seven steps, her ankle gave out and she slipped off the side of the shoe.

Mrs. Wilson chuckled. "They do take some practice. Your daddy might've been better off giving them to you last week. But never you mind, just take small steps and concentrate on staying in the center of the shoe."

Pookie nodded. She took a deep breath and grabbed the railing of the grand staircase. Slowly, she made her way down, one step at a time.

Welcome appeared from the kitchen, dressed in

his most dapper tux and chewing something he'd no doubt tested from the dinner menu. "Oh my, daughter. You take my breath away." He put his hand to his mouth, watching as she gingerly walked down the steps. He kissed her hand when she reached the bottom. "If you'll accompany me to the dining room, please."

The long, formal table was covered with a crisp, white cloth; eight place settings of the pink, rose-covered, fine china, that they only used for holidays were placed upon the table.

"Who is coming, Daddy? We don't know that many folks."

He smiled. "You'll see, my darling. Station yourself by the front door, so you may greet our guests as they arrive. I shouldn't have to tell you, but just in case: this is the time to use your finest manners. You are representing Naybor Manor in the best possible way this evening."

Pookie nodded. She stood nervously at the door, trying to imagine who could possibly make the trip thirty miles from town to come for her dinner. Eventually, the bell rang. She resisted the urge to throw the door open and took a breath. She thought of what Miss Dandridge taught her during manners lessons. *Count to ten before opening the door, Pookie. Guests expect to wait while you collect yourself.*

"Miss Dandridge! You never mentioned you'd be here this evening!" Her teacher was dressed in a plum-colored dress, with a pearl pin in her short, bobbed hair. "You look positively divine!" Pookie had never pictured her teacher functioning outside of their studies. It took her a moment to come to terms with her in a different setting.

"I outfoxed you then!" She winked and kissed Pookie's cheek lightly.

"How delightful you will be joining us!" Pookie quickly regained her senses and remembered her formal occasion lessons. Miss Dandridge nodded her approval.

Right behind her was Freddie, accompanied by his mother. He was wearing a brand-new suit and his hair was slicked down against his head.

"Freddie!" She hugged him tightly, his body stiff and unwelcoming. He didn't smell like old grass, his usual Saturday smell.

"He's feeling a bit uncomfortable in the new suit your daddy bought him." His mother explained.

"It itches!" He tried pulling at the collar, but his mother slapped his hand away.

"Behave!" she whispered.

Pookie counted. That was three. She resumed her post next to the door while Welcome ushered the guests to the living room.

The next time she opened the door, Raymond,

freshly washed and carrying flowers from the south field, smiled at her.

His mouth hung open. "Miss Pookie, I was wrong. You look like the pertiest grown-up woman I've ever seen!"

She blushed. "You fooled me this morning! Thank you for the flowers! Please come in and join the other guests." Freddie wouldn't be happy Raymond was joining them on top of having to wear an uncomfortable suit. She stared after Raymond as he walked into the living room. He and Welcome greeted each other like friends from town, not two people who had recently made a dirty deal in the moonlight.

Pookie stood, transferring her weight from one foot to the other. She looked at her father, trying to get his attention. When she finally did, she mouthed, "Can I sit down now?"

He shook his head no.

She sighed but dutifully maintained her post. Finally, as she was seriously contemplating removing her shoes with or without her father's approval, the doorbell rang once more. She counted to ten.

Welcome joined her, his hands on her shoulders. "Best behavior," he whispered in her ear.

When she opened the door, a gorgeous blonde woman with big green eyes, rosebud lips and a perfect, tiny nose stood on the grand porch, alongside a man who was equally handsome. They were both wrapped in furs even though it was spring and they were considered off-season, at least according to her fashion magazines.

Pookie didn't make any effort to let her in, nor did she greet her. Instead, she stood, mouth agape.

Welcome pushed by his daughter. "Tulip, darling. Greetings from our humble manor. So delighted you could make it to my daughter's celebration."

CHAPTER TWENTY-SEVEN

Lanie
Piney Falls

I LOOK ACROSS the street where a thin woman wearing glasses that have darkened to adjust to the sunlight was staring at the light pole beside her. It's so absurd, and yet she is hiding in plain sight so easily.

"You're brilliant, Vem. Stay here and I'll go talk to her."

"Oh, no you don't, Lanie. I wouldn't miss this show for all the dandelions in North America."

I look at her with dismay. There is nothing I can do to keep November Bean away once she sets her mind to something. "Okay but–"

"I know. Keep quiet and let you do the talking. You know I never speak unless I've got something brilliant to say, Lanie."

We approach Esmay slowly. I'm not sure if she will bolt the minute we reach her, or if she really wanted us to see her there.

"Esmay? We were looking for you out at the farm today. Mandy said I might find you here. I had a couple of questions."

"Why would you want to ask me anything? I'm just the help. I don't have the inside track on Naybor Manor." She pulls a cigarette from her purse with shaking fingers.

"Well actually, I think you do." I do my best not to wrinkle my nose in disgust. Cigarette smoke makes my entire body shudder, in part because my mother used to smoke while she drank her vodka. That was always followed by some sort of verbal abuse. "Can we buy you a cup of coffee at the bakery? There's just a few loose ends I need to clear up."

She looks around cautiously before starting to walk toward Cosmo's shop. I'm curious that she knows where to go, given Mandy said she never goes into town.

"No smoking, please. November Bean has the lungs of a twelve-year-old junior high track star and we're going to keep it that way," Vem chides. Esmay throws her cigarette on the ground and stomps on it and Vem promptly picks it up with one hand while plugging her nose with the other. "No littering either." She holds it at some distance before placing it in a community trash can.

We walk brusquely to the bakery. When we arrive, Piper looks at me anxiously.

"Yes, we had our talk. She has a new project on which to focus her unbelievable energy. I think she'll leave you alone now."

Her shoulders drop. "Oh good. Thank you, Lanie!" She turns her attention to our guest. "What can I get you today, ma'am? We have a special, Razz MaTazz berry hand pies, two for the price of one!"

"I'll just have a coffee. Black."

"You can take off your sunglasses inside." Vem chides Esmay. "You're not a fugitive." She leans in close and smells Esmay's jacket. "Wait, are you?"

I put my hand on her arm and shake my head. "Will you go find us a table, Esmay? Vem, what would you like? My treat."

She eyes the display case hungrily. "Do you have any Colossal Cosmos Cinnamon Rolls left?"

Piper nods. "You realize they're the size of a dinner plate, right?"

"You remember that I have the metabolism of a teen boy?" Vem retorts. "Maybe I'll come back for another."

I roll my eyes. "My usual Scorpio Scone, hon. And a latte, half-foam."

When we're settled in at the table, I fold my arms in front of me, trying to prepare for the third difficult conversation today. "We were so surprised to see you. Mandy says you hate coming to town."

Esmay clears her throat. "I never liked it here. Too many nosy people. I prefer to keep to myself at the farm." She looks around the room, examining each person seated at the other tables.

I scooch forward in my seat. "At Piper's party you were wearing the most gorgeous brooch. You told me you got it at a second-hand store."

Esmay chuckles uneasily. "I did. You said it was a good deal, so I'm thinking I should go back and see what I can sell it for."

Vem leans forward and pulls Esmay's glasses off, staring at her nose to nose. "I'm sorry, but I can't take this. The eyes are the window to the soul, and yours seem pretty black."

Esmay immediately puts her hands to her face, trying to cover the large black eye she has. Vem jumps up and throws her arms around her. "Did Delbert do this to you? I know karate and other forms of self-defense. I can take him."

"I don't want to talk about it." She looks at my shoes.

"We can help you, Esmay. You don't need to live in fear. Everyone here is broken in some way. Vem came from a cult and then an abusive marriage–"

November howls with her inside howl voice. Immediately the place is quiet, but then they realize it's just November being November, and they go back to their conversations.

"My husband didn't do anything to me. I live on a farm where there are hundreds of reasons to have a black eye. Is that all you wanted to ask?"

"Not exactly." It's going to be hard now to be blunt. "Look, I know why you're here. You and your husband. You came back to the farm because this is where you grew up."

Esmay chuckles uncomfortably. "Miss Anders, you couldn't be further from the truth. I didn't grow up on the Naybor property. Is that what the gals told you?"

"They didn't have to. I saw the drawings in the passageway. Your drawings. You documented your life so well. Even drawing images of the men who worked there. It was like a historical picture book of Naybor Manor. I read about them in your diary. You detailed it so well. I've got a note in my purse that you wrote and taped to a desk."

She is silent now, staring at the ground. I can't tell if it's in anger or defeat.

"But what gave it away was the brooch. You told me it came from a secondhand store."

"It did!" she protests weakly. "Why would I make that up?"

"It's the same one you're wearing in your lovely painting. We found it upstairs today in your secret passage, Pookie."

Chapter Twenty-Eight

Pookie
1947

"**D**ARLING GIRL, YOU look as if you've seen a ghost. Please invite your guests in before they wilt from boredom right here!" The feathery light voice commanded.

Pookie stared at the familiar face: the eyes, emerald green and almond shaped, the flawless skin and shiny, platinum blonde hair pulled back like Pookie's but much more regal. She was perfection.

"Miss Sloan, I'm…honored." She curtsied awkwardly, stumbling over the heel of her fancy shoes and falling face-first into the chest of her idol.

"Gracious, Welcome. You didn't tell me your sweet daughter was such a klutz!" She pecked a light kiss on her cheek before pushing Pookie to a standing position so that she could enter the house, handing Welcome her fur. "I like what you've done with the place. It's been ages since I've been here. Too long, in fact."

Pookie stared at her father incredulously. "You know her? Tulip Sloan? You never said a word!"

Welcome shrugged. "Tulip, please join our other guests in the living room. I'll get you a cocktail. And who might this stranger be?"

The man blushed slightly and offered a handshake. "Owen Pherson, of course. It's been too long. Thought I'd accompany Tulip on this venture and check up on my old friend."

The two men chuckled uncomfortably. "That last time we were together was before the war. Many things have changed since then." Owen remarked.

Welcome nodded without emotion. "Pookie, this man is one of those most powerful in Hollywood. Owen Pherson runs Golden Lights Studio and just about everything else in town. The president even calls to ask his advice."

Pookie stared at him in admiration and awe. Owen took her hand and brought it to his lips. "A delicate rose. How proud your father must be," he declared.

Pookie blushed. There was something both exciting and terrifying about Mr. Pherson.

"Darling, please show our guests to the living room and introduce them to the others. I'll join you in a moment."

Tulip grabbed Welcome's arm as he was walking off. "We must discuss business later."

Welcome nodded tersely. "When the other guests have gone."

Pookie took care to walk carefully, hoping to avoid another embarrassing event.

"You cut a pretty figure, my darling. My designer said she was making a dress for this occasion. When your father insisted I come for your birthday, I said, 'anything for you, Welcome.' I neglected to ask your age."

"I'm thirteen, Miss Sloan. An adult now." Pookie slowed but didn't stop walking. It didn't seem right to look her in the eye.

Tulip let out a loud guffaw. It sounded just as she did in the movie, *Joyous People,* when she had a mental issue that made her laugh uncontrollably whenever her mother was near.

Pookie stopped and turned around, facing her idol. She was slightly taken aback.

"Oh, dahhling girl, I thought that at your age too. I ran away the next year and began a hard life on my own. We must enjoy the impertinence of youth, mustn't we, Owen?"

His face, as beautifully-crafted as hers, remained perfectly still. He nodded slightly and followed behind them into the large living room.

Freddie's mother, Alicebeth stood up and dropped her tea cup on the jade-colored Oriental rug. "It's you!" Freddie scrambled at his mother's feet, trying to recover the pieces of china.

Oblivious to her mess, Alicebeth ran over to Tulip and knelt at her feet. "I never thought I'd have the privilege of meeting you, ma'am. You're breathtaking. To be in the same room –"

Tulip gently kissed her head and helped her to her feet. "No need for a woman to bow before me. Now men, they're a different story." She chuckled and the rest of the room responded in turn. "Tell me your name, dear."

"I'm...I'm Alicebeth Browler. And that's my boy, Freddie. He's a good friend of Pookie's. They go to the picture show every week, to see you. The owner mostly shows Tulip Sloan movies, but my boy doesn't mind. And listen to me, I'm babbling."

Tulip gently caressed Alicebeth's head. "You poor dear. You work hard to support your boy, your few extra pennies going to give him the luxury of a picture show. Is there no father?"

Alicebeth blushed. "No, ma'am. Freddie's pa didn't want the bother of a boy to care for."

"Then I shall make sure he sees his movie every week, without a worry. I'll make arrangements with Welcome to pay for a year's worth of movie tickets. And a sweet for each of you."

Pookie started to protest, wanting to say that her father paid for every movie and gave them money for sweets, but seeing how happy Freddie's mother was, she said nothing.

"Oh, thank you ma'am." Alicebeth kissed Tulip's hand.

Freddie moved to his mother's side.

Tulip's brow furrowed. "Pookie, darling. Please step closer to your friend.

Pookie obediently moved to her Freddie's side, towering over him in her fancy shoes. She clasped her hands behind her back, poking Freddie playfully from behind. He scowled at her in response.

"It's uncanny. The two of you share all of your features. If I didn't know Welcome better, I'd wonder if this weren't a delicious movie script. Owen, make note; we'll have a studio meeting about a movie with lost siblings."

Owen bowed slightly. "Of course. Brilliant idea, Tulip." He straightened his cuffs.

Pookie cleared her throat. "I'd like to present, Miss Tulip Sloan and her guest, Mr. Owen Pherson, of Hollywood, California."

Raymond stood up and danced on his feet nervously. "What a day. Reckon my ma would cry tears of joy, seein' me in the same room with the likes of Hollywood royalty."

Tulip moved to his side, reaching up and kissing him on the cheek, her lips lingering while she grabbed his hand. "What a delicious man," she said softly. "Tell me your name?"

"Raymond, ma'am," he stuttered. "You're just as perty as you are on the screen. More so."

Pookie pushed aside the jealousy that was welling up inside her. This was her idol, after all. Raymond couldn't help feeling just as overwhelmed by her presence.

"Welcome will get your mother's address and we'll have a photograph sent to her, dear Raymond." Tulip finally released Raymond and moved to Welcome's side.

A maid unfamiliar to Pookie appeared behind them. "Dinner is served."

The guests made their way to the formal dining room where place cards had magically appeared. There were roses of every color in tall vases up and down the long table with every piece of silver polished to perfection.

Welcome was set at the head of the table with Pookie to his right. Next to her was Freddie and then his mother. Miss Dandridge was next, then Raymond and Owen Pherson. Tulip flanked Welcome's left side.

As giant soup tureens were carried into the rooms and bowls were filled with a rich, brown broth, Pookie whispered in Freddie's ear. "Isn't she marvelous?"

"Looks older in person. Something funny about her eyes too." He sniffed the liquid in his bowl. "Am

I gonna have to eat vegetables tonight?"

Freddie's mother nudged his arm, both as a reminder to take it off the table and to watch his words.

While they made their way through pea croquettes, sweet-sour carrots and a giant turkey with Naybor Manor potatoes and gravy, Pookie watched as Tulip spoke intimately with her father.

She tried not to stare, but this motion picture image she'd seen on the screen for so many years was right here, in luscious full color, making animated gestures. Though it was definitely the same face and voice, there was a hint of sadness when she spoke.

Pookie waited patiently for a break in the conversation, taking care to make sure her napkin was in her lap before attracting her father's attention. "Miss Sloan? May I ask you a question?"

"What is it, sweet girl? My life is an open book." She shared a knowing glance with Welcome. "At least an open chapter."

"Your eyes display such emotion in your movies. What thoughts might you be thinking to achieve such intensity?"

Tulip took a deep breath. "Well, one must draw on their past to create their future. Your father may not have told you about my hardships growing up."

"It was in one of the magazines I read. You grew up without a father, helping your mother with the neighborhood laundry. When your mother retired to her bedroom at night, you began baking bread that you took to the neighbors with their laundry, making extra money."

Tulip smiled, her small, pearl-white teeth glistening. "Usually we have a dramatic story released to the rags in order to make our pasts seem more dramatic to the public. Half the people in Hollywood have perfectly wonderful parents but it wouldn't sell as many tickets if the public caught wind their lives were normal. I didn't have to plump up my story. In fact, it is much worse than I allowed be told in the papers."

The room was hushed, with only the faint sound of the dishes clattering in the kitchen heard.

"My father left my mother soon after coming to this country from Hungary. He found work in Philadelphia and didn't want to take a wife and child with him. He promised my mother he would send money. He never did."

She took a deep breath and stood up, as if she were getting ready to give a soliloquy in one of her movies. Tulip put her hand on the back of Raymond's chair, causing him to squirm uncomfortably. She looked down for a moment, composing her thoughts.

"Once my father was gone, my mother was forced to do unspeakable things to support us.

Eventually she went to work in the department store down the street from our tiny apartment, Blanchard's, selling perfume. But that didn't bring in enough money so we started taking in laundry. After that, Mother would sell cigarettes on the weekend at gentlemen's clubs. She would come home reeking of smoke and talking about the men who promised her a better life if only she'd send me to live somewhere else."

"A terrible thought." Welcome shook his head. "No mother should be forced to abandon her child."

Freddie's mother looked sharply at Welcome.

"Please continue, Tulip. Your story is a lesson for all of us." Welcome winked at Pookie.

She began walking around the room, pausing when she reached Pookie's chair. "By the time I was fourteen, my mother was completely worn out. I rubbed her feet every night when she came home from work but there was no ridding her of the pain in her back and her arms. I started to understand she would be much better off without a young girl to care for."

"No!" Miss Dandridge protested. "A child must never be considered a burden!"

"I assure you, these are different times. I discovered the address of her benefactor and went to see him. I told him that my mother was no longer capable of selling cigarettes, but that she longed to be by his side. I made a deal that day, to help my mother."

There was an audible gasp from the room.

"He gave me a healthy sum of money and bought me a train ticket to California. He promised to care for my mother. I left her a note, telling her I was living in a home for unwanted children. I requested that she not search for me because I was using a different name in order to mask my identity. I promised myself I would send her money when I made my first picture."

"Is she proud of you now, Miss Sloan? Does your mother understand you left for her best interest?" Alicebeth asked.

Tulip lowered her lusciously long eyelashes. "This is a tragic story, remember. When my first picture was a success, I sent money and a letter and they both came back. After some searching, I discovered my mother had died of consumption shortly after my removal. You see," she gestured across the room, her body and mind in a different place than Naybor Manor. "Her paramour moved her into a fine home and brought in his best doctor, who informed him there was nothing to be done for my mother. She had been sick for some time, keeping her symptoms well-hidden from us all. My leaving didn't save her. And that, my dear Pookie, is the emotion you see on my face when I am doing a scene of any dramatic quality."

Miss Dandridge wiped tears from her eyes. Alice-beth clutched her chest. Pookie looked over at her father, who displayed an odd smile.

"Shall we have cake now?" he asked, breaking the solemn mood.

"Yes, darling. We must celebrate," Tulip's stiff posture relaxed, bringing her out of a scene from her past and into present day 1947. "Our dear Pookie is a woman. A true aaah-dult."

The four-tiered cherry-chocolate cake, covered in tiny frosting roses, was carefully moved in front of Pookie's plate. Everyone stood, joining together in singing Happy Birthday to You.

Pookie smiled through eyes filled with tears. Tulip, her idol, somehow became a movie star despite a life full of misery. She rose above it all. she smiled, nodded her head and closed her eyes when it was time to blow out the candles. This year's wish would be much different.

When it came time to open gifts, they moved back to the formal living room where Welcome brought grown up tea to those who wanted it.

"I chase my drinks with drinks, darling," Tulip mused, adding, "a gin ricky please."

"I've never heard of such a cocktail, Mis Sloan. How does one make those?" Miss Dandridge asked.

"I can answer that." Owen Pherson put one hip

on Tulip's chair, leaning his arm around the top. "It's one shot gin, 1/2 shot fresh squeezed lime juice and seltzer water. Tulip finds them refreshing. Especially the morning after," he looked at the children in the room and then at Tulip. "After a night of, shall we say, exuberant festivities."

Welcome chuckled from the bar area. "Tulip does enjoy her next-day beverages."

Pookie began unwrapping the mound of gifts, thirteen from her father to start. He usually gave her things that were more practical and less exciting, but she always remembered to appear gracious. "Thank you for the gold-plated pen, Daddy!" she said with fake enthusiasm as she reached the end of his pile.

"Open mine now!" Freddie commanded.

She picked up a small, unwrapped box and opened it to find a delicate pearl necklace. "Freddie!" she gasped. "It's delightful!" Pookie put it around her neck, Miss Dandridge assisting with the clasp.

"I need a stretch!" Tulip declared. "Who shall accompany a weak-kneed woman so she doesn't fall in a very unladylike way?" Welcome and Owen jumped up and held on to either side of her while they walked to Welcome's study, chattering about a Hollywood party they had all attended.

Raymond nudged Pookie and pointed to the foyer. Carefully, she stood and wobbled her way to the other room, hoping her father wouldn't notice her leaving her guests alone and chastise her later.

"I've got nighttime chores, Miss Pookie. Wish I could stay longer, but oh golly, the thought of my Ma's eyes shining bright while she reads about our fine meal with a movie star will keep my spirits up for many days."

Pookie looked down at his scuffed boots. "Thank you for coming, Raymond. Especially after last week. I–"

He clasped a rough hand over her mouth. "This ain't the time or place for that kinda talk. I brought you a present. A nice one too." He released her mouth, reaching into his pocket for a burlap-wrapped object. "Open it now, 'fore your Daddy comes back. He might not approve."

She carefully unfolded the material, to find an emerald brooch made to look like a flower pot. Three daisies sprouted from the pot, each flower made from a different-colored stone. "Oh, Raymond! It's the most exquisite thing I've ever seen!"

"Not all a them stones is real. You'll have to figure that out on your own. I was gonna give it to my girl, and when that didn't work out, Ma said to take it with me on my travels. She said to give it to the finest woman I ever had the pleasure to know. That'd be you, Miss Pookie."

"But Raymond," Pookie protested. "What about your future wife? What if she is the person you find on your next adventure? In your next town? What if you gave away your beautiful brooch before you found her?"

Raymond shook his head and looked toward the study, where Welcome had gathered the adults, save Freddie's mother to smoke cigars. He took her hands in his. "No wife in my future. I can say that with some certainty, Miss Pookie. I'll feel satisfied knowing Ma's brooch ended up with a good woman. You'll pass it along to your youngin and that way a part of Ma and me will always be in your family."

Pookie's eyes filled with tears. "Even more than seeing Tulip Sloan, this is the best gift I've ever received. She put her hands on his face and reached up to kiss him. She was almost to his lips when she heard someone clearing their throat.

"Pookie? You have guests in the other room. Let Raymond get to his chores now. Thank him for attending your celebration and tell him goodbye." Welcome stood in the doorway of his study, hands on his hips.

Pookie's cheeks turned bright red. "Daddy, I was thanking Raymond for coming and for being a good friend."

Raymond took his hat from the top of the coat tree and placed it on his head. "Thank you for the delightful celebration, Mr. Naybor. I'll tend to the important events of the evening then. Miss Pookie." He nodded in her direction.

"I'll send someone down with extra cake for all the help later." Welcome said, not waiting for his response. "Come Pookie." He commanded.

Pookie lagged behind her father, carefully slipping the brooch in the drawer of a wooden desk in the hallway.

She stared out the picture window as her guests visited, disappointed that Tulip found her father much more interesting than the guest of honor. The two whispered and giggled while Owen sat awkwardly nearby.

Freddie nudged her side. "Pookie, guess what? Can you guess your last surprise?"

"I'm exhausted, Freddie. I think I've had quite enough surprises for one evening." She laid her head back in the chair, closing her eyes as she strained to hear the conversation between her father and Tulip.

"I'm staying the night! Your Pa is sending my Ma back to town and tomorrow there is an order for Naybor Manor coming in at the store. I'll go home then."

"Oh. Wonderful Freddie. It really is." She was slightly disappointed. She needed time to absorb all that had taken place: Tulip, the real Tulip, gorgeous but unable to carry on a conversation, Raymond and his secret brooch, Daddy's ordinary dismissal of Raymond after their intimate conversation.

"You can show me your notebook. Let me see what you've learned in your investigation."

CHAPTER TWENTY-NINE

Lanie
Piney Falls

"NO, NO YOU'VE got it all wrong," Esmay's voice quivers.

"You killed those men to keep Naybor Manor for yourself. To keep strangers away so that with the property restored, you could begin your life over. I can understand you had hard feelings when your father, Welcome Naybor, was caught selling drugs, but this land belongs to someone else now, Pookie."

She makes an exasperated sound. "Honestly. Do I look like an elderly woman to you?"

I hadn't stopped to consider the timeline. Esmay may not look like she's aged well, but there is no way the girl who made those paintings in 1947 is sitting in front of me.

"More coffee anyone?" Piper asks cheerfully, oblivious to the unfolding drama right here in Cosmic Cakes and Antiquery.

"I'll take a little more coffee, if you don't mind."

Esmay looks up at her and smiles. "You're a cute little thing."

Piper giggles. "Thanks. People always think I'm a teenager. Guess all of the years I spent hiding in one house or another did wonders for my skin."

As she pours Esmay's cup and returns to the counter, I try to re-work the timeline in my head.

"This doesn't make any sense. If you aren't Pookie Naybor then who are you? How did you really obtain that brooch? Don't think I believe for a minute you found it at a second-hand shop."

Esmay runs her hands up and down her pants. She takes quick breaths in and out. Vem uses this opportunity to jump up behind her and squeeze her shoulders, guiding her in deep breathing exercises.

"Think of the last thing you ate. Now push it out through your nostrils. It's the best release you'll have today," she instructs.

After what seems like an hour but is more likely two minutes, my irritation level reaches its peak. "Esmay!" I half-yell. "Can you please tell us what is going on? What is your game?"

Esmay, whose eyes were closed while November was instructing her, snaps to attention. "The name I was born with was Carlene. Carlene Petrie."

Vem gasps. It's unusual for air to be going inward with her, she's more of an exhale in a dramatic fashion type of woman. "You're Gladys's lost daughter?"

Gladys has mourned for her lost daughter for decades, searching every corner of the internet for information. "Did you know her, Vem? From your time inside the cult?"

"No, she left when I was still a kid. Wowie." Vem clutches her chest. "All sorts of stories were told about her. She was the rebel who couldn't be tamed. When we heard our leader, Zion, was pushing people over Piney Falls, I started to wonder if they were all to cover up the fact that Sister Carlene had been given a good shove."

Carlene's face twitches. "That's funny; Zion having the guts to push me. He had his hooks in my family but would never have dared to do that to me. Did you know that my mother had an affair with him?"

It's my turn to clutch my chest. "What? Not Gladys!" I think back to conversations we've had, where she gushed about a young, handsome man who came to town and charmed everyone before he started his cult. Many families left to join his group, and she became resentful of them. "How long did this affair go on?"

"It was brief. When I decided to join Fallen Branch, she looked at it as a betrayal. Like he was only interested in her for whatever family members she was willing to release to him."

None of this is making sense to me. "Esmay, how long were you there? And why did you disappear? Does your mother have any idea where you are?"

"Lanie, give the poor woman a minute." Vem puts her arm on mine, much like I would normally do to her. "We can't expect her to give up all of her secrets." She turns to Esmay. "Can we?"

"Just like my Cosmo and Vem, you've been through a lot. I can understand why you wouldn't want contact with your family for a while."

"My mother and I were always like oil and water. She wanted me to fulfill all of her dreams and I just wanted to get away from her and figure out my own. She was so nosy, I couldn't even have a friend without her knowing more about them than I did."

"Well that certainly hasn't changed over time. Gladys is the snoopiest person in this town. I caught her out in my garbage once. I asked her what she needed for her soup, but I guess she just wanted to know what I paid for cable," Vem remarks with a nonchalant shrug.

"If you've been here all of these years, then you've seen what happened with the neighbors. You know what's going on with Truman Coolidge. I'll bet you knew who was killing people too."

Esmay's brow is tightly knitted. "I joined the cult because my mom admitted her affair to me. It made me angry and the only way I could think of to make her pay for her transgression, for the sake of my dad, was to join. I was in Fallen Branch for a year. At first, I was all in. *'Stay up all night and copy my stupid rantings, Sister Carlene.'* Of course, I did. Whatever Zion wanted was my command. Then one night when I finished whatever menial task he gave me, I was on my way back to my quarters when I saw people digging holes. I asked what they were doing and they said burying everyone's personal items so they would forget about their worldly goods. I saw they had taken all of the things that were precious to me and put them in a bag."

Vem nods vigorously. "That was all normal to me growing up. Now, I can't imagine living without my Fabulous Frother and my rock collection. You'd have to pry them from my cold, dead hands." November reaches over and touches Esmay's hand in support. "They were your things, not his."

"Right next to the hole where they were trying to bury my identity was another one with items they had obviously just dug up. I demanded my things back and wanted to know why they were digging up the other hole. Someone finally admitted they kept them buried for six months until a person forgot what they'd owned. Then they dug them up and sold them. It was Zion's personal bank."

"We discovered bags of money." I feel guilty now, given that the remaining members had decided to give that money to Cosmo and I to build our dream home as a thank you for all we've done to help them. A home I'm not sure will ever be finished until the day Cosmo can return to his normal routine and mind-state full-time.

"I demanded my things back and threatened to go to the police. I realized I'd made a horrible mistake. They reluctantly agreed. But I could no longer stay there, knowing what I did. I left that night, on foot."

"Why didn't you go back home? I've seen the scrapbook your mother keeps. She misses you terribly." *This is all I have of Carlene, Lanie. Prettiest girl you ever did see.*

"My whole family would have been in danger. The cult was capable of just about anything. By then, I'd heard my sister was married to a cop. We were told Zion bought them off so I didn't really know who to trust. I had to leave town quickly."

"Where did you go?"

"I bummed rides all over. Worked in truck stops up and down the coast. One night, an ex-con came in right before closing. I could tell he was down about the world, so I locked up and asked him to tell me his story while I cleaned."

"Delbert?" I ask.

Carlene nods her head. "His world was even more messed up than mine. Lost both of his parents, had to live with his grandmother, moving from place to place because they lost their land. When he was grown, he learned the truth about his dad, who was considered some sort of hero in their small town in Oklahoma."

"Why?" I ask, though my suspicions are rising that I may know exactly who Delbert's father is.

"His dad teamed up with the government to bring down a drug dealer. He was just an uneducated drifter looking for revenge for his best friend's death. Then he got in a bar fight one night and it happened to be an FBI agent he was fighting with. Turned out they'd each been wronged by the same person."

"This is getting good." Vem sits back, folding her arms.

"Delbert's father had been working on a ship, going back and forth from a port near here to Canada during prohibition. They were supposed to be hauling maple syrup, but it was really whiskey."

Esmay stands up and begins to pace around us. "Delbert's dad didn't care one way or another, but when you agree to do work that shouldn't be done, you end up with people you shouldn't be with. The man they were working for was evil. If anyone got out of line or tried to drink the profits, he made sure they were tossed overboard."

"Is that what happened to his friend?" Vem asks.

"Yes, we do believe so. He sent letters to his

mother every week, but sometimes she felt he left things out, so she wouldn't feel any more misery than she was already feeling."

"So, Delbert's father was upset and wanted revenge." I continue.

"His whole life. He never forgot the friend who came with him from Oklahoma, the two men with little more than the shirts on their backs and dreams of money and a good life. He was just a poor drifter, with no way to find the man who killed his best friend though he vowed he'd never stop looking. Every week he sent his mother letters, telling her how he would come home once he had exacted his revenge on this evil man."

By now, the bakery has cleared out. The only people left are the three of us and Piper. I wish Cosmo were here, not only to hear this but to help Piper as she washes pans in the back.

"One day, as he was clearing tables in a bar where he was working in San Francisco, he overheard a well-dressed man on the phone talking about a drug kingpin who needed to be taken down. A man with three fingers on one hand and a voice like velvet. Delbert's father tried asking him about it but the man pushed him away. They got into a fight and Delbert threatened to kill the man unless he told him everything."

I gulp. "Did Delbert kill him?"

Esmay shook her head. "The man agreed to explain. He'd been telling his boss for years that there was one man who should be arrested. He supplied an entire town with morphine, growing the poppies himself."

"Delbert's father found someone to help him!" Vem says excitedly.

"An FBI agent, to be exact. They hatched a plot together, to bring down the biggest morphine dealer on the West Coast. All they needed was a way to get inside."

CHAPTER THIRTY

Pookie

1947

Dearest Ophelia,

I can only write briefly for now. This has been a magical and tragical evening, all at once. I got to meet my idol, Tulip Sloan. She was just as beautiful in person as she is on the screen. Her hair was silken and her face exquisite.

After our dinner she got up and gave a performance. As to whether her memorable words were truthful or just a movie script she created in her head, I'll always wonder. At one point I noticed her looking at the men in the room for approval.

It mattered little to those who were enthralled by her passion. Remarkably, she had little to say before or after. I'm beginning to wonder if she isn't like the paper dolls Daddy bought me when I was eight. They were so pretty to look at when I placed them on the floor, but when I picked them up, they were blank on the back.

Please, dearest Ophelia, don't believe I am ungrateful for all I have been given. Any forlorn child would give her left braid to have half of what Daddy has given to me. It may be time, as an adult woman, to put my foolish dreams to rest and start thinking about what to do with my life. I don't need movies or magazines; I need to concentrate on my future. Maybe I will run Naybor Manor myself. I don't care what Raymond says, it's a lovely farm and I can continue on just as Daddy has.

Yours with resignation,
Pookie A. Naybor

There was a soft knock at the door. "Come in!" Perhaps it was Tulip, there to tell her an inspirational story about her Hollywood life.

"Can I lay in your bed for a bit?" Freddie asked timidly. "Ma and I sleep together in one bed at home. Don't know if I can sleep without someone beside me."

Pookie had never slept in her father's bed. Not once. It seemed like something only babies did. She pulled back the covers. "Come on."

Freddie crawled in beside her, smelling of the soap he was forced to use in the bath he was forced to take by Welcome. "Naybor Manor rules," he replied sternly when Freddie protested that he'd taken one just the night before.

"Tell me everything you've written in your notebook. You promised!"

Pookie pulled her notebook from underneath her pillow and read out loud, as if she were Tulip Sloan recalling the tragic story of her childhood. When she finished, she looked over at Freddie, who's eyes were tightly closed. "Freddie? Did you hear it all?" Nothing. She rolled over and put her notebook back under her pillow. She was just about to drift off when she felt a tapping on her shoulder.

"Pookie? Can I tell you something?"

"What is it?" It was irritating enough he was here in her bed, not listening to her reading from her notebook. But now as she was about to drift off, he was bothering her.

"Your present – that pearl necklace? Your pa bought that. We couldn't afford nothing like that."

Pookie sighed. "I know. Why do you have to ruin it for me? You could at least pretend you picked out something nice."

Freddie poked her shoulder. "Can I tell you something else?"

"One more thing, and then we need to sleep. Now that I'm a woman, I can't skimp on my beauty rest."

"There's a story about your ma. I thought maybe this one was made up, but after seeing your place, I think it's true. All the – what do you call them – details is right."

"I'm too tired for this now, Freddie."

"Can we get a snack before you sleep at least? I'd like another piece of that cake or my stomach might be growling before morning. And getting up in the middle of the night, it'll be harder to get back to sleep then just taking care of things now."

"Fine. Just fine, Freddie." Pookie threw the covers off and stood up. "We'll have to be quiet, though. Daddy and Miss Sloan are likely already asleep. We don't want to wake them."

"Quiet as a mouse, I promise."

They crept down the long hallway, to the grand staircase where they could hear hushed voices. "Daddy's still awake. We'll have to be very sneaky," Pookie whispered. Freddie nodded. One step at a time, they went down the steps until the living room was in plain view.

Pookie motioned for Freddie to sit beside her as they peered into the room, waiting for their opportunity to sneak past it and into the kitchen. Welcome was bending over the high-backed leather chair he sat in to smoke his cigars. When he stood, they could see Tulip sprawled across the chair in a very unladylike manner, her eyes barely open.

"Do it now," she commanded.

"Are you sure? You've had more than—"

"Do it, Welcome. Give me some peace."

Welcome picked up a large syringe and shot something into Tulip's arm. Pookie and Freddie watched as her body relaxed. He then moved over to Owen Pherson, who lay in a similar position on the green velvet couch. "Another?" he asked.

Owen groaned and rolled over. Welcome injected him and then stood up, looking around the room.

"I think he sees us!" Freddie whispered.

Pookie put her hand over his mouth and shook her head furiously. Welcome paused momentarily before walking into his study and shutting the door.

Pookie motioned for them to hurry down the stairs. Freddie, instead of going into the kitchen, walked over to Tulip and bent down to view her face. Pookie pulled on his arm, but couldn't help but notice the open mouth of her once-favorite person. As she lay slack-jawed, the drool dripped out of her mouth. The dark lines on her eyelids were partially smudged. The jewel-studded clips in her hair fell haphazardly onto her face. Tulip Sloan, the screen siren voted Most Sensuous Hollywood Star 1946 and 1947, looked no better than the down-and-out characters she played on-screen.

Pookie couldn't take it anymore. She dashed to the kitchen, where she cut Freddie a big slice of cake, neither of them knowing the right words to describe what they had just seen. They both scurried back up the steps and to her room, closing the door gently.

"I didn't know your daddy was a doctor!" Freddie proclaimed.

"He's not! My daddy does help people, but..." A sickly feeling crept through her body. "My daddy helps people," she repeated. She turned to face Freddie. "We must never speak of this again. Ever. Do you agree?"

Freddie nodded his head. "I'm not sure what I saw, so how would I know what to speak of?"

"Pinkie swear?"

They wrapped their pinkies around one another and bounced them three times on Pookie's lap, neither looking the other in the eye.

The next morning, the two ate their breakfast solemnly. There were no adults other than the help around to question them. It was an unusually sunny, spring day; the rains abating for at least a time.

Mrs. Wilson appeared, looking somewhat shaken. "How was your big night? Did you enjoy having a famous movie star as your guest for dinner?"

"She wasn't my guest as much as Daddy's," Pookie began. "I mean, it was lovely to meet her and all. I'm glad I can say I've met someone who is a genuine movie star. Right, Freddie?" She kicked him under the table. Instead of joining in the conversation, he nodded his head silently.

When it came time for Freddie to leave for town, there were still no adults around. Unless Welcome was away on business, he was always in the middle of whatever was happening on his property.

"Remember last night, when I told you I knew something about your mother?" Freddie asked, as he drug his suitcase down the stairs, carelessly bumping it on each one.

"Yes, you said you knew something to be true."

"The stories go that she's a ghost who haunts this place. But my ma knows her. She's not so bad. Could be your daddy got that part wrong?"

"Maybe," Pookie said noncommittally. It wasn't a day to start new problems. There were already too many to be solved. "Let me help you get your things in the truck." She lifted his small tattered bag into the back of the truck and closed the door after he hopped inside. One of the new hired hands got into the driver's seat and waited patiently for them to say their goodbyes. "I thought Raymond was driving him into town?" Pookie asked.

"'Nother project came up. Your daddy needed his help." The man started the engine and stared straight ahead.

Freddie leaned out the window. "About what you wrote in that notebook: Raymond should be arrested, along with your daddy. Oh, and Pookie, to be honest, I'm not sure I've got the will to see another movie for a while."

Pookie nodded. "You wait. Things will be back to normal soon." She wasn't at all sure they ever would. As soon as the truck was no longer visible, Pookie made her way down to the bunkhouse.

She didn't want to make the mistake of getting caught snooping around inside, so instead she stood on the porch, hoping someone would come out. When no one did, she walked around back where Raymond was cleaning a shovel. She thought she heard him crying, but when he turned around, his face looked normal to her.

"There's the newly crowned woman. Feelin' like you've earned your scepter, your highness?" he chided in his usual voice.

Pookie looked at him with unease. "Raymond? Can I ask you about something?"

He set the hose down and came over to where she was standing. Shading his eyes, he looked at her with concern. "What's got you worked up, Miss?"

She didn't hesitate before telling him everything that had happened the night before. He nodded his head, but as usual for Raymond, he waited until she finished speaking.

"That's all of it, then?" He asked when she ran out of breath.

"Isn't that enough? Is Daddy really a doctor? Or

is he something horrible instead? I didn't think Tulip was sick during dinner. But maybe she has some exotic illness and Daddy is the only one who knows how to help her."

Raymond wiped his hands on his pants and looked around. "Let's walk a bit and talk, shall we?"

They headed over the little hill, over past Barn Two and toward a pasture. "I think it's time I show you something. Are you feeling brave?"

"I can do anything if you will help me, Raymond." She took his hand and they walked further away until they reached a familiar spot.

"Do you think I'm old enough now?"

"I do, Pook. Take a few more steps with me."

They walked to the top of the hill where a valley full of tall, open, red flowers, dotted with black in the centers was visible.

"THIS is the forbidden field? It's lovely! I've never seen such beauty!"

"They are pretty. But they can also be deadly in another form. They're what your daddy has been using to make a drug. These flowers, when crushed up, can cause people to lose their minds. These flowers cause people to get real sick."

"I don't understand."

"These things is called poppies. Your daddy has a whole entire operation where he's growing them and then turning them into a drug that makes people, like your Miss Sloan, real sick."

"I don't believe you, Raymond. Why would he do that? And why did she tell him to give her the shot?"

"Cause people's minds get real twisted once they've started using it." He rubbed his palms together. "Do you remember the first time you had ice cream?"

Pookie thought hard. "No, but I do long for it every winter. It's creamy and smooth and when it's warm out, there's nothing better."

"So, you got yourself a longing for something. But this particular longin' can't wait till summer. You got to have it now. That's the problem. It makes you feel happy and warm inside, but then your mind gets twisted into thinkin' you need to feel happy and warm all the time."

"What else does he do with it?"

Raymond took off his hat and scratched his head. "Well, that special grown-up tea that he won't let you drink? That's got some of these bad flowers in it. He gives it to all of his new employees 'round here to keep 'em indebted to him."

"Daddy drugs them? My daddy? And why do the drifters always leave?"

"Pookie, they don't. They just get to the point they can't work anymore. That's when your daddy has to dispose of them. I told you this would be a hard day."

Pookie bit her lip, failing to keep the tears from rolling down her cheek. "You don't know everything, Raymond. You don't."

"I know it's hard. I'm worried for you. Now that you've seen things, it may be time for–"

"It's not just Daddy. You're doing bad things too. I heard you making a deal with him. And Daddy didn't kill Paulo. You did."

"No, Pook. You've got it all wrong. Ah, geez." He rubbed his face hard before staring at her. "I'll tell you the entire story. But first, you have to agree to leave here forever. Things is gonna get rough and you can't be any part of it. I'll buy you a ticket to go down to Oklahoma with my ma and son. You'll be safe there."

CHAPTER THIRTY-ONE

Lanie
Piney Falls

"Y OU'VE EXPLAINED DELBERT'S father, but what about him? How did he end up all the way up here?" I lean forward on my chair, starting to wish I'd skipped the extra hike up Piney Falls yesterday that Vem insisted would bring us clarity and relieve the body of excess gasses.

A smile flickers across Esmay's face. "I was tired of waitressing. Tired of running – from what? – I wasn't sure anymore. He came in that night all smiles and handsome. I knew he was a bad boy, but something about him seemed so vulnerable. He told me he was passing through, trying to see the country as a drifter would."

"Like his father?"

"I didn't know it then, but yes, just like his father. He wanted to find a way to be closer to him. He told me he'd been to prison for killing a man and if that scared me, it was okay to leave. As you can see, I didn't."

"That's so sweet. My husband and I had a similar love story," Vem clasps her hands behind her head, cradling her neck. "He was a wealthy toilet paper magnate who was transfixed by my unusual look. We dated for two months before deciding to marry and moving to California. The Toilet Paper King, as he was called. Let's just say, my life really fell into the crapper." Vem shakes her head. "It's hard to start over after living that life. I know."

"That's nothing at all like what she said, Vem," I respond softly. I don't want this to lead into another story and get us sidetracked. "Why did you and Delbert end up at Naybor Manor?"

"Delbert wanted desperately to find out what happened to his dad. By that time, the property been sitting empty for many years. Overgrown and wasting away. We went to the bank and said we'd take care of the land, living in a little shack if they'd let us live there for free. We never worked in the main house. Delbert thought that place was cursed. We've been there for fifteen years, living peacefully."

"Just thirty minutes from your family?" I ask incredulously. "How did you do that? And why?"

"I did it for my husband. He needed to make things right in his head. He never found out what happened to his father, but we kept strangers off the property."

I start wiggling in my chair. My muscles are definitely starting to seize up from so much time sitting still. "Shall we get up and walk somewhere? Piper is ready to close, I'm sure."

"You can stay as long as you like!" Piper calls, seemingly listening to our every word. "Cosmo promised he'd come in after closing today so we could go over next week's menu."

"Cos! I completely forgot. We were going to hike together today. He got out of bed again and I promised him I'd be back." I glance at my watch, discovering that it is almost four o'clock. He'll either be walking in the door any minute to discuss tomorrow's lunch menu with Piper, or stuck in bed because I never came home to keep up my part of the bargain.

"Ladies, I'm going to go outside and make a call." I get up too quickly, grimacing as my thigh muscle seizes once again. In order to think clearly, I'll need to spend a few minutes pacing around, working out my thoughts. When I took the seminar *Working Out the Kinks Completely Non-Kinkily,* an after-hours fun seminar for the business elite needing to blow off steam, I learned that sometimes working to put a person at ease was the best way to get information from them. Twins Dan and Stan Landy taught the course. I slept with one of them twice. At least I think it was just one.

Once I reach the door, I can see Cosmo walking down the street with his motorcycle helmet in his hand. I wave vigorously, hoping he doesn't find it unusual that I don't hurry to greet him.

"I'm so sorry!" I say when he is close. I study his face for anger or sadness, but I find neither.

"We were at the winery and then we met up with Esmay, who is really Carlene. We've been sitting in the bakery and–"

"Lanie, slow down." He grabs my elbows. "It's okay. I got up today and looked outside to witness a rare sunny sky and a beautiful day, and I appreciated both. Piper actually texted me to ask if I was coming, and she told me that you were here. That was my extra incentive." He leans down and kisses me deeply.

"It's so good to have the familiar Cosmo making his presence known," I reply breathlessly.

"I needed to talk to you anyway." He stands up tall, touching my shoulder. "You know I mentioned that Delbert and I made an agreement not to communicate again? Well, I received this." Cosmo hands me his phone so I can read a text.

Mr. Hill, we were both guests at the state correctional facility together. Not gonna tell you who I am, but I just heard from Delbert Dockley. Sounds like he's in some sort of trouble. I remember you two had your issues,

but I'm pretty sure you're the decent type.
Don't know anyone else in that area to check
on him or I'd ask them.

"I can have Gladys look up this number, if you like. She can find just about any information with a little time and a scone for incentive. Should we show this to Esmay er, Carlene? Cos, I've got so much to tell you."

Cosmo glances over my shoulder and I turn around to see Vem's arms are moving up and down while she bends at the waist like a tall balloon at a used car lot. I'm not sure if this is a ritual she's done before. Carlene is chuckling.

"She doesn't seem too broken up," Cosmo comments. "And Piper told me the whole story about Gladys' long-lost daughter."

"That is odd. She made a trip into town for something unimportant and she's been visiting with us all afternoon like she doesn't have a care in the world."

"Maybe I should make a trip out to Naybor Manor and see for myself what's going on with Delbert." Cosmo begins rocking on his heels as he does when he is nervous. "Don't like the man, but I can't sit back and do nothing if he's really in trouble. Can you keep Esmay busy for a while longer?"

"You could…" The wheels in my head begin to turn. "But let's try something else first."

CHAPTER THIRTY-TWO

Pookie
1947

Dearest Ophelia,

Daddy once told me the only place for dreams was in one's head. The minute they are forced to exist in the real world, they have no chance of living up to our standards.

My greatest dream, meeting Miss Tulip Sloan, my idol, began my worst nightmare. Raymond tried telling me all about my father – that he was a drug dealer who killed people and my life would soon be in danger. Like a child, I ran from him.

Later that night, as I sat in my window watching, Raymond left for his meeting one more time. I followed him again, insistent upon proving it was Raymond who was selling drugs to his mystery man.

This time, I boldly crouched so close I could pick up every word.

"I done buried another one for that evil letch. This time it weren't no drifters; weren't no fancy black plum root concoctions involved. This one was an important man from Hollywood. Don't know how he'll explain this one. You can't just throw them types away without consequences."

"We'll be taking down the target soon, Mr. Dockley. There will be plenty of consequences," Mr. Bowler assured him. "You'll need to stay clear, as soon as you have everything in place. You've done all you could to make things right for your friend."

"I done all you asked. Now could the government see clear to give me and Ma our land back, seein' as how it didn't have any oil?"

Mr. Bowler said that was a definite possibility. In the moonlight there was a mark visible across his face. A long scar. It suddenly occurred to me that I'd seen that scar before. Months ago, when Freddie and I were leaving the theatre and the man stopped me and warned me to be careful. That was Mr. Bowler!

Ophelia, he is a government agent who clearly has Raymond under his spell. That explains it all! I will tell Raymond about how he accosted me at the theatre, himself full of *theatrics. Raymond will understand how things have gotten blown out of proportion. I can stay on my farm with Daddy. Poor Raymond is a simple man; he doesn't understand that some people don't have his best interest at heart.*

In Relief and Embarrassment,
Pookie A. Naybor

"What did you hear? A familiar voice spat in her ear. Raymond grasped her tightly around the back of the neck.

"All of it. I know the government man is threatening to take your land in Oklahoma and you must hurt Daddy in order to get it back."

"Get up, Pookie. We have to get you home before your daddy figures out you're gone. It would ruin everything we've worked for."

"I've been following you every time you leave, Raymond. I'm much smarter than you give me credit for," she retorted. "We need to talk. This is all a big misunderstanding. I've already met your friend; Mr. Bowler, I call him. He's just full of his own importance. He doesn't understand Daddy at all."

They began walking at a furious pace, Pookie finally pulling on his sleeve to slow him down. "One or two minutes isn't going to make a difference."

They stopped so she could catch her breath,

though Raymond looked around anxiously. "They already done took it."

"What?"

"For the war effort. They said they thought there was oil underneath our land, so they might need it. Ma fought to keep it through the depression. Then, when we both thought we were safe, the government came in one day and said we had thirty days to vacate the premises. By then, I'd come back from working on the ships without my buddy. It was too much to lose my farm as well. Realized I'd need to find a way to get it back so my son could grow up there." Raymond looks off into the distance. "But this ain't as much about the land as about my buddy. Your daddy killed him."

Pookie began to protest, but Raymond put his hand over her mouth tightly. "I worked for your daddy on a ship. We hauled all kinds of things never meant for proper business dealings. He didn't like anything to be out of his control. Not one thing."

Pookie struggled against his grip for a minute and then gave in.

"A man must put in an HONEST day's work. That's the truth. My buddy, Len, was gonna go back to Oklahoma with me where we'd build a real farming empire. We figured after the dust bowl ended and lots of folks up and moved to California, we'd become big farmers."

He let go of her mouth and she looked up at him.

"That sounds nice. You would be an excellent land owner, Raymond." They started walking again, this time at a more relaxed pace. Pookie shone her flashlight on the ground as they went.

"Well, Len resented what he thought was grunt work. He'd been on the ships for a while and wanted to do more above deck. So he asked for a raise in exchange for more responsibilities. Your daddy banished him to slop buckets. That's when he started pokin' around in the cargo, to see just what was being carried. Yep, your daddy, even back then, was selling morphine. Len thought he'd try it, just to see what the fuss was about. He was just as good as 'em rich people."

"Did your friend get shots just like Tulip?"

Raymond nodded. "Oh, he was mighty sick. The more he tried to forget it, the more he craved. Purdy soon, it was hard to get him moving at all. I started doing his work and mine, but a feller has to rest at some point. Your daddy called us both into his office one day. He wanted to know why I was covering for someone who was too lazy to work. Said he'd thumb his nose at a no-good employee. They'd end up with nothing cause nobody took advantage of his good nature."

"What happened next?" Pookie thought back to all of the drifters Daddy told her had disappointed him with their laziness. *One must always put in a productive day to earn their keep, Pookie.*

"Len told your daddy that maybe he didn't need to have thumbs then. He grabbed his hand and instead of biting his thumb, he bit off the next two fingers. Poor Len was crazed from the drugs. That's when your daddy threw him overboard."

"That's what happened to Daddy's fingers?" Pookie gasped. "He's never told me that story!"

They were almost back to Naybor Manor.

"Can you tell me what happened to Paulo?"

"Got himself in the same predicament as my buddy. I told him he was gonna end up dead like the others. He didn't listen. Mr. Jones of the F.B.I. even promised he'd find a place for him in the agency." Raymond sucks in some of the early morning air and puts his hands on his hips. "None of it mattered. Paulo was too afraid your daddy would find him. He took some of your daddy's drugs and did himself in."

"Oh, Raymond! That's terrible!"

"Didn't want to give your daddy the satisfaction of knowing it was his doing. Mr. Jones brought his remains and I buried him proper."

Pookie thought about Mr. Bowler—Mr. Jones – creeping around their property. Even if he was a good guy, it gave her a feeling of unease to know he'd been there, undetected.

"Purdy soon it's not gonna be safe here, Pookie.

Like I said before, you can go live with my ma and son in Oklahoma and I'll make sure you're sent for when it's all over with."

"And what about you, Raymond? Where will you be?"

Raymond bent down and grabbed hold of her shoulders. "Your daddy is one of the most powerful drug dealers in the country. I seen what he does to those who cross him. I'm not making any plans for myself. As long as I finish what I started."

Chapter Thirty-Three

Lanie
Piney Falls

"Are we both on the same page?" I ask Cosmo, though I currently don't trust that we share the same wavelength. I put my phone in my pocket after speaking briefly with Piper and also with Gladys.

"Like we share one beautiful brain." Cosmo touches my back lightly as we enter Cosmic Cakes and Antiquery.

November is still waving her arms around dramatically as Carlene sits, entranced.

"You two seem like you're having a lovely time."

Carlene jumps at the sound of my voice and turns around. "November was showing me how to pull my stress down to my fingertips. Sometimes it gets stuck at the collarbone and she's forcing it out."

November, as if on cue, turns in circles waving her arms up and down like an erratic car sale balloon caught in gale force winds. She opens her eyes and stares hard at me and then at Cosmo. "I SMELL DECEIT!"

I swallow hard. "You said the same thing the other day when I asked if you wanted tuna. Sometimes your sniffer is out of whack."

She nods and purses her lips. "I concede. I do make mistakes occasionally."

"Carlene, Cosmo and I feel so badly that we've been delaying our wedding plans. We've been talking it over outside and we've decided to donate pastries for your guests this weekend."

"I...I should probably ask Mandy about that. I care for the property and she's in charge of the food."

"I just called her. Well, Cos and I did on speaker phone. November and I visited Sassy Lasses this morning and I mentioned the possibility but I needed to speak with Cos first. Mandy asked me to track you down and tell you if we went through with it. I knew my wonderfully giving man wouldn't hesitate to say yes!" I kiss him passionately, completely for the benefit of those watching.

When we finish our display, I wink at November as blatantly as possible.

At first, November's face is lost in confusion. Her pea-green ensemble, including her headband and glasses frames, makes her look like a giant question mark from a 70s game show. "Yes? Yes! SHE told us to find you. With my newly developed keen sense of smell, I'm practically a bloodhound. You do give off the aroma of cigarettes and stale cheese puffs, Carlene."

I turn my body so it isn't facing the women so I can let out the breath I've been holding.

"Carlene, Mandy called a few minutes ago and said I should show you our scone menu. Would you like to come in the back and we can go over everything?" Piper asks sweetly, just as we instructed her to do.

"I don't feel right about this," Carlene looks around at all of our exceptionally cheery faces. "Okay, I guess if it's free, there's no way I can screw it up."

Once the two women are in the office with the door closed, I rummage around in Carlene's purse until I find her phone.

"Can I ask what you're–" November whispers.

"No!" Cosmo and I hiss in unison.

I get my own phone out and download the code Gladys sent me before installing an app on Carlene's phone. When the two women return to the room, I've already returned her phone to her purse.

"We'll have the Pluto Plum and Cosmic Cream Cheese. If she doesn't like it, I guess she should've made the decision herself." Carlene gathers her purse. "I need to head back. I was only planning to be in town for an hour or so."

I nudge Cosmo.

He clears his throat. "I'll be following you out there. I got a message earlier from your husband. He wants my help."

Carlene jumps, her hand hitting the table and causing it to become unstable. The remainder of my coffee spills on Piper's freshly-mopped floor. "He what?" she asks.

"Yes, Cosmo and Delbert were in prison together, so they go way back. Didn't he ever mention that to you?" I ask innocently.

She looks at Cosmo with uncertainty. "Never heard his name until you two started planning your wedding, or whatever it is you're doing."

Cosmo gazes out the door at the few people walking up and down the sidewalk. I'm fearful that any minor hiccup may send him back to bed. Any hurtful comment that wasn't intended that way.

"We're taking that process slowly, so we get it just right. It's the only time either of us will ever be married, so it has to be perfect." I squeeze his formerly firm bicep, trying to bring him back to the present.

"Yeah, Delbert's an old friend. We were in prison together and being two ex-cons, we try not to announce our relationship to the world. He was sworn to secrecy, so that's why he didn't tell you,

Carlene."

She looks at Cosmo and then at me. "Delbert's awful busy right now. There is an event coming up next weekend that he's working on for the ladies. They also wanted Barn Three painted. I don't think he has time for visitors."

Cosmo puts his hands in the front pockets of his jeans. "I feel pretty strongly that I should go see him. He said it was urgent."

Carlene fumbles with her purse. "Let me go outside and call him. I'll let you know what he needs. It might be something I can just pick up in town and bring back." She slings her purse over her shoulder and walks outside quickly.

"Was that good enough?" Cosmo looks at me and asks.

"Perfect, dear."

CHAPTER THIRTY-FOUR

Pookie

1947

Dearest Ophelia,

Sometimes the best decisions are the hardest. The truth is, I can't imagine a life away from Naybor Manor, other than one in Tulip Sloan's fantasy Hollywood world, but here I am, contemplating just such a venture.

Raymond has proposed I spend time with his family. I can tell he cares for me deeply and by the time I am of proper marrying age, I will have already become enveloped in his loving family. It may not be the ending I planned, but it will all work out in the most glorious way.

This I've discovered: People in the magazines are just characters. All of my Saturdays spent with Freddie at the theatre, we were just pretending. Freddie will never be a leading man and I will never be a glamorous star, no matter how many fancy dresses Daddy buys me.

After whatever ugliness Raymond thinks will happen here at Naybor Manor is finished, he and I will come back home. Maybe his family members will join us. They can fall in love with Oregon the way Raymond did. I'm sure Daddy will approve. Though he's never mentioned it to me, I can tell Daddy longs for more Naybors. Our long table has been a lonely place during Thanksgiving feasts. The Dockleys and Naybors – we'll all be a happy family. I have a good feeling about this.

Yours in Wisdom and Peace,
Pookie A. Naybor

"I've decided to take you up on your offer." Pookie sat on her usual bale of hay, this time unraveling her brown braids and letting her hair flow freely.

Raymond leaned on his shovel and looked her deep in the eyes. It still made her shiver.

"You made the right decision, Miss. Things ain't gonna be safe here."

"Hold on," Pookie put her index finger in the air. "I have some conditions."

"'Course you do," Raymond smiled slyly. "You want carried out on an elephant with gold tusks?"

"No, I'm serious. This is about Daddy. And you."

"Well, okay then," Raymond continued raking

the old hay into a pile. "Go ahead."

"First, I want to make sure Daddy is safe. I don't want these—what did you call them? –government agents to harm him. I'm sure this is all a simple disagreement of some kind. They just need to sit down and enjoy a proper chat over some tea."

"I told you, this is serious, Miss Pookie. Ain't nobody having tea. But if you like, I'm glad to request that they give him time to say his piece. Will that do?"

Pookie nodded. "Second, I need to be able to explain everything to him before I go. So he doesn't think I'm angry with him. He's a wonderful man who's given so much to the community, and–"

Raymond let out a loud honk. "Now Miss, we had a deal. No telling your daddy. That will get me in some real trouble and you don't want that, right?"

"No, I...you're right, Raymond. I don't want you to get into trouble. I won't say anything to Daddy for now. I'll send him a letter. But that leads me to number three."

"There's three? C'mon now!"

"I want you to come with me."

Raymond itched his muscular chest. Pookie tried to look away.

"You know I can't do that. I'm here to do a job for the sake of my friend. I have to see it through 'til the end."

Pookie stood up and put her arms around his waist. "I can't bear the thought of leaving you. I just know if you'll come with me, I can help you. I can teach you everything I've learned from Miss Dandridge so you can be educated. Then one day, we'll come back to Naybor Manor, where you and Daddy will work side by side. We'll all be family."

Raymond pushed her away. "Those ain't things I want, Pookie. I'm a simple man. Just tryin' to do what's right. For now, that's making sure I make sure my buddy's death don't go without consequences. The cherry on top will be gettin' our land back from the government. That's what my head tells me to do. Don't need an education more'n what comes from hard livin', or a fancy dinner for that matter."

"But you want to see your son. You'll come to Oklahoma. Your mother must miss you so." Pookie insisted.

"Tell you what." Raymond took her soft, white hands in his stained, weather-worn palms. "You go down, get settled with my family and a'fore you know it, I'll be there. One day you'll be chasing my boy 'round the yard and a stranger, all gussied up in his best clothes, will be ready for one of your hugs and one of your delicious pies."

Pookie threw her arms around his neck. "Thank you, Raymond!"

Four days later, she was lying in a field of tall

grass, chewing on one particularly juicy piece. She was daydreaming about the windswept prairie of Oklahoma when Raymond found her.

"Miss Pookie? Your daddy sent me to town for supplies, so I got you a ticket to San Francisco. You'll have to get on another train there. I wrote it all down, and I've got a note for you to take to Ma. She'll understand everything. I've been sharing with her all the trials and tribulations in my life. She knows what a special young gi—woman – you are. Always wanted a daughter of her own. She'll be right pleased to entertain you under her roof."

"I'm still not positive this is the right thing to do. What if you're mistaken and Daddy isn't really involved in all the things you say he is?"

"Well then, I'll make sure'n tell your daddy I done him wrong and tell him where to send for you. You'll be together with him in the blink of a squirrel's eye."

"We'll have a glorious reunion." Pookie's eyes glistened. "You and me, Daddy and your ma and your son. Maybe she'll make her famous fried okra, cornbread and barbecued pork?"

"And you'll make a sweet, berry pie for dessert."

"Wait," Pookie looked down at the ticket. "What day do I leave? I must say goodbye to Freddie."

"Next Thursday. You'll have plenty of time for goodbyes. Heck, you can even tell your daddy

goodbye in a secret way. I did that with my son."
Raymond pulled his cap off and wiped his brow.

"Wasn't he just a baby the last time you saw
him?"

"Sure was. That's the best kind of goodbye. I told
him all sorts of things I'd never tell another soul.
With your daddy and your friend, you'll have to be
more careful. Tell them goodbye in code. The way
you learned from all of them Tulip Sloan movies."

Pookie pushed Raymond's pile of hay around
with her foot. "Well, I'm done with Tulip Sloan.
After seeing how she acted at my birthday party, I
don't want any part of her ever again."

"We all have to pretend sometimes. At least she
came to your party and made you feel special for a
little while. Do you know how many people would
give their good teeth for her to look in their direction? My ma, fer one. She'll want to hear all about
it."

Pookie nodded noncommittally.

"Look, if you're gonna say goodbye to your
friend, you'll have to pretend you're still over the
moon for Miss Sloan. Go to your movie and tell him
all the things about him that make you happy. That's
the finest goodbye the boy could ask fer."

That Saturday, Pookie hopped into her daddy's
fancy car for likely the last time. She ran her fingers
up and down the smooth seats, taking in the feel and

smell of the grandest car of all time. She wanted her senses to drink in every bit of this experience.

"Pookie, you seem morose today. Are you struggling with your world history studies again?" Welcome reached over and patted her shoulder. She grabbed his hand and kissed it, fighting back tears.

"Now what's all this? You're on your way into town to see your favorite actress with your best friend. There isn't a finer Saturday activity for a young woman of your age."

Pookie let her breath out slowly. "I've been thinking that maybe I don't really want to be an actress anymore."

"Oh? Did Tulip say something to change your mind? She works long hours, but the reward is beyond compare. She is adored worldwide."

"I want to….help people. Like you do. Run the farm for myself and give away our produce to those in need. Isn't that a better use of my life?"

Welcome was silent for several minutes, tapping his pinky finger of the hand missing fingers on the steering wheel.

"Daddy? Did I say something to upset you?"

"There's no finer compliment, daughter. Your becoming a benefactor for some lost soul is such a fine reward for spending my life in service of those less fortunate. You've made me truly happy today, dear."

"I'm glad, Daddy." She turned her head toward the window, so he couldn't see the tears running down her cheeks. "You make me happy, too."

When they arrived at the theatre, Pookie hopped out and didn't face her father. "See you at three."

"Aren't you forgetting something? The money you'll need for today?"

"Tulip gave Freddie money for the movies, remember? Bye, Daddy." She walked away quickly, not giving him a chance to question her further.

Freddie was waiting for her in front of the theatre. "You're late today," he grumbled.

She bit her tongue. She didn't want their last day together marred by grouchiness. "Daddy drove slow. I wasn't sure you'd come."

"Thought about it. Ma said we shouldn't disrespect a gift giver and I agreed. I can suffer through her movies if I think of things that way."

Freddie insisted that today they buy a big popcorn and two Tart Chewie boxes with his riches.

"You don't want to blow all of your money at once. If it's going to last and we can go to every…" Pookie stopped herself. "Buy what you want, Freddie."

She held his arm, studying his face intently before closing her eyes. Committing every irritating morsel of her friend to memory. "Freddie, you are the best friend I've ever had."

Freddie shook free of her grasp. "I'm the only friend you've ever had, far as I can tell." He walked to their usual seat.

"I just wanted you to hear that I have been lucky to know you. Someday, when we're grown up, we'll have delightful conversations about our days in the movie theater. How we discussed all the problems of the world and decided us two kids could solve them."

Freddie shrugged. "I guess so. Why are you bein' so serious?" He starting shoving popcorn in his mouth, even before he was fully seated.

"It's important to tell the people we care about just how we feel. There's a real uncertainty to life."

Freddie's normally serious face broke into a big smile. "I know what you're doin' Pookie Naybor. You're retelling the movie *The End of Millie*. I don't remember the next line, but French Tolbert drove off to meet his secret girlfriend. That's right, ain't it?"

Pookie sighed. "I thought this would be easier. Raymond made it seem like it would be."

"Today is *Love's Last Wish*. Too squishy and lovey." Freddie, oblivious to her pain, dug further into his large container of popcorn. "You gonna open the Tart Chewies or should I?"

"Do you remember when you told me I'd only seen rainbows and sunshine? Well, now I can safely say I've seen the rain and the terrible storms. Too many of them. Freddie Brower, I'm just as worldly as you. Don't ever forget that."

Freddie rolled his eyes. "I s'pose."

"And one more thing: I'm tired of silly fantasies. I thought we swore we were both done with them after what we saw the other night. You should concentrate on your future. What do you want to be when you grow up? Think about that."

Freddie stared at her. "What'r you sayin'? You're throwin' away a movie star? Just cause she had one bad night? I just got scared was all."

"I'm saying that you—we—should find someone else to pattern our lives after. Not her movies. They aren't real. She isn't real. Don't you remember how awful she looked after Daddy gave her the medication? Like she was possessed!"

"When I asked my ma about that, she said–"

Pookie gasped. "You told your mother? You pinkie promised me, Frankie!"

Freddie shrugged. "It ain't no worry. Ma don't have many friends."

"But what if she tells Daddy we were watching? What then?" Pookie tried to fathom Welcome's reaction when he figured out that they knew about his dark secret.

"You said people getting medicine like that wasn't a normal thing, but Ma told me that ain't true."

"How does she know?"

"Guess I never paid attention before. Ma showed me on her arm where she gets shots too. They're like vitamins to help a person have more energy. When I'm older, I'm getting 'em too."

CHAPTER THIRTY-FIVE

Pookie

1947

W ELCOME DIDN'T ASK her about the movie or what she thought of the plot. They drove in silence all the way home. When she stepped out of the car, she could take it no more.

"Daddy? Did I do something wrong?" Pookie reached for the car door handle.

Welcome clutched the steering wheel. "We're going to have a lovely dinner tonight, Pookie. I've been guilty of reading my paper and not giving you a chance to talk to me. I'm sorry about that."

Pookie turned and studied her father as he drove.

"Why the seriousness?" he asked.

"I'm memorizing your face. I never want to forget one inch."

He chuckled. "Oh, Pookie. Even in the most dire times, you've always been able to make me laugh."

"It's okay, Daddy," She looked at him with affection. "About dinner. I get lost in my own world.

That's a silly thing to do. I promise not to wander off in my mind again. You mean the world to me." She reached into the car and across the seat and hugged her father hard. He pressed her head into his chest tightly.

"I'll go wash up for dinner."

"Yes, daughter. Please do."

As she carefully removed her Saturday clothes, she pulled out the satchel from underneath her bed and placed them inside. There were most assuredly movie theatres in Oklahoma. They probably played movies of all sorts. She'd learn those scripts just as easily as she'd learned the lines to all of Tulip Sloan's movies.

When she rejoined her father, the fine china with the tiny roses was sitting atop a burnt orange table runner. "What's all this?"

"We're celebrating. It's been quite a year of growth, don't you think?" Welcome raised his glass filled with wine in a toast. "To you, Pookie Naybor. For all that you have accomplished and to your future success as my partner at Naybor Manor."

Tears filled her eyes as she sat down at her place. "Do you mean it, Daddy? I can be your partner?"

"There are terms we'll need to work out first. But for now, let's enjoy our celebratory dinner."

They feasted on roasted chicken, mashed potatoes and gravy, and creamed corn canned from their own fields. Welcome leaned back in his chair and smiled once again at his daughter. "I have a surprise for you, my darling."

"Oh, Daddy, I don't deserve another surprise."

Welcome called for Mrs. Wilson to bring dessert from the kitchen. She emerged, her face without its usual pleasant expression. She set the tray, containing two teacups and a plate of applesauce bars, in front of Welcome. "Take my daughter her tea, please," he instructed. Mrs. Wilson paused, looking at him with uncertainty. "Go ahead," he pointed his remaining fingers toward his daughter. "It's time."

Mrs. Wilson set the steaming cup in front of Pookie. "Careful," she warned. "It's hot. You'll want to drink it slowly."

"Grown-up tea." Welcome announced. "It's high time you joined the grown-up world."

Pookie swallowed hard. "I don't like the taste of tea, Daddy. You know it makes my stomach sore."

"Oh, you'll like this kind my dear." His voice lowered an octave. "Take a sip."

Pookie put the cup to her lips and took a small taste. "Mmmm," she agreed half-heartedly.

"I had a conversation with Freddie's mother today. She said the two of you saw something you ought not have."

Pookie sucked her cheeks in. "Yes, Daddy. Freddie wanted a snack. I tried to tell him."

"You know my feelings on snooping. Being nosy only gets one into trouble. We keep to ourselves at all times. Punishment will be required."

"No, Daddy! I'm so very sorry. I didn't mean to disobey!"

"Drink your tea, Pookie. You'll feel so much better."

This time, Pookie put the cup to her lips without actually drinking. "Oh, so good," she said with all the gusto she could muster.

"If you're going to engage in grown-up activities, you must learn that above all, I am in charge. Those who mistakenly thought they could make changes, to alter the daily workings of Naybor Manor, had to learn things the hard way." He called once more for Mrs. Wilson. "Bring me the other item, please."

She came out of the kitchen carrying one more silver tray. She didn't look at either one of them as she set the tray in front of Welcome.

Welcome picked up a familiar item and held it above his head. "Those who work for me are constantly being tested to prove their loyalty. Mrs. Wilson knows what can happen to her family, rest the good soul of her departed husband, when you disobey Welcome Naybor. When she uncovered your blasphemy, she brought it to me immediately."

"It's just a silly notebook of... observations." Pookie stammered.

"It's proof you've been deceiving me, Pookie Naybor. Now how will I ever trust you? I can't have someone who goes behind my back, watching private meetings as my right hand, now can I?" He began tearing the pages out, one by one until there was a small pile of paper in front of him.

"I'm so sorry, Daddy. I didn't mean to–"

Welcome's face was a strange mixture of anger and calmness. "My brother, sister and I came here as wards of the Wormlys. Terrible, controlling people. I had to free us from their grip. My brother and I returned some years later. He begged for partnership in my business interests. I gave him explicit instructions to achieve that end. Instead, he ingratiated himself with the townspeople and forgot his loyalties. He, too, deceived me. That's when I knew he, too, must be dealt with."

Pookie gulped. "What happened to your brother, Daddy?"

"Met with a horrible harvesting accident. Poor soul."

Pookie stood up. "I'm going to my room. I've got to complete my geography lesson. Miss Dandridge will be cross with me if she finds I've forgotten."

Welcome sat up abruptly. "But I haven't finished telling you about your new responsibilities! Sacrifices have to be made, you know. One of the more difficult, but necessary, tasks of ownership." His eyes were cold and hard. "You have no idea the secrets this land holds. I've always done what was necessary to keep Naybor Manor thriving. Someday you'll do the same."

Pookie moved quickly to the stairs. "I need to finish my homework." Without giving her father any time to respond, she ran up the steps and into her bedroom. She pulled her satchel from under the bed and opened it, surveying the items. She had forgotten to include the one thing that mattered most. There was a light knock on her door and she jumped out of her skin. She shoved her bag under the bed and cracked the door.

"Miss Pookie? I just wanted to check on you. That tea's not meant for young ladies. I don't understand what gotten into your father," Mrs. Wilson's eyes were red. "I'm sorry."

Pookie let out a sigh of relief. "I'm fine, thank you. But you're right, Daddy isn't quite himself." She wouldn't allow herself to be angry with Mrs. Wilson for her betrayal. There wasn't time.

"He's threatened my family, Miss Pookie," she whispered, as if reading Pookie's mind. "You should know. He asked me to search your room. He's been wary of you for some time after hearing you leave at night. When I found your notebook, I found your bag too, but I didn't tell him. You need to get to safety as soon as possible. Welcome Naybor doesn't take kindly to those he thinks have gone behind his back."

Pookie sighed in frustration. If only Mrs. Wilson had come to her sooner – helped her see through her father's lies. "I didn't know he heard me sneaking out. He never said a word. I'm leaving now. But I need to get something out of the hall table downstairs. Can you distract him for a few minutes while I do?"

She nodded solemnly. "He's in his study smoking his after-dinner cigar, but that won't last long. I can go in and ask him about the menu for next week, closing the door behind me. That will take a few minutes. You can't leave out the front door. He'll be able to see you through the study window."

Pookie closed her eyes and tried to commit Mrs. Wilson's face to her memory forever, just like Miss Dandridge had instructed her to do with her other memories that she painted with such detail. "I'll never forget you, Mrs. Wilson."

Mrs. Wilson touched Pookie's face with her wrinkled hand. "Be safe, my dear girl. Count to twenty before you come downstairs."

Pookie hugged her tightly. After counting to twenty, she carefully snuck down the stairs, where she could hear Mrs. Wilson speaking clearly and slowly through the door. "Spring is a pleasant time for fiddlesticks and pot roast."

Pookie opened the drawer where the flower-patterned brooch Raymond gave her on her birthday still remained. She put it in her pocket and turned to go back upstairs. She walked over to the study door and placed her hand on it. "I love you, Daddy," she breathed.

When she reached her bedroom, she placed the pin into her bag and opened her closet door. She looked around her room one last time; at the girlish, rose-patterned wallpaper she used to pretend was actually endless fields of real flowers, and the window seat where she watched Raymond come and go.

She turned on her flashlight and headed into the passageway, stopping to sit down and open her diary one last time. When she finished, she kissed the cover and left it there as she continued on.

Pookie had only followed the passageway outside once before. She had been running when she reached the end, and when she burst through the door, she hit one of the drifters who had been doing back yard gardening squarely in the head.

"Oh, I'm so sorry!"

He rubbed his forehead and then looked at his hand to see if it was bleeding. "You should be. What'r you doin' coming out of a secret passageway like that? Don't you know the ghost stories?"

Pookie shook her head.

"Rumor is that a woman comes in and out of that at night. She lived here long ago. She's looking for her lost baby. Nestor said he even seen her one night."

"Like a ghost?" Pookie shivered.

"Not like, it is a ghost. You don't want to find yourself face to face with one of them spirits. Never can tell if they're good or bad."

After that day, she only went in far enough to leave her paintings, and then hurried back out. Today though, she didn't have time to think about ghosts of any kind. Carefully, she snuck around the side of the house and behind the enormous evergreen trees until she reached the bunkhouse.

She opened the door slowly. "Raymond?" she called. "Daddy knows!" There was no answer.

Pookie crept into Raymond's room, where to her surprise, there were no sheets on the bed. When she opened the dresser drawer, all of his underthings were gone. The picture of his mother had disappeared too.

She heard the door close and she hid behind his bedroom door.

Soon she heard voices and smelled food. As she walked into the main living area, the men were sitting down at the long table, preparing to eat. One of them turned around.

"Looking for something, Miss?"

"Raymond. I have something to give him. Do you know where he is?"

"Left in the night, Miss. That's the way our kind operates."

Pookie ran out the door and continued until she reached the field where she had watched Raymond so many times. Maybe Mr. Bowler would come looking for him again. Someone would know what happened. She lay down and waited.

CHAPTER THIRTY-SIX

Lanie
Piney Falls

"NOVEMBER BEAN, IF you step on my foot one more time, I'll take those boats you're wearing and grind them up for soup." Cosmo glares at Vem as we all huddle around my phone, waiting for the information from Carlene's phone to come in.

"Your animal magnetism is not all that you think it is, Cosmo Hill. These boats are looking for something sturdy to rest on," Vem retorts.

I stifle a giggle. It's such a good sign that these two are at each other's throats again. "Quiet, you two. She's making a call." The complicated app, that Gladys tells me all the police are using now to track phone calls, has connected me to Carlene's phone.

"What do you want me to do about it? They know. I could tell by that smug expression on his face."

Vem elbows Cos, who in turn elbows her.

"I'll take care of it." A gruff voice on the other

end of the line says. "Just get back here and make sure you're not followed."

Click.

"That voice sounded familiar. I can't quite place it." Vem remarks.

"I'm starting to think Delbert really is in trouble." Cosmo puts his hands in his pockets and rocks back and forth. "But how do we get to him to find out?"

"We set up a catering event for real with Marveline. I could show up with a car full of pretend food and say I got the date wrong." Piper offers.

"Hon, we don't want to put you in any danger. That's so brave of you to offer though." I touch her arm and she smiles at me.

"When we were at the neighbor's house, I was drinking in the world as he spoke. You know that's a new class I'm considering—Drink It All In?"

"Point please, Ms. Bean!" Cosmo snaps.

She glares at him. "There are several places on his property where you can clearly see the winery."

A picture begins to form in my head. "Piper might actually make an excellent decoy. Cosmo and I could go in through the trees on the Coolidge property and search for Delbert. Vem, you'll go with Piper and make sure those women don't pull any funny business. Block their view of the field in front of their house and make conversation."

"What are we waiting for?" Cosmo huffs. "As much as I hated Delbert in the good ol' Gray Bar Hotel, we're both out now and trying to put that behind us. He deserves a good life as much as I do."

The trip out to the Sassy Lasses Winery is tense and takes much longer with both of us lost in our own minds. I feel just a smidge guilty for insisting Piper ride with Vem.

As I pull into Truman Coolidge's driveway, his big dog comes barreling out to greet us. Cosmo puts his hand on the door handle.

"Wait. That pup is a little erratic. I'll call Truman and ask him to come get his dog," I warn.

"Doesn't look like a threat to me." Cosmo opens his door despite my warning, standing up tall as the big dog jumps on him, licking his face. "Good boy, aren't you?" He coos, stroking the sides of his slobbery head.

Truman appears on the steps of his house and commands the dog to come in before greeting us himself. After one more big lick up the side of Cosmo's face, he galumphs back to his master.

"When you called, I wasn't sure if we were going in for an actual mission or if this was some flim-flam, girlie situation. I see you brought the big guns, so you're serious." Truman thrusts his hand in front of Cosmo. "Truman Coolidge. I can tell you're a no-nonsense guy. Those're the kind our presidents would appreciate. You know Lincoln liked a straight shooter, though he was prone to off-color humor. Also think you're that type, young man."

Cosmo chuckles. "Sounds about right. Me and the lady would like to get ourselves situated on your property so we can get a visual on our subjects."

I'm trying to avoid feeling offended by this entire man-centric situation. It won't help. "Can we, please?" I ask.

The three of us head to the back of his property, Truman explaining his love of wood and presidential knowledge to Cosmo as if I don't exist. "Don't have a political affiliation myself. Our best presidents have a respect for all of their people. Can't tell you how many folks judge me for that. An outsider's what I am."

Cosmo slaps his back. "Right there with you, Truman. Been an outsider my entire life."

"Chatty Charlies, Vem and Piper are in place!" I snap, tired of this two-sided conversation in a group of three. I point to November, who is gesturing animatedly with her hands, taking care to make sure the women's backs are to us.

"Let's go!" The three of us walk briskly across the open field, though now my muscles are spasming fully and I'm doing more of an enthusiastic gallop as we reach the back of Barn One. I gaze at Cosmo, who seems to have become so enamored of Truman that he can't glance in my direction. "We didn't discuss where we'd go from here. This is a large piece of property."

"Oh, that's the simple part. I set up surveillance on this place when they moved in. I have cameras in all the outbuildings." Truman pulls his phone from his pocket, where he opens a program with several cameras.

"And you haven't been a threat to these women? This is entirely unaccept–" I begin.

Cosmo touches my arm and shakes his head. "Do you see Delbert anywhere?" he asks.

"No, but I got a good visual on Carlene." Truman replies. "She's outside of Barn Three." He puts his phone down and stares at us. "What'r we waiting for?"

When we reach Barn Three, Carlene's voice is loud and angry. "How do they know? Did someone tip them off? You promised nothing would happen!"

We continue walking until she is in view. There is no one with her.

"Who are you talking to Carlene? Or should I start calling you 'Carlene' now? Where is Delbert?"

She jumps when she hears my voice. "My actual name is Carlene Esmerelda. After my grandmother on my father's side." She is oddly calm.

"You didn't answer my question. We're worried about Delbert. Can you help us find him? We have information that leads us to believe he is in danger."

Carlene looks at the shiny wood floor under her feet and shakes her head. "My sweet, sweet Delbert isn't in danger anymore."

Cosmo runs to either side of the building, looking for any evidence of danger. "Nothing, Lanie." he yells.

"Where is he, Carlene?"

She stares at me blankly.

I grab her arms and begin shaking her out of frustration. "Tell me, Carlene! We want to help you both!"

"Do you understand that poor man's whole life was about seeking revenge for his dad's death?" Her voice falters. "He was cheated out of his parents. There was no way I could go back to mine when he was suffering like that."

I release her arms and touch her gently. "That makes sense. But we need to see him."

Carlene sighs. "We came here so he could make his peace. That's what he said: we'd stay long enough to put his father's ghost to rest. Then he came home and told me he'd caught a drifter wandering through the property. He was sure they were looking for Raymond Dockley's remains. He wouldn't allow that to happen."

"Delbert killed the drifter?"

Carlene nods. "That was supposed to be it. Then

a year later, he told me he caught someone else at Spoonback Creek. They were looking for Raymond, too."

"Delbert killed the two men who died here recently, too?"

Carlene begins to cry. "Enough is enough. I thought about telling the police, but that would mean risking my identity being discovered. There was only one way for it to end. For the curse of Naybor Manor to end."

I am crying too. I can see she has been tortured by Delbert's pain without knowing how to end it. She and I are soul sisters of the worst kind. Cosmo's pain is tearing me up inside too. "You loved him so much, but you didn't know how to make him better," I sob.

"Ms. Anders?" Truman clears his throat. "We need to turn this over to the proper law enforcement. It's the right thing to do."

CHAPTER THIRTY-SEVEN

Pookie

1947

Dearest Ophelia,

I had the most horrid dream. I was running up the staircase, in fear when I heard something behind me and turned to see Daddy dressed in his neatly pressed striped pajamas. The look of concern on his face seemed genuine.

"I didn't know, Daddy. I thought the world was a beautiful place. But all I saw was this room, the pretend world you created for me. It wasn't until Raymond opened my eyes I realized how ugly things really are."

"Put that suitcase down and change into your nightclothes. There will be no more talk of things you don't understand."

Then I realized I was carrying a suitcase. "I understand perfectly well," I said calmly. "You got rid of Raymond and you'd like to get rid of me. Why couldn't you just let him be? He was good and kind. He only wanted things to be right in the world."

"He was a drifter, dear. Just like all the rest. He was never going to stay and become your friend. He didn't have the breeding for long-term relationships."

Tears poured down my face once more. "He didn't deserve to die like this."

"Oh, poor Pookie. You're always living in your movies."

"Was it all a lie, Daddy? Were you ever good to people?"

Daddy shook his head. "You're talking complete nonsense now. Maybe you weren't ready for grown-up tea."

"Daddy, come with me," I begged. "We can start over in Oklahoma. You can farm good things there, you can help people. Really help people. There are so many people without."

Daddy sighed. "This is our home. Let's get you to bed."

I woke in a cold sweat, fearful of what was ahead.

In "Can't Stop Me Now," someone trapped Tulip Sloan in a miserable marriage. Her husband didn't allow her to have friendships outside of the postman who spoke to

*her through the glass of her front window.
One day, when she could take her husband's
incessant chatter no more, she looked over at
the lamp beside her bed, picked it up and hit
him over the head. It was both her beginning
and her end.*

That is what I fear for myself.

*In Overwhelming Loss and Sadness,
Pookie A. Naybor*

"The train ticket isn't for four more days. I can
exchange it for another one. I could still go to
Hollywood and visit Tulip Sloan. She'd be happy to
have me as her guest." She smiled, daydreaming
about a life where Tulip was exactly as she imagined
all of those years.

As she walked down the dark road, slapping at
the hungry mosquitoes feeding on her neck, it
occurred to her that when the hired hands tried
walking to town; it took them at least one full day to
walk the thirty miles. Her heart sunk.

There had to be a neighbor, somewhere she could
go to ask for help. Someone her father hadn't
changed with his drugs. But who? Now that she
thought about it, when they came to visit, she was
sent up to her room. *Grown-ups need to talk now,
Pookie. We'll have some tea and discuss important
matters. It would bore you.*

She stopped in the middle of the road, stunned by the revelation. "It was everyone. There isn't one person in this place untouched by Daddy's evil."

There was nowhere to go now. If only she knew Raymond's government agent friend, Mr. Bowler. He would understand.

The sound of a car driving down the road made her stomach drop with a thud. Welcome was coming after her. Probably with strong men from the farm who would force her into the car and back into her old life.

She did the only thing her brain could fathom. It would all be over quickly.

Someone got out of the car and walked around it. "Are you all right? It's too late to be out here by yourself."

It was the voice of a woman. An unfamiliar voice. Her face was blurry. "We don't have much time so if you can, you need to get in my car." She instructed.

"Hurry up!" another voice said; a voice she knew all too well.

CHAPTER THIRTY-EIGHT

Lanie and Pookie
Piney Falls

"I WISH YOU would have told me sooner." I cross my legs uncomfortably, the muscle spasms unimproved since this morning at Sassy Lasses Winery.

Gladys shrugs her shoulders and looks away. "It's been so many years since I thought about her. That little girl with the brown braids and the funny ideas."

"When I showed up looking just like Tulip Sloan, you didn't say a word. How did that not trigger you in some way?"

She removes her orthopedic shoes from the table with a clunk. "That's the thing. In order to move on from something so scary, you have to lock it away without air. I'd hoped those memories had suffocated." She crosses her arms over her saggy chest and turns her chair away from me.

"You were such a brave girl." I cluck my tongue

sympathetically. "I'm sorry I didn't realize it when I first read your diary. Can you tell me what happened the night that you left? Did your father hurt you?"

"Oh, no. I snuck out without him knowing. I was planning to make my way to Oklahoma, to be with Raymond and his family. I was sure he'd finished his business at Naybor Manor and left before Daddy could hurt him. Unfortunately, he never came back for me." She coughs loudly and clears her throat. "Get me a glass of water, toots."

I move quickly to the watercooler, not wanting her to lose her train of thought to some weekly gossip. "Raymond wasn't there, so what did you do?" I start to hand her the glass, but she grabs it from me, almost causing it to fall on the floor.

She takes several large gulps. "Ahhh. That's better." Gladys hands the glass back to me. "Take a drink. It will clear your cobwebs. We can share a glass, I don't think either one of us has the cooties."

Instead, I sit back down in front of her, eager for more information. "And?"

"I started walking down the road. Thought either wild animals would get me, or Daddy would send one of the remaining farm hands to fetch me. Either way, my hours were numbered. That's when I heard a car rumbling up behind me. Did something impulsive and stupid at that point."

"You ran?"

"I jumped into the middle of the road with my hands up. If Daddy wanted me dead, I'd give that to him on my terms."

"Oh, Gladys; you poor thing."

"The car lurched to a stop, just tapping me. Being a girl full of dramatics, I fell down anyway. Didn't think that one through," she chuckles, putting her hand to her mouth. "I heard a voice that sounded like silk. When I opened my eyes, the most beautiful woman I'd ever seen was standing over me. She had dark brown eyes like mine and cheek bones Tulip Sloan couldn't muster."

"It was your mother?"

"Yes, indeed. I did not realize she'd been watching out for me all of those years. She snuck into that secret passageway many times and saw all of my artwork. I wondered if Miss Dandridge knew that when she encouraged me to paint?" She spins her chair around for a second. "I guess I'll never know." Gladys turns back around without giving me a chance to respond. "That night, she read my diary and came looking for me. She couldn't allow me to suffer any longer."

My heart aches for little Pookie; for elderly Gladys who still carries these scars.

"Daddy had been torturing her, too, you know. He tried to get her hooked on drugs, like he did everyone in town, but she was too smart for him.

When that didn't work, he forced her to give me up, paying handsomely to assure she never came around. Welcome Naybor wanted complete control of his offspring with no interference from anyone else. He had no concept of that woman's determination."

"It runs in the family," I chuckle. "Where did she take you?"

"Texas. She'd been planning our escape for at least a year, waiting for the right moment. We lived a grand life. My cousin Freddie visited every summer. She didn't tell me about Daddy's death until I was almost eighteen. She knew I'd already been through enough."

"You'd seen more than a child should have," I feel tremendous guilt that it took me so long to take her – Pookie – and her diary seriously.

"Everything about Welcome was a sham. He started his life as Filmont Naybor. Plain old Naybor, not Nah BOR. During a picnic at Spoonback Creek, he ambushed Mr. Wormly and drowned him. He ran away and changed his name to Welcome Naybor. Filmont, Welcome or *whoever* he chose to be, made up stories wherever he went. It didn't matter to him whether they had a kernel of truth or not. The story he told me about being named 'Welcome' to remind him to be kind and giving? Completely fabricated." Gladys rolls her eyes. "I think it was a way to thumb his nose at his adoptive parents and their outward appearance as a charitable couple. You know, 'I'll show *you* who feels welcome.' He never felt like anything more than a drugged-up captor.'"

"He really played the townsfolk as fools, didn't he?" I remark. "Manipulating them like a puppet master pulling their strings."

Gladys nods. "After Filmont's disappearance and alleged death, the Widow Wormly adopted his two siblings, Larry and Pookie. When he heard they were being subjected to the same workhouse environment and drugs that were used on him, he decided to rescue them. He killed Mrs. Wormly with the same mixture that was used on him as a child. Nobody figured out that's what caused her death. Nobody would have ever known if he hadn't bragged about it to my mother."

I nod. "I read the stories put out by the library, and Cedar checked adoption records for me. But none of this information was included. What happened after Mrs. Wormly's death?"

Gladys folds her hands across her chest and leans back. "Pookie reinvented herself as Daisy Devine. She ran a house of prostitution for several years out of Wormly Manor, though she branded it as some kind of 'house of health'," she scoffs. "Daisy was selling and using morphine. That didn't end well. She and her best customer, the sheriff, were murdered by the sheriff's brother. He was madly in love with

Daisy and wanted her to end her relationship with the sheriff."

"Daisy, Larry and Welcome, all worked together? They were drug and prostitution kingpins?"

"Yes. While Daisy was running things at Naybor Manor, Daddy and Larry supplied drugs for the uppity-ups. Got themselves invited to all the best parties in big cities so they could sell drugs to rich, powerful people. That included movie stars like Tulip Sloan. Sorry to upset you, if you didn't know."

"I know all about her drug addiction. She must've been the perfect accompaniment for Welcome Naybor." I say sarcastically.

Gladys crosses her legs and kicks one nervously. "When Welcome and Larry got word that Daisy had died, they showed up in Flanagan once more. Now they were the Nah BOR brothers, ready to set up shop in Wormly Manor. Nobody seemed to know they used to be Wormlys; or if they did, they didn't care."

"I don't picture your father – Welcome – as the partnership type. I did read an article about 'Lisping' Larry. Another strange disappearance." I lean forward, straining to see her face. I search Gladys' face for signs of distress. The last thing I want to do is overtax her today, when I know there are much worse things to come. She seems to be fine.

"Oh, he wasn't interested in a partnership. More

of a dictatorship. Larry made himself at home and that really upset my father. He wanted to be in charge of all of Larry's comings and goings, and Larry was sneaking around and making friends. That didn't sit right with Welcome."

"He tried to kill him, but Larry escaped," I offer. "At least that's the lore. But with so many unaccounted-for deaths, who knows?"

"Who knows?" Gladys repeats softly, though her eyes tell a different story.

"And Raymond? Did you find out what happened to him?"

She spins her chair around once more to look me squarely in the eye. "Never. During one of my summer breaks from college, I went to Oklahoma looking for his mother and son. I wanted to apologize for never showing up when Raymond told them I would. The government promised to return their land after Raymond worked undercover. Never happened. His mother died, destitute, some years later. Couldn't find the son."

I gulp. "And why did you end up back here? The place that held all of those memories you tried to suffocate?"

Gladys adjusts her glasses. "The memories took place in Naybor Manor. I'd never spent much time in town. I guess I wanted a chance to do things over again, the right way. I got a job here, right after college, and married my cousin Freddie's best friend. Guess I got that one right. I miss that man every day. Never told him or anyone about my sordid past."

"Whew." I rub my hands on my legs nervously. There is still tension in the room – emanating from me. "That's quite a story. You've kept that bottled up a long time. I'm glad you finally let it out."

She grumbles in agreement.

I reach into my pocket and pull out a small piece of paper, pushing it over to her side of the desk. "I found a note you left taped inside a table. Your hopes and dreams: brave, strong and beautiful. Gladys, you've achieved them all and more. You've triumphed over your past."

"Guess so," she says noncommittally, looking briefly at the three words scribbled on the page before sliding it back to me. "All of this is out in the open now. What's next, do you think, toots?"

What's next will be tricky and I need to take care that I don't wound her any deeper.

CHAPTER THIRTY-NINE

Tale of the Brown-Eyed Woman
1947

"FREDDIE! WHAT ARE you doing here?" Pookie asked in astonishment.

"I wanted to go with you to the big city. I ain't gonna live here no more. I don't care what you tell Ma, Auntie." He pushed a blanket aside, one he'd evidently been using to cover himself up.

Pookie looked at the woman in astonishment. "You're Freddie's aunt?"

The beautiful woman lowered her dark eyes. "Alicebeth is my sister." She looked at her nephew with dismay. "Freddie, perk up and listen."

Freddie reluctantly sat tall.

"You've really put me in a bind. You'll have to ride with us for now. I'll call Alicebeth when we get there and tell her I'm putting you on a train. We have to get Pookie to safety."

"How did you know my name? I didn't introduce myself."

"I know quite a lot about you, Pookie. I'll explain while we drive. Let's get going."

Pookie opened the back door, motioning for Freddie to slide over.

"No, you'll be up front with me. And you—" she pointed to her nephew, "will stay in the back seat. And not a word. Not one. Do you understand?"

"Yes'm." He saw Pookie's suitcase. "Where ya goin'? This have something to do with that Raymond? I told you he was bad news!"

"Not one word, Fred!"

The woman got in the driver's seat and started the car. She turned to face Pookie. "We've never been properly introduced. I'm Salome. Freddie's Aunt."

"Pookie Naybor. Very nice to make your acquaintance, ma'am."

Salome shook her head, her dark curls static under her hat. "What a horrible name for a girl. He could've at least called you Mamie, or…"

"I'm named after my aunt, Miss. Daddy says it was her nickname. We never spoke of her given name, but Daddy said she disliked it so."

"Josephine. It's not such a horrible name. She also went by Daisy later in life. Your middle name is after your aunt on the other side. Alicebeth."

Pookie's eyes opened wide. "I never knew that. Daddy said my mother gave me a middle initial and nothing more. He said it was just another way she was careless in her mothering. How do you know–"

Salome tilted her head as she put the car in gear. "We have much to discuss on our way to Portland. This is serious, Pookie. Grown-up talk. Are you ready to hear words that might not be pleasant to your ears?"

Pookie nodded. "I'm thirteen. I'm practically grown." She regretted those words as soon as she said them. Being grown wasn't at all what she'd envisioned. "I've decided I'm not terribly fond of grown-up talk, but I've learned many awful things and I've handled them just fine up till now." She glanced in the back seat where Freddie was fiddling with the handle of her bag.

"I'd rather wait to tell you, until you're ready. Unfortunately, with all of the events of this evening, we simply don't have time." Salome glanced at her worriedly. "You do understand, don't you?"

Pookie nodded solemnly.

"I used to live on the farm next to Naybor Manor. My father had peach trees, blueberry bushes and many fields of corn. We had a lovely life. When the depression hit, my father was beside himself. He'd only farmed his entire life, and he didn't know how to do anything else. We had trouble selling our crops because no one had any money to buy anything."

"I learned about the depression. My teacher,

Miss Dandridge, told me all about it. People starved."

Salome smiled. "I'm glad you've learned so much from your teacher. For the rest of your education, you'll be learning in a classroom with other young women. You need to experience the world, with all of its harsh and beautiful facets."

"I'm going to Oklahoma. To live with Raymond's mother and his son. That's just until he's done here, and he and Daddy can come and get me." Pookie looked down as she remembered what had just transpired. "I'm sorry to interrupt, please continue."

"My father decided it would be best if my sister and I went to live in town with his cousin. He promised we would be seamstresses and be able to send money back to him. That's not at all what happened. His cousin sold pleasures to the men who docked in the harbor. He locked us in the house and sent money to our father himself, so he wouldn't understand what was happening."

"Oh, Miss Salome." It was hard for Pookie to imagine such a glamorous woman in such dire circumstances.

"One day, a finely-dressed gentleman came into his establishment. He paid for time with me, but only asked to hold my hand. I hadn't experienced such tenderness before. I told him everything, how we'd spent months as the captives of our cousin. He was so kind.

"The next day, he brought several powerful men with him who threatened to burn the place down if we weren't allowed to leave. He drove us back to our parents, who were so sad for what we'd gone through, but still unable to care for us. That's when the man offered to take us in, as caretakers for his home."

"Was it Naybor Manor?"

"Yes my dear, it was. When we arrived, it wasn't the grand castle it is now. It was in a state of disrepair and neglect. We worked long, hard hours restoring it. It wasn't easy work, but Welcome paid us well for our labor."

"Daddy told me how difficult it was to fix it up. How it took over a year."

"Eighteen months. By the time we'd finished, Alicebeth and I had calloused hands and permanently sore backs. But we were proud of what we'd accomplished. As the months went by, working side by side, we'd developed an affection for the man who'd rescued us and taught us his trade."

"You fell in love with Daddy?"

Salome nodded. "The man we admired was so kind and caring, but also a bit overpowering. He told us of his childhood, where he was controlled by a mother who drugged him to keep him in line. He vowed never to lose authority over anything again. He wanted us to check out when we traveled to visit our parents. He asked that we not develop friend-ships with the other workers on the property, not for any reason."

"Kept in servitude. I learnt that word last year in class." Freddie piped up from the back seat.

Salome looked in the mirror. "Yes, Fred, it start-ed feeling that way. Though, I'd let myself fall in love and didn't listen to the voice of reason speaking in my head."

"What did you do?" Pookie asked.

"The wrong thing. I allowed myself to be courted by this dashing man who was the age of my father. We enjoyed walks in the hills filled with flowers, we had picnics by Spoonback Creek. I spent so much time with him that I forgot to go visit my family, and gradually they became less important to me. I didn't even listen when Alicebeth told me that her high school boyfriend had been sharing Sunday dinners with them and she'd fallen in love too."

Salome looked into the back seat where Freddie was laying with his head against the suitcase. His eyelids fluttered quickly. "I know you're not sleeping, Fred. These words are things you're not to share with your mother. Grown-up talk, right?"

He didn't respond, continuing his sleeping ruse. Pookie knew just how well he kept secrets, but she didn't want to upset Salome.

"The series of events that happened next were as awful as being held captive at my cousin's home." Salome glanced at the innocent girl for a moment before returning her eyes to the road. "In my head, I would marry my prince and live on this magical property forever. I planned to visit my parents the following Sunday to tell them of my decision. I got halfway there and realized I'd forgotten to bring the rhubarb-strawberry pie I'd made. When I got back to Naybor Manor, Welcome was injecting Alicebeth with drugs."

"He did that to Tulip Sloan and Mr. Pherson! Freddie and I watched!"

"Those were vitamins. That's what my mom said," Freddie retorted.

"I felt so angry, so betrayed, that I went right to my parents and told them what Alicebeth had done," Salome said, ignoring Freddie. "My father marched over and yanked Alicebeth from Welcome's home, threatening to tell the entire community exactly what he was doing if he didn't let her leave for good. And that's just what she did."

"Oh, my!" Pookie gasped. "Why didn't you leave, too?"

Salome sighed. "My father demanded I pack my things, but I informed him I couldn't go with them. I told you this would be hard to hear, Pookie," she began hesitantly. "I had to confess to my father that Welcome and I were expecting a baby. I told him a story I'd made up about the wedding we were planning, so he wouldn't think any less of me. But after seeing what I did, Naybor Manor was the last place I wanted to be."

"Did you marry Daddy? He never told me that." Pookie tried to imagine Daddy gazing lovingly at a bride. Sometimes she fantasized about Miss Dandridge and her father getting married, always shaming herself for thinking such thoughts about her teacher.

"We talked about a wedding but it never happened. Truth be told, I think he was as disinterested in marriage as I was. He wasn't really capable of caring for someone as his equal."

"Marriage ain't for the weak. Tulip Sloan's movie husbands end up flat as a pancake, or buried alive, or..." Freddie's voice drifted up from the back seat.

"That's enough from you, Freddie!" Pookie snapped, not bothering to turn around.

"As the time of my child's birth grew closer, Welcome became even more controlling," Salome continued. "I couldn't go anywhere unless he was right beside me. I felt as if I was having the life choked out of me. Each minute brought me closer to losing my sanity. As the days passed, it became obvious to me that I couldn't spend the rest of my life in that prison. But I knew Welcome was a powerful man in a dangerous world – those who wanted out, didn't live. He tried everything to keep me under his control. Even trying to get me addicted to his tea."

"Daddy isn't–" Pookie stopped herself. "How did you leave?"

"I was of little value to him, so if I wanted my freedom, I would need to find something he treasured to use as a bargaining chip. I'm not proud of this, my darling. I traded my child for my life." Tears appeared on her perfect cheeks, though she didn't make any crying sounds.

"Are you saying that you're my…"

"Yes, Pookie. I'm your mother. And Pookie isn't your proper name. It's Gladys. Gladys Alicebeth. It broke my heart to leave you, but it was the only way to keep my sanity and maybe even my life. I had to promise never to see you again and he sent me off with a large sum of money. I outsmarted him though. I snuck in through the secret passageway and watched you at night when I could."

Pookie thought about the legend of the ghosts roaming the passageway. It was always her mother. "And what about your sister? Did she have a happy life?"

"Alicebeth and her husband separated when Freddie was four. She had no choice but to go back to Welcome to ask for help. She began selling drugs for him."

Pookie mulled over these facts. "Miss Salome—there are people coming to hurt Daddy. Shouldn't we go back and help him? Even after all he's done, he's been a very good father to me. He'd be very thankful to you, wouldn't he?"

Salome pulled the car over and took her daughters hands in hers. She looked her directly in the eye. "Gladys, my dear sweet girl, from this moment on, Welcome Naybor is nothing more than a series of tall tales. Your new life begins right now."

CHAPTER FORTY

Lanie
Piney Falls

"GLADYS, I HAVE two things to tell you. They will be hard to hear. But first, can you tell me why you've been pretending to be much older than you really are?"

"What? For heaven's sake. Why would you ask that?"

"Because I have your diary right here." I pick up the navy-covered book. "Indisputable proof of your age."

"Oh, toots. I've been caught red-handed, haven't I? I guess the jig is up." Gladys taps her fingers rhythmically on the desk in front of her. "One day, me and my grandkids were at the park. Some nosy little booger comes over and asks how old I am. Being a smart aleck, I told him I was nearly a century. Thought that might shut him up. He ran right over and told his parents and I chuckled to myself. You should have seen the looks on their faces. Gawking at me like I was the largest zucchini at the county fair."

"I can imagine."

"Thought that was the end of it and I didn't give it another thought. But, you know this is a small town, Lanie. Word gets around."

Usually It's through the Gladys grapevine.

"Next thing I know, I get a phone call that the fire department wants to give me a cake to celebrate my being the oldest person in Piney Falls. Well, it offended me at first. Who wants to be told they're the oldest this or that? Then I remembered that time in the park. I picked up the phone to call them back and tell them it was all a misunderstanding. I stopped myself before I made the call." She slams her hand on the table. "That nice man told me they were makin' me a big cake. Whatever flavor I wanted and three layers! A woman can't turn down good cake."

I shake my head enthusiastically. "No, she certainly can't."

"The next thing was the parade. 'Gladys, we want you to be the grand marshal.' I never got my moment in Hollywood like I dreamed, so I thought, why not? Gave me a crown and a nice orthopedic pillow to sit on. I felt bigger than Tulip Sloan herself. Oh my, was I somebody." She interlaces her hands behind her head and stares at something far away, maybe dreaming of young Pookie as the grand marshal of a Hollywood parade with Raymond watching from the street.

"Your family went along with all of that? It was a big ruse for them, too."

"They like their cake, Lanie." Gladys says matter-of-factly. "Well, you know all except for Carlene. She was never one for cake. She was long gone, anyway. Wish that was the worst of our problems. We left things on harsh terms, she and I."

I take a deep breath and let it out. "That's the other thing I wanted to talk to you about." I lean forward, placing my folded hands on the desk in front of me. "What if I said you could see Carlene today? Even though you had bad blood between you, wouldn't it melt away if you could hold her in your arms one more time?"

"You're being silly, toots," she scoffs. "Carlene's long gone. No matter what my real age, I'll never live long enough to see that."

"Okay. Here comes those two hard things to hear. This won't be easy."

Gladys leans forward across the desk, so close I can feel her breath on my face. "What's this game, toots? Are you havin' me arrested for parade fraud? Can't sweeten that act by throwin' Carlene's name in front of it."

"Both Raymond's son and Carlene have been here, living on your old property for many years.

Your daughter was right under your nose this whole time."

Gladys sits back, grasping her chest. "Don't be fooling with an old lady's heart."

"It's true. There are many complicated pieces to this puzzle." I don't dare tell her that Carlene's phone was the one she helped us bug. That might send her over the edge.

"What kind of complicated?"

"Raymond's son is dead. Drugged the same way your father killed so many people all of those years ago. They discovered his body earlier today, right where the killer said it would be."

"Oh, no. That's just terrible. Just terrible." She sits for a moment, composing herself and then clasps her hands together in front of her. "Is Carlene out there now? At that winery? Does she know what happened to Raymond? How does she know his son?"

My face is the wrong color of red. The kind that happens when its mimicking what my stomach feels. "She's down at the police station. With Boysie. I'll let them explain it to you. Would you like me to take you to her now?"

Chapter Forty-One

Lanie
Sassy Lasses Winery

"THANKS FOR COMING with me today, Cos!" I yell. "We needed some time to talk things out!"

"I can't hear you!"

We've both got the windows rolled down to take in all we can of this gorgeous, late-spring day. We're driving out to the Sassy Lasses Vineyard, on the invitation of Mandy and Marveline who wanted to thank us for all we did to finally end the murders once and for all.

Gladys went to the city jail, one floor above the city library, where she reunited with Carlene. She shed quite a few tears when she learned Carlene was being arrested for her husband's murder. There even more emotion when Gladys learned that her only connection to Raymond, his son Delbert, was dead at her daughter's hand.

"I said–"

"Hold on!" He reaches over and pushes the buttons, rolling up our windows simultaneously. "Go ahead, Lanie."

"Just going to throw it all out on the table, Cos. You've been out of bed three days this week. It's a wonderful sight to see; you're acting like your old self." I glance over at him with concern.

He stares out the window as we rumble down the road, almost to the former Naybor Manor. "Three days is better than no days."

"It's excellent, really. But if you want the bakery, your dream, to be your business and not Piper's, you need to get some help."

"I'm not hiring anyone else. Piper already has those irritating high school girls who giggle their way through every order. That's plenty."

"No, Cos. I mean help for YOU. Seeing a therapist might be what you need to get out of this funk."

He leans forward in his seat and rubs his hands back and forth on his jeans. "So you're thinking I'm crazy? The type of crazy where I need to be supervised?"

"No, it's more of a pre-crazy state," I joke. He doesn't laugh.

"There's no way I'm telling my problems to someone in this town. I miss my sister. That's normal."

"Oh, Cos." I pull off the road, just short of

Naybor Lane, and grab his hand, pulling it close to my side. "It's okay. You've gone through so much in your life, it was bound to hit you at some point. Your life in the cult, life in prison, and now having to face a world without your beloved sister. You're allowed some down time, Cos. You just don't want to let it get you so down you can't get up again."

He pulls my hand to his face and kisses it. "There have been so many days I wanted to get up and tell you how much you mean to me. But the darkness just came in and grabbed ahold of me by the throat."

I reach over and pull him close, drinking in the scent of his freshly-washed face. "I understand." We hold our embrace long enough that I start to wonder if someone driving down the road will think I'm being kidnapped. With so many ugly tales originating from this general location, I should take care not to be the source of one more. With regret, I pull away.

Cos reaches over and touches my face. "I was thinking, we should start planning our wedding. I would be ok with doing it at the winery. The day is about being with you. If this place makes you happy, I'm all in."

"Really? I mean, Delbert is gone so there's no threat of any more surprise bodies. And we can invite whoever you want. Even if it's just the two of us–"

He lets out a loud laugh. It startles me, this sound that hasn't come from him in months.

"Do you think November Bean would let you get married without her there to witness it? She'd do some kind of voodoo dance with empty egg cartons and curse us for the rest of our marriage."

"I suppose you're right. And we'd want Piper there. Gladys won't come, but Urica could give her all the details."

"So it's settled then?"

I start the car again, pulling into the long drive that is Naybor Lane towards the big, imposing house. The one with all the stories that almost kept me from seeing the truth of Welcome and Pookie Naybor. "Yes. We'll tell the women today."

Cosmo leans forward and drums his fingers on the dash nervously. "It worried me you might not want to stick around. I'm glad you're still here. I don't know what I did to deserve you, Lanie Anders. Something I slept through, I'm sure."

He always manages to make me smile. "We're both in this for the good, the bad, the ugly and–"

"November," we say together, before sharing a giggle.

I'm surprised by all the vehicles parked on each side of the driveway. Maybe things have finally turned around for them. When we reach the house, there is a large gathering on the lawn, people are laughing and drinking. The faces appear very familiar.

"Cos? What's all this?"

"No idea. Looks like our friends decided to have a party without us."

We get out of the car and walk, hand in hand up the driveway. To my surprise, November is standing there, dressed in her formal peach jumpsuit with matching glasses and headband, holding a large glass of wine in one hand and a hunk of cheese in the other.

"Vem? What's going on? You never mentioned you'd be here today!"

She turns around when she recognizes us, dropping her cheese to the ground with a thunk. "Pickles and Pork rinds!" She exclaims as her face turns white as a sheet.

I bend down to pick it up and notice she's even wearing formal-looking peach shoes.

"Those twins were supposed to be the lookouts. Now everything is ruined." She pushes me to the side and waves to the large group of people milling around on the lawn. "Everyone! They're here! As we practiced! Mandy! Marveline! It's time!"

Vem lifts her arms to direct.

"We're so happy for you both," the group sings in poorly executed harmony. "Your engagement we will toast. Please enjoy this special day, to your nuptials we will say," they take a collective breath and then not in any form of unison, yell, "Good wishes Lanie and Cosmo!"

Mandy appears hurriedly on the porch, carrying a large cake, followed by Piper who is toting the utensils.

Piper looks crestfallen. "How did we miss the surprise?"

"Nobody has explained anything to me yet. Piper, would you like to give me a clue?" Cosmo sticks his hands in his pockets and starts rocking back and forth.

"This is your surprise wedding shower. It was Vem's idea. We weren't sure you would feel up to this sort of thing, but Vem was adamant." Piper gazes at Cosmo hopefully. "You're up to it, right?"

We all hold our breath, waiting for Cosmo. He could decide we have to turn around and go home right now. Even though that would disappoint me, I would support whatever he needs. We're a team through the dark clouds and the blue sky. "Cos? We can go if you like," I whisper.

He turns to me, still displaying his serious face. "Can't think of anything better to do today than celebrate with the woman I love." We embrace tightly and a cheer goes up from the crowd. Marveline, appearing from behind Mandy, directs Piper and Mandy to set their items down on a long table adorned by many vases of colorful begonias.

"Come sit over here, in the honored guests'

chairs." Mandy ushers us to a shady spot on the lawn, where a table covered in a lavender cloth and a vase bursting with bright, pink begonias await us.

"I'll get you two some wine."

Mandy turns to leave, but I grab her arm. "I'd like to talk to you later, just to clear some things up."

"Sure. When things wind down, I'll come back and we'll talk." I look around at the crowded lawn, where it seems almost everyone in Piney Falls is in attendance.

"Excuse me, could I have your attention?" Piper is standing in front of us, holding a microphone. "They asked me to say some sharp and witty things about Cosmo today." She looks him directly in the eye, apologetically, if I'm not mistaken. "I didn't want to say anything mean. I'll leave that for someone else. But I can tell you a funny story. One day, after I'd been here for six months, Cosmo asked me to leave a special package out in the alley for Lanie. I thought it was kind of cute. I thought, 'Well, he's a man, so he probably needs some help to say the right thing.' Because just a package isn't enough to tell someone you care." There is a murmur of agreement in the group.

"I wrote out a long, sappy note and signed it from Cosmo. It disappeared two days later. I never thought anything of it until one day, a stranger came in with a serious face, looking for Cosmo."

I know this story well and look for Cosmo's reaction to see if he finds the humor in it as well. He catches my gaze and winks.

"The man said he'd found Cosmo's package and note and he was so touched. No one else pays that much attention to the garbage men, but for someone to say they 'don't go a day without thinking how empty this world would be without them,' well that meant a lot."

The guests roar with laughter.

"Cosmo had no idea I'd written this note, or that I'd made an actual package instead of leaving the cat toy and can of food out in the back for Lanie Bug, the stray cat he'd been feeding. He looked at the trash man and said, 'Buddy, I meant every word.'"

People are slapping their knees and laughing so loud I worry that Truman Coolidge will come out and fire a warning shot. When I gaze toward his property, I can see he is seated in the furthest table back, wearing his finest red-white-and-blue overalls and a freshly washed red shirt. He waves enthusiastically and I wave back.

"In all seriousness, that's the kind of guy Cosmo is. He wants everyone to feel like it's their best day." Piper looks behind her and then straight ahead, where she sees something that makes her smile. "Well, Cosmo, we want this to be your best day."

I can feel someone walking up behind me. Before I can turn around, I smell the familiar scent of her rose and cinnamon perfume as Cedar Hill clutches her brother around the neck. He jumps up and hugs her, lifting her off her feet.

"You're really here? I can't believe it." He whispers.

"I wouldn't miss this for the world, brother."

I lean in and hug them both, wanting to be a part of this circle of love.

When he puts her down, he takes her face in his hands, each sibling sharing tears in their matching blue eyes. "Why didn't you tell me you were coming?"

"Vem just called me the other day. She said she was planning a surprise showery thing for you and asked if I would be here. I got on the earliest flight. I wouldn't miss a celebration for the two most important people in my life."

An hour passes like a minute as we laugh and joke with Cedar about her new job and old times in Piney Falls. When Cosmo gets up to refill our wine glasses, Cedar turns to me.

"Have you convinced him to get help yet?" she asks.

"No, but that hard nut is beginning to crack. We'll get there." I smile broadly at her. "It's so good to see you looking well."

Cedar's face, radiant even on a bad day, displays a sense of peace. "Thanks. I just love my life, Lanie. Oh, and I didn't forget about the information you wanted. You asked me about the Pherson deaths? They are actually classified as 'unsolved.' There was some kind of suspicious substance found on both bodies. A derivative of opium from the poppy flower mixed with black-plum-flower root was what the autopsy said. Like something homemade."

A chill runs down my back as I remember my conversation with Nate Cadbury, the coroner. "And they had no idea if these people were forced or if they took it on their own?"

"Even more troubling is the disappearance of Mandy and Marveline's grandfather, Owen Pherson. Unbelievably, the last place he was seen alive was in Flanagan. During a big parade downtown. The newspapers all said he died in a plane crash, but there was never a plane or a crash that I can find on that day." She bends over and whispers into my ear briefly before there is a sharp tap on both of our shoulders.

CHAPTER FORTY-TWO

Lanie
Sassy Lasses Winery

"**S**ECRETS ARE JUST plain rude," November has poked her finger directly into Cedar's back. "We need you three. This is the most exciting part of the day. I contacted the world record people and they sent someone to record the momentous occasion about to occur."

Cosmo returns with our drinks and sets them on the table in front of us. "November Bean, whatever cockamamie plan you've cooked up–"

I put my hand on his arm and look him directly in his eyes. "Cos, she's doing something special for us. Relax and enjoy."

He stands up straight, his shoulders still tense.

"We're doing a group moan session. I contacted the world record people and they believe this may be the largest group moan to occur. They sent that little man over there who resembles a turtle."

I gaze across the lawn, where a short, bald man

with round glasses and a humped back is standing. "We're setting a record today? That's what this is all about?"

"I told you. Cockamamie," Cosmo growls.

"While we're here, we might as well accomplish something extraordinary. Probably good publicity for the winery too, right Lanie?"

"You've got me there, Vem. Cos, are you going to join us, or just sit and giggle? Either way, you will be a part of history whether you like it or not." I stand, reaching my hand out to the only man I've ever loved.

"Can't believe I've lived long enough to see this day." He mumbles.

We move to the center of the lawn, where Vem has already begun gathering people. Cosmo takes my hand and squeezes it, hard, before grasping the hand of the one person who got him through his life in the cult.

"If you'll all follow me, please. This must be done precisely if we're going to make it into the books. We get a practice round, right Mr. Turtle?" Vem points to the small man, who shrugs his shoulders.

"I guess we have to make this one count." She looks at me with uncertainty and I give her two thumbs up. "You've got this!" I mouth.

"Okay Exquisite Piney Fallsisans, dig down to your toes, feeling the very tips. Now, take a deep breath from that point and pull it all the way to the tops of your blessedly beautiful heads."

Everyone breathes in except Cosmo, who is standing with his arms crossed. "You look even more beautiful when you're doing something completely ridiculous," he says, far too loud for this semi-somber moment. Cedar bends forward, catching my eye and winking.

"Cos! Stop it!" I hiss.

"Now we will begin with a baby moan, starting with our mouths open slightly and building to a monstrous moan that will rattle the grapes right off the vines."

A low hum begins. At first it sounds funny, like a group of a thousand bees conferencing on their next major hive project. But as it builds, I start to feel a strong energy around us, enough that the ground may possibly be moving.

Cos is still planted firmly in place, looking skeptically at the large group of moaners. "Do this for her," I mouth. "Please?"

Cosmo rolls his eyes before beginning a moan. He starts slowly. I close my eyes and squeeze his hand in thanks. Several minutes go by as I relax into the peaceful energy of the group. There is a deep, bellowing moan that shakes me out of my solitude. It sounds like someone is in pain. I look around to make sure no one is injured.

Instead, I find the strange, powerful sound is emanating from my partner. What comes out of his mouth is so loud and fierce, everyone around me stops and stares. He leans his head back, eyes closed and lets loose a fog horn sound full of rage and energy. It's like all the sadness and anger he's been experiencing are escaping from his body all at once. There is so much moaning coming from Cosmo, no one else bothers anymore. His mournful voice is the only sound on the spacious former Naybor Manor lawn and it's echoing throughout the property.

The man I love is in another world. Cosmo's body begins to shake violently as he sobs in between moans and finally just stops moaning altogether. His muscular shoulders are shaking so hard I pull him in close, wishing I could make his experience easier.

"It's all right. Let it out. As long as it takes." I stroke his head, trying to keep him in a protective cocoon where he won't hurt anymore. As I do, the emotions begin to flow from me as well. Those I've kept hidden from him so as not to burden his already heavy soul. I can't seem to stop the tears and maybe I shouldn't. "As long as it takes." I repeat. "We're going to heal."

Cedar comes to his other side and kisses him on the cheek, pushing the hair from his eyes. "Cos, it kills me you've been so sad." She hugs us both until his eyes open.

"If it helps, my life in San Diego couldn't be more perfect. This is what we dreamed of all those years ago in the cult. Finding what makes us happy. When you're sad think about those days. Not to make it worse but to remember where we were on the path and where we are now. We're in the sunshine, brother."

He nods. "I know, sis. I guess I needed to let this all go." He looks at me with love, as a new sense of peace creeps over his face. "We both did."

Cosmo wipes the tears from his face with the back of his hand before tenderly wiping mine with his fingers. He ever-so-lightly kisses my nose. Vem, from out of nowhere, appears with a tissue. She puts it to his face. "Blow!" she commands. He does so willingly. When she tries to do the same with me, I politely decline.

Marveline walks to where we're standing, looking Cosmo up and down. "That was quite a performance."

He shrugs. "That's what you get when you invite this bunch to a party."

The air somehow feels lighter now. Things have miraculously become clear in my mind, details that had to be pushed aside earlier. Moaning is the magic pill Vem has always said it was. "I've got to find Mandy. Does anyone know where she is?"

"Kitchen," Marveline says without emotion.

"You know I don't like people in my house, though."

"This will be the one exception." I turn to Cosmo and Cedar. "If I'm not back in ten minutes, please come look for me."

"Should we come with you now?" Cedar asks with concern.

"No, I need a few minutes to clear some things up with her. Things I'm sure she'll be able to explain."

I walk briskly to the kitchen door where I can see Mandy through the screen, cutting up strawberries. My muscles are tense again, something I haven't taken the time to deal with. "Got a minute?"

"Sure." She wipes her forehead with the back of her hand and opens the screen door, bringing the knife with her. "What's going on? Do we need more wine?"

"I need to apologize." I say, searching her face for signs I may have missed.

"Why? You did your best trying to solve that mystery. It wasn't your fault Delbert killed all of those people."

"No, not to you. To Carlene."

CHAPTER FORTY-THREE

Lanie
Sassy Lasses Winery

"WHY WOULD YOU apologize to her? She tried to destroy our plans for this place." Mandy returns to the chopping board, and I follow her into the kitchen.

"Because it never occurred to me the day I confronted her that the black eye she received came from you, not her husband. She changed her mind at the last minute."

Mandy doesn't look up at me.

"You did quite a lot of searching on the internet for drugs made from plants in this area," I continue. "That's in addition to extensively researching Naybor Manor."

"Yes, I think I told you that already. My sister and I dreamed of running a winery. In our free time, we researched on the internet to find the best place."

I fold my arms in front of me, protecting my chest just in case the knife gets too close. "I was surprised to learn a few things from my future sister-in-law, who did a little digging for me. The first fact was that your grandfather, Owen Pherson, was in the motion picture industry. He owned Golden Lights Studio, where Tulip Sloan was his biggest star and his biggest source of income."

"Lanie, I have things to do." Mandy pushes an imaginary piece of hair from her eye.

"Tulip Sloan was a known drug addict. By all accounts, her love affair with drugs began when she attended a Golden Lights Studio party thrown by Owen Pherson, also attended by Welcome Naybor, a wealthy shipping magnate. It was in 1932, I believe. Welcome supplied all of Owen's stars with drugs to keep them happy and productive. He wanted his actors working as many hours as possible."

Mandy's brow is furrowed. "None of this means anything."

I put my hand up. "Please be patient. It took me far too long to figure this out. It would stand to reason that Owen, himself, partook."

"Are you accusing my grandfather of being a common addict?" she asks, continuing to avert her gaze from me.

"Owen and Tulip Sloan came to Flanagan in 1947. There was a parade down main street, all documented in the local paper. In Pookie Naybor's diary, she talked about Tulip and Owen attending her birthday party that very evening."

I wait for a reaction, but her face is made of stone. "Your grandfather was in this house the last time he was seen alive. Pookie Naybor witnessed her father administering morphine to Owen and Tulip." I take a deep breath before I dive in. "The story of him dying in a plane crash was all made up for the press. No one actually knows what happened to the poor man. But we can certainly use our imaginations, can't we, Mandy?"

Mandy's face is scarlet. "My grandfather disappeared. He was scheduled to fly in a private plane. That's all we know for sure."

"That's when things start to get complicated," I continue. "His son, your father Owen II, couldn't bear to stay in Hollywood after his father's death, so he bought into a pharmaceutical company. Your father and mother manufactured the same drugs that killed your grandfather. That must've been very upsetting for you."

"Wouldn't it upset you?" she retorts. "They were spitting in his face. He was a sweet and loving man, from what I've heard. I never got the chance to meet him. Thanks to Mr. Naybor."

"And what better way to get revenge than finding someone to help you right the wrongs of Welcome Naybor. You emailed Delbert to ask about the property and then started asking him about the deaths here. He bragged that he'd killed two people, drowning them in Spoonback Creek as revenge for his father Raymond's death. Delbert wasn't afraid to do it again. That's when you came up with your plan."

"What plan is that?" Cosmo asks, opening the screen door and motioning for me to join him on the step.

I can't say I'm unhappy to see him. "The plan to continue Welcome's legacy and keep this place forever cursed. Remember how I told you that Welcome Naybor killed his adopted parents, the Wormlys?"

"I remember." He squeezes my arm once I'm by his side.

"Mandy here couldn't use morphine to kill. That would be too obvious. Doing some research on Welcome Naybor she discovered he'd made a deadly concoction using the poppies he grew here, as well as dark plum plants. That's how he poisoned the people who wouldn't take his morphine." I glance at Cosmo, making sure he's following, but he is watching Mandy to make sure she doesn't try to harm me.

"She enlisted Delbert to help her harvest the plants before she even moved here," I continue. "The first time she experimented was on her parents. They needed to be out of the way so she could move to step two: buying the Naybor property. Mandy used the same mix to kill Delbert that she used to kill Bill Bogus and Gene Yardley."

Mandy laughs nervously. "You have no proof I killed Delbert, or anyone for that matter. Carlene already confessed."

I fold my arms in front of me. "Here's the thing. Carlene told the police she knew her husband was dead. She didn't say she killed him."

"Sounds like you did a good job of convincing her otherwise," Cosmo quipped.

"The poor woman is so traumatized, she's spent the last two months in jail afraid to say anything. You must've scared her good." I add. "My guess is that Delbert readily agreed to help you drug Bill Bogus and Gene Yardley, these 'no-good drifters' who only came here to work because they wanted to see if the legend was true. At least that's what you told Delbert. He helped you place the bodies in the field where they would be found by guests. He had no idea you were perfecting this deadly mix to use on him."

"I told Carlene it was for the best, after all trouble he's caused," Mandy says confidently. "She only had to help me drag Delbert's body into the field. If she kept her mouth shut, I wouldn't implicate her in Delbert's crimes, even though she knew about them. Believe me, she was tired of his behavior. I did her a favor. As for Delbert, he was a murderer. He bragged about it. I don't think he really had a reason other than his anger at the world. At least I had a mission."

"But it was you who did the dirty deed." Marveline is directly behind me, so close I can feel her breath on my neck. "Why would you ruin everything we've worked for? It doesn't make any sense."

"My real dream, sister," Mandy's head wobbles defiantly, "has always been to rid ourselves of the stain of Welcome Naybor. If you would ever listen to me tell you about my research into our family history, you would know that he killed our grandfather. I didn't want this property to become anything great if it meant it would somehow make Welcome Naybor appear in a positive light." She stops and sniffs, staring down at her feet. "That's why it was so important that we purchase it; that I get rid of our parents so we would have the money to do so. Then I connected with Delbert and discovered his mind worked just like Naybor's. He was evil to the core. It was history repeating itself and I couldn't allow one more remnant of that awful time. I had to end things."

"You didn't end things. You continued them." Marveline's voice cracks. "You added more misery to an already weary story. We could've had such a lovely life here."

Mandy is crying now as well. "Do you remember when we were little and you showed me the family history book? It meant something to me to be a Pherson. I looked at those faces and I saw myself." She stops to wipe her eyes on her shirt. "There was a paragraph about Grandpa and how he destroyed the family legacy by joining forces with Welcome Naybor. After all of his great accomplishments, all the careers he launched, he was remembered in the family lore as a drug addict in the service of a no-good grifter. That awful man was his downfall." Mandy looks down at her hands, curling her fingers around the knife.

"There are too many witnesses for that, lady." Cosmo moves quickly into the kitchen, grabbing the knife from her hand. "I'll be happy to monitor her while we're waiting on Boysie."

"There's really nothing left for me to do." Mandy's shoulders sag. "This was my dream. I'm sorry, Marveline." She slips around Cosmo, moving toward her sister and me. As she walks, she reaches into her pocket and takes out a small bag filled with a crushed, dark substance. "Don't bury me here, sister."

"Grab it!" Marveline yells.

I lurch forward, jerking Mandy's arm downward. The bag slips out of her hand and onto the porch. Mandy attempts to push me aside to grab it but I hold her small body tightly. My legs once again begin to spasm as we struggle; I lose my balance and fall backwards onto the cement step, bringing her on top of me.

There is instant pain like I've never felt before. "Ahhh!" My voice is disconnected from my body, but I can hear myself say, "get the drug, Cos!" before losing consciousness.

In my mind somewhere there are unattached sounds that may or may not be real. "Call an ambulance!" "Call Boysie!" "Lanie, I can grind up some beetles to fix your…"

⇒⟫⟪⇐

IT SEEMS LIKE it's been days when my eyes willingly open. I recognize the institutional smell of Piney Falls Community Hospital. Once, Piper was trying to learn to skateboard when she ran into my car and I had to bring her to the emergency room for an x-ray. I gagged for those two hours inhaling that overpowering scent.

"Her eyes are opening. Lanie? Are you in there? They weren't sure if all the lights would be blazing upstairs. Are they blazing?"

"Go get a nurse, November," Cosmo growls.

I can feel his rough, cool hand on my forehead. "Are you okay, babe? You took a nasty fall."

"A-OK." I force a smile as my head begins to throb.

A nurse arrives to check my vitals and looks into my eyes. "You have a subdural hematoma, Miss Anders. We'll need to monitor you, but you should be able to go home tomorrow."

"And what about her back?" Cosmo asks.

"Just bruised, but the doctor will come in and talk more. Relax, Miss Anders."

The more alert I become, the less I want to be. Everything is sore. "Tell me what happened. Did they arrest Mandy?" I ask groggily.

"She's in jail. She confessed to everything again with her sister there encouraging her. Almost feel sorry for her, she never had a moment of peace with her controlling sister and now she'll have others telling her what to do."

"Maybe it will be a relief for her to be away from Marveline and her overbearing behavior. What about Carlene?"

"She's talking to a good lawyer and cooperating with the police. Having conversations with her family. Who knows what will come of that. I suspect once she spends a few days with Gladys, she'll remember why she ran off."

"Cos..." I protest weakly.

I can hear footsteps coming in from the hallway. Footsteps that seem to be coming from a very noisy giant. "Lanie! Oh, thank goodness! I wasn't going home until we were certain you would be okay."

"Cedar? I'd forgotten you were here. This really messed up your visit with Cos. I'm so sorry."

She leans in and kisses me lightly on the cheek. "We are all family. Through good and bad."

I smile briefly before the pain in my head overtakes me. "Ooh. I hope this goes away soon."

"We'll let you get some rest. I'll make sure Cos stays out of trouble."

"Thanks, sis!" Cosmo's booming voice, normally a source of comfort, is too much for me right now.

"I'm going to head over to your house. Piper's there holding down the fort and she is a wreck; worried sick and baking up a storm. But first, I've been dying to know, how did you figure all of this out? All I told you was that Mr. Pherson attended a parade here." Cedar asks.

I smile weakly. "I have an encyclopedic knowledge of Tulip Sloan. The rest just sort of came to me. I thought Mandy would tell me none of it was true, but she never did, so I kept making it up as I went."

Cedar smiles. "Piney Falls is lucky to have you here, sister. But we already knew that."

CHAPTER FORTY-FOUR

Three Months Later
Piney Falls

"Cos? Can you come in for a break?"

"We'll be there in a minute!"

There is a loud clattering from the roof of V*em's Stretch and Moan* studio. Ever since November broke the world record for the most moans in one place, interest in her classes has skyrocketed. She needed a place to house everyone during inclement weather, so Cosmo (reluctantly) agreed to build one for her if she found someone "halfway decent" to help him.

Cosmo comes down the ladder and stands, keeping an eye on his new friend as he descends as well, and wipes the sweat from his brow on his shirtsleeve. "I think we're just about done with the shingles."

We all move to the center of the unfinished but already welcoming room where we've set up a card table. "I baked these sugar cookies and frosted them with stars, just the way you like, Mr. Coolidge." I hand him the plate proudly, hoping Piper's tutelage on decorative frosting has paid off.

Truman Coolidge, dressed in tattered jean overalls and a blue-and-white-striped polo shirt, takes a red handkerchief from his pocket and blows his nose with a honk loud enough to rival Vem's. "Thank you kindly, ma'am. Properly festive cookies."

"When do you boys figure we'll be ready to welcome our first moaners?" November asks. "They kicked us out of the city park last week for some reason."

"You scared off the tourists is the reason." Cosmo gives me a knowing glance. "Piper had to chase after some of them and promise they weren't about to be abducted by aliens."

"Shouldn't be more'n a couple of weeks. I thought I was eager to get projects done. This boy'll wear me out if I let him." Truman elbows Cosmo. Cosmo playfully elbows him back, setting Truman off balance. We both grab him and bring him upright.

"I'm just happy you work so well together. Have you had a chance to look at the plans for our house?" I offer him a glass of lemonade before handing one to Cosmo.

"Yes ma'am. Sure have. Cosmo says he'll hire out the worst of it. I think the two of us can handle the rest, when he's not busy at his bakery."

Cosmo smiles at Truman and crosses his once-again muscular arms. "As long as you keep the details of President Taft's bath time to yourself."

Truman removes his cap and wipes his balding head on his sleeve. "Hope to see you three at the winery soon. Carlene has some nice summer events planned. Sounds like she won't serve more'n a few months, since she cooperated with the police. We'd miss her if she was gone too long."

"It's so nice you're all working together. Sassy Lasses is on its way to success." I pat Cosmo's back and slide the cookies in front of him.

"That's what was missing all along. Mr. Naybor pitted the community against each other for too many years. Didn't matter that he passed; his anger kept flowing like Spoonback Creek all these decades. Now that Marveline handles the business end, Carlene plans the events and I'm in control of the grounds, we're a force to be reckoned with. A détente of warring nations, if you will."

Cosmo raises his glass to Truman. "To a most successful cease-fire."

The four of us clink glasses.

"Now here's a toast needs saying," Truman announces. "To Cosmo and Lanie, who found the end of old legends and the beginning of new tales. Can't wait to see what happens next with these two."

Check out all of my books at Amazon.com
Be the first to hear about new releases! Sign up for
my newsletter here!
http://www.joannkeder.com

Made in the USA
Coppell, TX
01 November 2020